THE FORGETTING FLOWER

KAREN HUGG

ADVANCED PRAISE FOR THE FORGETTING FLOWER

"A lush mystery with the underpinnings of a fairy tale shot through with magic and tragedy. Karen Hugg is the rare author who can blend wonder and suspense."

— EMILY CARPENTER, AUTHOR OF
UNTIL THE DAY I DIE

"The delight and grit of Paris, the desperation of poverty, the love of plants and family – all beautifully and authentically told. The literary side of the novel brings sensitivity and texture to the struggling characters and their surroundings, and the thriller side kept me up late, anxious to find out what happens next."

— SUE BURKE, AUTHOR OF SEMIOSIS

"Intriguing and atmospheric, The Forgetting Flower has a fairytale quality, a journey into the sensuous magic of plants. The florescent beauty at the heart of this eerie story of sisterly love and redemption is the extraordinary mountain hybrid Violet Smoke with its scent of burnt apricot, as dangerously potent in Paris as it was in its beginnings in Poland."

— DEBORAH LAWRENCE, AUTHOR OF
THE LANTERN

Cover Design by Dionne Abouelela

Edited by Nicole Tone

Digital Edition ISBN: 978-0-463-01860-6

Print ISBN: 978-0-578-48407-5

Ethan

CHAPTER ONE

Renia doubted her sister would answer, but every week she called anyway. That Friday, as the clerk packed up the plants, she stood at the wholesale counter waiting through the rings: one . . . two . . . three. By four, she knew chances were slim. When the voicemail clicked on, she knew nothing had changed in eight months. At the tone, she said warmly in Polish, "Steri, the fall perennials are in. New cultivars you'd find interesting. And the city, it's still hot, but beautiful. The flowers in the squares have such bold colors, there's even a palm tree. So . . . if you'd like to visit, please visit. Come. Let's talk things out, okay?" She ended the call and headed to the métro, carrying her heavy crate of mums.

She went down the stairs into the dim subway, smelling the stale air, ripe with dried urine and rotting food, telling herself Estera hadn't meant what she'd said. "Never" was a long time. Still, Renia couldn't escape the ache in her chest, so as she sat on the train, she focused on the little perennials she'd purchased: ten 'Misty Secrets,' four 'Javelins,' six 'Ruby Gems.' They were lovely chrysanthemums in fresh bloom without dry leaves or disease. They had been arranged in neat rows with newspaper in between to prevent tipping and keep the soil secure. Their tidy cheeriness gave her relief from the untidy aspects of her own life.

As she came out of the Saint-Germain-des-Prés station, she vowed to leave her longing behind and enjoy the summer day: the ornate buildings, cobbled sidewalks, the welcoming shade of a tree. At the café, a young couple read a book together as they ate lunch. Three businessmen climbed into a taxi, laughing about a missed flight. A grocer helped an elderly woman untangle her dog from a post. The scenes lightened her spirit though she couldn't fully relax, couldn't fully exhale, not yet. But at least she lived in Paris.

She was about to cross the street and go into her plant shop when she noticed a dark spill on a building wall. Paint had rolled down the limestone in streaks, tarnishing the façade. Such a strange color. Not bright like the Polish flag or carmine like military coats, but scarlet like the Kordia cherries she ate as a girl in Kraków. She paused, shifted her crate, and touched the liquid, rolling it between her fingers. It was thin with a weak metallic scent. Looking up, she saw it had spilled from a *deuxième étage* apartment. The balcony door was open and a Rachmaninoff concerto stormed in the air. Through an iron railing, orange petunias jittered in the wind.

That was Alain's apartment.

Odd. He never opened his balcony door.

She called his name, set a hand on her forehead to block the sun, waiting for him to come outside and apologize for knocking over a can of paint. Laugh off some clumsy thing he'd done. But he didn't. Instead, the trumpets blared, the piano banged. The violins swooned over rolling tympani. It was as if the music answered in a language she couldn't understand.

"Alain! It's Renia!"

No response.

A rising panic swelled inside. Last month he'd had that relapse. And he'd switched medications. He had wanted a natural cure. He'd tried St. John's Wort and saffron and who-knew-what, but Renia knew there was no magic cure. Sometimes one simply had to change their attitude. She had, more or less. He'd wanted what was hidden in the atrium and she'd helped him with it before. But she wasn't a doctor, and his condition was too serious for amateurs and—*oh lord, was it still there?*

"Alain!"

Come to the door. Please.

The blue sky sat like a giant shroud. The concerto roared, the No. 2, his favorite. The liquid streaks, so scarlet red. He couldn't have done it, he couldn't . . . but he might have. She strained to see through the balcony railing. There seemed to be a hand with fingers, an arm stretched out on the cement floor. Difficult to . . . *was that an arm?* Yes, it was an arm.

Oh Hell. She turned and darted to the street, paused for a scooter to whiz by, and hurried to the door of Le Sanctuaire.

She fumbled in her bag for the key to the shop and after a moment dropped the crate to better search. With dirt at her feet, she found it and stuck the antique trinket in the hole, jiggling while pulling the door in a stiff hold. Finally, the lock opened and she raced around the counter to her phone by the computer. She dialed 112 and waited. The fountain at the room's center, a cement bowl with a goddess and her urn, trickled water like a pep talk. When the dispatcher answered, she explained that her neighbor, who lived at 35 Rue Sereine, was bleeding and needed emergency care.

The dispatcher asked questions about location and her name, but when the dispatcher asked how the man had been injured, Renia went mute, staring at the phone, unable to speak. *How had he been injured?* Renia knew how, at least she thought she did, but how to explain it? And did she want to?

The goddess of the fountain stared with graceful ease as she poured her steady waterfall. Renia decided she better not, because after all, she didn't know how or what had happened exactly, whether he'd gone mad or fallen asleep or done the one thing he'd agreed not to do. No, she didn't know how he'd injured himself but she had an idea.

"Please come," she said. "There's blood."

MINUTES LATER, a siren whirred, its brassy cry growing louder. Swirling red lights saturated the shop like a ghoulish theatre. A medic truck and police car arrived, blocking one side of the two-way traffic. Renia was about to go outside, intending to cross the street and show them where Alain's apartment was but stopped. The paramedics marched straight in as if they knew. Maybe someone else had called too. Maybe Alain had called, just before he'd used . . . *it.*

She knew the proper thing to do—the innocent thing —would be to appear at his apartment. Check on him. Talk to the police. But that was a risk. Instead, she went to the back of the shop. There, the answer to a more pressing question waited.

At the shop's rear, a door in the back wall opened to an atrium. It was a long, narrow lean-to built of wood and windows. A potting counter lined the windows with a sink, tools, clay pots, and twine. Along the upper shelf attached to the store's outer wall, Renia felt blindly until she found the crow bar. *Thank God, it's there.* Under the counter she pushed aside a clump of hose and a handful of signs she used for pricing, shuffled through newspapers, knickknacks, boots, and bags of soil. Finally, behind a stack of metal buckets, she found it: the gas mask.

It smelled rubbery in the heat. She put it on, tightened the belt and made sure the mouthpiece covered her jaw. Feeling like a creature from an old horror movie, she dragged the stool to the false wall she'd built. In January, she had cut a piece of paneling to fit from the shop's outer wall all the way across to the windows, and all the way from floor to ceiling. Anyone who came in the atrium thought the room was six feet smaller than it was. Only two other people in the world knew what was hidden there.

She climbed on the stool, remembered the bar, and came down to grab it from the counter. When she was up again, she set the short curve of the crowbar into the thin seam between the shop wall and panel and pried back the board. It creaked and heaved. After some more gentle yanking it finally shifted.

The entry bell jingled in the shop.

Renia froze and listened. *Relax, it could be a customer.*

The door clicked shut. The glass hummingbirds tinkled against the windows.

"*Allô?*" a man said.

Not a customer. They didn't call out. She scrambled down and whipped off the mask.

"*Allô?*"

In a flurry, she searched for a box or tub, then spotted a wicker basket filled with dead flowers and stems. She dropped the mask in and with a foot slid it beneath the counter.

"*Police,*" the voice said.

She held the bar behind her back, straightened up, and smoothed her hair with her free hand as an officer came in view.

"*Oui?*" she responded.

In French, he said, "Ah. Excuse me, Mademoiselle, my name is Officer Kateb. I was wondering if I could ask you a few questions."

He looked to be an Algerian-Frenchman, with wavy black hair and black eyes. In his late 20s, he was skinny with a sparse goatee, as if he'd been a teenager a few years ago. His blue short-sleeve shirt made him look like a traffic controller but his patch denoted Brigadier. So did his stern expression.

She slid the crowbar into the back of her dress pants as she inhaled a calming breath.

"Yes?" she said.

"Are you the owner of this shop?"

"No, I just . . . I'm the manager."

"Did you make an emergency call?"

Relax. "Yes."

He opened a notepad. "And your name?"

Slowly, casually, she spelled the words "Renia" and "Baranczka."

He scribbled it, omitting the *z*. "So, were you here about an hour ago?"

"No, I was out running errands."

He looked up. She held his surprised stare, worried he'd hear her heart pounding. "I went to lunch. And I went to the plant market." Then, so as to squash any suspicion, she added, "Le Chasseur and Petit Rungis."

"I see," he said and wrote on his pad.

The iron bar felt heavy and cold against her back. She imagined it sliding through her pant leg and clanging on the floor. She pictured his alarmed expression, her muddled explanation.

"Okay, so . . ." he flipped a page to check his notes, "do you know any of the people who live across the street?"

"Yes."

"Do you mind giving me a list?"

"Eh . . . I know João, the owner of the bistro."

"Which bistro?"

"There's only one. Across the street."

He waited.

"Vida Nova."

He wrote that on his pad.

"And there's a couple, young, who live in the building beside the bistro. They live on the second floor. I don't know their names. Alain Tolbert lives across the hall from them. He's my neighbor."

"Your neighbor?"

She blinked, swallowed her fear. "Well, I mean, no, their neighbor. But yes, my neighbor as well. He's a friend, a client. I noticed his balcony door open."

Kateb wrote "friend and client."

She yearned for him to say "thank you" and leave, but he didn't.

"So, I hear a slight accent," he said. "Were you born in France?"

She held her breath. "No. Does it matter?"

He didn't answer, only wrote on his notepad.

She didn't want to be a suspect. She couldn't be.

"Is he dead?" Renia said.

Kateb looked up. "Who?"

"Alain. Tolbert."

"Dead?"

She nodded.

"Perhaps."

She lowered her head, cringed. That meant yes.

He watched her.

"When's the last time you spoke to him?" he said.

Alain, dead. She expected it and yet didn't.

She gave a slight shrug. "I don't know. Last Tuesday, I think."

"How did he seem?"

She closed her eyes to remember. He'd sat on the very stool she stood beside. He'd come from a luncheon he'd organized. His suit coat was off, tie loose. Alain had a narrow, clever face. He wore his hair gelled back, showing a widow's peak, though the hair was soft and fresh. His long nose pointed to a wily grin and his deep-set eyes were both melancholy and bright at the same time. He had twirled the stem of a fading aster. "He was happy."

"What was the purpose of his visit here?"

"He put in an order for flower arrangements." Who would deliver them now? And Madame Palomer was still working on them. Who would tell her? She felt agony at thinking she might have to. "I, we, sell him flowers. He's a, eh . . . he coordinates events." Her face warmed. Her hands shook. *Alain, lost. Not him. Why him? This happened too quickly. We texted yesterday.*

The bar slipped down and she straightened up. The hook caught on her waist band.

"Are you okay?" he said.

"Yes," she put a hand to her back and held it. "I'm . . . upset."

Kateb nodded, took a card from his pocket. "If you remember anything unusual, anything suspicious, or if he did anything out of the ordinary, talked to someone he normally doesn't talk to, please call me and let me know."

She took the card. "Yes, okay."

He held out his hand. "Thank you very much."

She moved her left hand to her back so her right could shake his. She didn't want to ask Kateb and yet she wanted to know. She needed to know. "Was his death a suicide?"

He studied her.

Her heart raced. She forced her face to remain placid but concerned. She would not allow herself to cry in front of this man, this stranger, no matter how much her heart was breaking.

"We don't know the details of the situation," he said. "That's what we're hoping to find out."

AFTER KATEB RETURNED to Alain's building, Renia locked the shop door. She considered pulling the shade but decided that looked suspicious, so she backed away from the window far into the shadow of the room and unhooked the bar from her waist. This time, once she was in the atrium, she closed the door. She wanted to collapse on the floor and cry. Alain, gone. Forever. *Oh God.* She wanted to scream at him, berate him for doing what he'd done. For the hole he'd now left. She dropped her head in her hands and as the heat of tears came, she allowed herself to grieve for a minute, then inhaled a huge breath and told herself to get it together. What was done was done. *He'd* done it. Not her. Right? Maybe. Sniffling and shivering, she dug out the mask from the trimmings basket. With it on, she pried out the panel far enough to slip past and yanked on the metal handle to scoot it behind.

There, in a six-by-six-foot space was a potting table made of old whitewashed wood. Atop the table was a small antique greenhouse without a floor, a Wardian Case from the Victorian era, about as big as a large cardboard box. It had a steel framework with little glass windows, dotted at the roof with sweat. She lifted the house to reveal the plant at the heart of her and Alain's dispute.

It was a small shrub in a large pot that could be mistaken for a bonsai, two feet tall with twisting branches and round, dark leaves whose surface sported a light fuzz. One trunk gave way to three woody branches that divided into thinner papery branches. Amidst the leaves were clusters of pinkish transparent stems with blooms. They resembled African violet flowers but larger with a color between purple and magenta. Estera had nicknamed the plant *Violet Smoke*.

A gangly awkward sight. Stupid plant. She leaned over the foliage, careful not to brush the blossoms and release more scent, and counted. Three days ago, eight blooms. Now . . . five. Five. Alain *did* do it. She put a hand to her head but hit the mask. What had he thought? If one did the trick, not two but three must be better?

Last Tuesday, he'd stopped by to chat. She had to make a deposit at the bank before Palomer overdrew the account. But the store had a wealthy customer, a regular, browsing. She didn't want to lose a sale. He offered to watch the shop. He said it was no trouble, he'd done it once before for Madame. With a long line at the bank, an excursion that usually took five minutes took twenty. But Renia had only told him about the secret nook, never shown him where it was. Apparently, he'd figured it out.

She slumped onto the stool, her face turning hot. Her only friend in Paris, dead. A friend who could make her smile. No one could make her smile; she never allowed it. Never let anyone control you—a lesson she'd learned long ago from schoolyard bullies, a boyfriend who'd conned her out of money, and even her own father. But with Alain she could forget caution. Now she sat, a chunk of clay, fighting tears that clouded her mask and the view of what might be her future.

LATER, Kateb's police car was still double-parked across the street. Another squad car and an unmarked van had arrived. The balcony door was still open and bursts of light flashed inside the apartment. Renia watched from the shop window. Those missing flowers were in Alain's kitchen or on the dining table, she knew it. Of course, shriveled and useless by now, the scent dissipated by time and air. The question was whether the police would see the flowers as any kind of evidence. Probably not. But an autopsy . . . that could reveal a clue. She had to get inside. Exactly when was the question. How long would the investigation go on?

Relax. Wait for the right time.

She imagined a customs official escorting her onto a flight bound for Poland.

You're not going anywhere. You're an EU citizen.

She saw herself in a police interrogation room, answering questions under a bright light.

It was an accident.

In the shop, Palomer's disgusted face, firing her.

The dream won't die. You've done nothing wrong.

But she *had* done something wrong. She'd made the wrong decision. Instead of keeping the plant a secret, she'd not only blabbed to Alain about what it could do but *shared* it with him. What a fool.

She went to the counter as if ready to tally an order for a customer, as if business was usual. She was surrounded by plants: hefty leaves and delicate branches, ovals, hearts, fans of dark green or light bluish tones, yellow echoes. They smelled of moist soil. There were soaps and books

and linens too—but the plants, the plants came at her with
their loud silence. They crowded around for attention, for
watering, for clipping, for dusting. But all she thought of
was the one plant she wished had never come into her life.

The Violet Smoke had lived amidst the same plants she
saw now. Orchids, ferns, ficus. She'd first seen it in an enormous greenhouse. A plain but large structure, without
finials or décor but heated, on Pan Górski's estate, the
estate with the white home called Biały Manor. Kraków
had had a hot August and that day, Estera harvested abun-
dant cucumbers and tomatoes in the kitchen garden. Renia
weeded the perennial border. Her knees hurt. Sweat rolled
down her back. As she checked her watch, she noticed
Estera approach, her gloves off, smiling.

"Come," she said and touched Renia's shoulder.

She remained kneeling, tossed dandelions on a pile.
She felt satisfied that she'd pulled the last three fully by the
root. "I'm not finished. There's a lot more to do."

"He's waiting for us."

"Who?"

Estera tilted her head as if the answer was obvious.

Renia stiffened, eyed the greenhouse. She was a
seasonal worker, unlike Estera, who was permanent. She
guessed she was about to be fired. "What does he want?"

"He said he needs to speak with us."

Inside the greenhouse the air was warm and dense. It
smelled of rich, moist soil. The tall oval leaves of the bird
of paradise dampened the weak light. Renia had never met
her employer. For a plant aficionado, he rarely went
outside. As she pondered whether that was unusual, she
passed a table of orchids, their wiry wands rising up to
explode in red sculptures. She wondered what Pan Górski
looked like, knowing he was one of the wealthiest men in
Kraków. A tangle of exposed roots bumped her face from

an orchid hanging from the ceiling. Its bent rubbery strings felt like fleshy fingers about to grab and choke. She hurried on, passing a table of moth orchids. Some were sprinkled with specs, some solidly pink. One was white with scarlet veins. The veins' delicate interweaving pattern was visible, reminding her of a human brain.

"Girls, come closer."

A man waited at the back wall. He was on the shorter side, slim, in a corduroy coat and trousers, and a tweed cap. Renia realized she had seen him before, walking in the field by the pond. With his weathered face and bony hands, she'd assumed he was the farm caretaker, not the descendant of a noble family.

"Now which is which?" he said.

Renia and Estera were born two minutes apart. The twins shared the same large green eyes and roundish face, straight gold hair, long nose, puckered mouth. But their personalities differed. Estera's name meant *star*, and she was a star. Outgoing, easy to know, emotional. She liked to express her opinions. Renia struggled to be open and friendly, she found it easier to be closed. Hesitation was her specialty and hesitation had not only saved her more than once, it had saved Estera a few times. But Estera always saved Renia too by being her voice, her advocate, her best friend.

"I'm Estera." Estera put her arm around Renia, a reassuring side hug Estera always gave her when she knew Renia felt shy. "This is Renia."

Górski nodded. "Girls, you've worked hard over the years so I want to give you something." His wide nose and full mouth announced a confident presence, but his tiny eyes showed mischief. "My favorite plant, a plant I . . ." His expression darkened, his body sagged. "See here, someday, I will leave God's earth."

Renia was about to ask if he was ill. Estera stepped in and reached for his hand. "Are you well?"

He took Estera's hand, smiled at her as a grandfather smiles at his granddaughter. "Yes, yes. For now, yes."

Renia knew Estera had met Pan Górski but didn't know they were close. She speculated they'd grown close because they shared a passion for plants. And perhaps because of their relationship with their own father, Tata. He was mildly interested in plants and had encouraged Estera to become a gardener but wasn't otherwise inter-ested in either girl's life—except to make sure they attended mass on Sundays and wore modest clothing and didn't giggle foolishly in public. Otherwise, as he worked long hours in construction, they saw him little. He was more of a father in name than action.

Górski patted Estera's hand, then cleared his throat with a snort and swiveled to a small plastic closet in the corner. It had a zipper and a flexible tube attached to vent moisture out the wall. Inside, on a metal shelf sat a squat twisted shrub.

It was the ugliest plant Renia had ever seen. It had no grace like a rose or symmetry like a hydrangea. Not even alluring flowers like hibiscus. The branches zig-zagged back and forth while shedding bark as if struggling against disease.

"Estera, you're the one who's taken care of it," he said, "and I know you love my dear miniature, so I want you to have it."

Estera's mouth opened. She clapped her hands. "Oh, wonderful! Are you sure?" Her face tightened. "But your wife. You made it for her, it's hers."

"Yes, but," he said quietly, "she can no longer walk out here to enjoy it."

Estera's eyebrows wrinkled, her face contorted in sympathy. "Poor dear."

Pan Górski's face softened. He gave a slight nod and loosened a crooked smile.

Renia envied how Estera could connect with such ease. She wasn't scared of his deep wrinkles or the humped way he stood or that he cleared his throat like an animal. Of the feelings he shared openly in a way Tata didn't think necessary. Estera only saw the soul and embraced it.

"Yes, well, she gets on as she can." He pointed to Renia, "Now, I want you to share it with, with . . ."

"Renia?" she said. Estera smiled as if to let him know she understood his difficulty in remembering.

"Yes, yes." He looked at each twin. "She wears the hair up, you wear it down, I must remember." Renia's hair was often in a smooth ponytail, Estera's loose and wild. "You know what my little dear needs, but remember to remove the blooms at the first sign of buds. Very important. Then, in autumn and spring, allow it to bloom but cover your face and secure it in this closet when it does."

Estera gazed at the plant, her eyes shimmering. "It's beautiful," she said. "Thank you, Pan. I'm very, very excited. How did you make it? Tell me. Tell me exactly how so I can make another for Renia."

Renia thought creating another weed like that was a ridiculous idea.

Górski's lips wrinkled. "I . . . I'm unable to remember. *Saintpaulia* and . . ." he gave a slight shrug, "so many hybrids, so many experiments and many, many failures, but this one, this was my favorite success." He repeated a soft grunting, which Renia realized was a laugh.

"Yes, of course," Estera said. "I understand." She looked at Renia. "We're honored to have it, aren't we?"

Renia straightened her shoulders. She opened her mouth to say, "No, not really. We don't need an exotic plant that only grows in warm humid conditions. Where will we keep it? At Mama and Tata's? We don't have the money to take care of it. And we certainly don't have the time to baby it. Besides, it looks like a bonsai that went wild." But she didn't say that.

"Well," she said. "I don't know where we'll keep it."

Estera's smile dulled.

"You may leave it here, as long as you care to," Górski said. "It likes its chamber."

"It's an amazing specimen, one of a kind," Estera said. "I assure you, I'll take good care of it." She squeezed his hand.

He nodded in a shaky bob. "Yes, good," he said. "My body tells me I no longer have much time here, but you two are young and have many years to enjoy plants. Now remember, be careful with it or dangerous things will happen that you can't undo. Here," he took a folded hand-kerchief from his pocket and handed it to Estera, "follow me and I will show you why it's so special."

IN THE ATRIUM, Renia mourned how that special quality was also the Violet Smoke's curse. After a year, so much had changed. Pan Górski had passed away. Renia was in Paris, Estera in Poland. When Renia remembered how she and Estera had parted, she warmed with anger. Estera had paid such a terrible price. Had Alain gone the way of Estera? Renia wouldn't forgive herself if he had.

She remembered how thankful she'd felt only a few hours ago. How she'd smiled at seeing a young boy on the Rue Sereine, playing with a yellow balloon, how it had almost floated away when he'd jumped at the last second and grabbed its string. These were Alain's last terrible moments, alone, as she approached the apartment. Maybe if she had returned sooner, she could have saved him. She might have texted him, called him, waved to him, jolted him from his depression. But she hadn't. The regret ate at her. She shook her head. She couldn't let herself fall apart, not when there was still work to do.

Wiping her tears, she went outside. There, on the cobbled sidewalk, she picked up the overturned crate of chrysanthemums, scraped the soil together, and tried to set each little pot of green life upright again.

CHAPTER TWO

On Saturday morning, after the men carried their metal suitcases out of Alain's building and left in the unmarked van, Renia went across the street to speak with the landlord. She pressed the buzzer and waited, checking the street to see who might notice her. An elderly woman in a straw hat stumbled along, pulling a cart of groceries, occasionally glancing her way. The wheels squeaked in a foreboding, rhythmic tic. Renia retreated into the doorway. A young man in a leather jacket eyed her as he passed. Even a cluster of pigeons, perched on a shady ledge, strutted and cooed anxiously as if they suspected her involvement in Alain's death. Agitated, she considered walking away when a blank voice crackled on the intercom, "*Qui est là?*"

She inhaled to calm her pulse. "Excuse me for bothering you. I'm a friend of Alain Tolbert's. I left my phone in his apartment and I need it."

Silence.

The blank voice said, "Tolbert is dead."

She swallowed, gathered courage. "I know, it's horrible.

And I don't want to bother you, but I have to get my phone."

Silence.

He must've seen her before. Once, she'd gone to the movies with Alain and François and afterward had passed the landlord on the Rue de Rennes outside the L'Arlequin theater. "That's Jojo, king of our building," Alain had said, referring to an old television show about a goofy-looking dog.

"I'm his friend," she said. "I assure you. My name is Renia Baranczka. Has he ever mentioned me? I manage the plant shop across the street."

"What shop?"

"Le Sanctuaire." She pointed at the storefront, as if he could see through the intercom.

The shop's terrace display reflected its name. Renia had worked hard to make it romantic and inviting, outlining the large windows in an olive trim that harmonized with the rusty cursive of the sign. She'd put the plants in antique terra cotta to evoke ancient times and ordered extra hydrangeas to extend the blooming season. A teal bistro set she'd picked up at a flea market popped against the dark-leaved camellias and underneath, a stone cat poked its head out. Right now, despite her work, the shop, with its door wedged open, was void of customers. Minh, her assistant, was working on fixing the air conditioning, which had only worked intermittently for a week. Not even Vivaldi Concertos playing on the outdoor speaker would draw in customers looking to escape August's heat.

"You are from Le Sanctuaire?" he said. "Where is Madame Palomer?"

"Oh, she only arranges flowers at home nowadays."

"Who is there now?"

"Another worker. Her name . . . look, I just need my phone."

Silence.

The lock buzzed. The door clicked.

The foyer, with its white tiled floor, smelled like bleach. He emerged from a door at the left. He was on the short side with a wide belly and wore a wrinkled tan suit. His hair was thin, charcoal colored. A gold wedding ring glowed in the dim light. With deep lines around his mouth and large nostrils, his face reminded her of a sad hound.

He gazed at her raincoat.

Earlier, the sky had clouded and sprinkled for a half-hour despite the rough heat. Enough to justify wearing a raincoat she could slip the flowers into. Feeling self-conscious, she shoved her hands in the pockets. "It rained earlier."

"Did it? I haven't been out."

They stood an awkward moment, he not seeming to remember why she was there.

"So, Monsieur . . .?"

"Armand."

"Armand. I'll be very quick. Could I?"

He held out a hand toward the stairs.

She hurried at a brisk clip, her heeled sandals clicking up the marble stairs. When she realized he was slowly trudging behind her, she slowed her pace, waited for him on the landing. She tried to sound light and cheery. "We were having coffee the other day and I left without remembering my phone."

"Well, the police removed the tape this morning," he said, "but the cleaning crew has not come. We must be careful." His eyes shifted to her shoes. "It's . . . messy."

She knew the police were finished. In fact, she knew it

had been two hours and seventeen minutes since the police had removed the tape.

When he reached the first floor, she stepped back and allowed him space. He took the keys from his pocket and paused. As if giving her a test, he pointed to the two apartment doors on opposite walls. "Which is Tolbert's?"

"Apartment 3." Her mind flashed to the first time she'd knocked on that door with a delivery of flowers for a concert reception. Usually, Alain picked up the flower arrangements that Palomer would drop off at the shop, but that day in February, Palomer had asked Renia to deliver the two boxes. Renia never suspected Alain would become her friend. And she never thought he'd kill himself. Of course, he might not have. The idea that the Violet Smoke had killed him squeezed her heart.

Armand must have read her silence because he said, "Yes, it's very sad. He was too young to die, a nice person, always paid on time—and quiet."

She recalled how Alain had blasted music on the day he'd died. Armand must have been out.

"Yes, he was only forty-two years old," she said.

Armand unlocked the door and opened it. The apartment was a comfortable, modern place. Large sitting and dining areas. A sleek galley kitchen with a counter facing the dining table, a counter where Renia had drank her first martini, made with potato vodka in honor, Alain said, of her Polish heritage. It was eerie to see the mustard sofa and peach pillows without him, smartly dressed and chattering away, perched upon them. His favorite white rug. The dishes in the sink he'd used less than three days ago. Loosely stacked mail. And there, near the balcony door, in the dining area on the Midcentury desk facing the wall, was his biweekly bouquet of freesia, dahlias, and tiger lilies —always lilies—that Palomer had made. In a standard clear vase wrapped with a ribbon, the flowers leaned in murky water, brown and curled with fallen petals. They, like Alain, had expired.

No sign of the Violet Smoke.

"I may have left the phone in the bedroom," she said.

Armand's eyebrows raised in a slight twitch. She hurried down the hall so she could enter before him. In the bedroom, there was evidence of Alain's final mood. An ashtray with cigarette butts. Four empty glasses, one half-filled with water, one rimmed with salt. The sheets were mussed, the pillows askew, a comforter tangled around itself. The dresser mirror doubled the jammed collection of colognes, hair products, and portable speakers. A brush full of Alain's brown hair lay at the edge, angled and about to fall in the crack behind the dresser. A distant smell of body musk. A magazine lay open on the bed, as if he were about to come back from the kitchen with a cup of coffee and read. A collared shirt was tossed on a chair near a stuffed laundry basket. Dress shoes were scattered. All evidence of Alain's private daily life lay in a fit as if they were angry at his abandonment.

Renia's head swayed. Nausea grew.

Armand lumbered into the room with a slow gait. "Maybe it's in the kitchen," she said and flew past him, jogging down the hall. Nothing. A breadbox, toaster. Crumbs. Old baguette. In the sitting area a few feet from the sofa, a large irregular puddle of blood shimmered on the parquet floor, crusted at the edges from the summer air. Another smaller puddle had pooled at the threshold, a puddle from where his blood had dripped down the building. The blood Renia had thought was paint. Now it was dark and dried. But there was so much blood. Had he stabbed himself?

The Midcentury desk had a sheet of glass to protect

the wood but was missing a large chip at the corner. She went to it, careful not to step on the blood, and searched the floor for the glass chip. It wasn't there. Instead, she spotted three flowers in an aperitif glass behind the bouquet. The police hadn't taken them as evidence. As she swiped the glass from the table, Armand came in the room. She slipped the glass in her coat pocket, making sure to angle it upward so the two inches of water wouldn't spill.

"Here it is." She leaned forward to block his view of the desk and pretended to pull her phone, already in hand, from behind the bouquet. "It was hiding in the papers."

His expression was staid. "Alright."

She thanked him and headed to the door, her hand in her pocket, careful to steady the glass. The motion of walking jostled it. Water spilled and soaked the inner fabric of her coat. As he followed her into the hallway, she prayed it wouldn't drip on the floor.

"I can see myself out," she said.

He closed the apartment door and checked the knob to make sure it was locked. "Wait."

She stopped, the wetness soaking into her skirt.

He moved in close, glancing at Alain's door. "You know, we all have secrets."

His breath felt hot on her collarbone. "Yes. We do." She held his gaze to show she wasn't intimidated by his proximity. She'd learned that as a child growing up in Poland, to never show fear and have a plan. She gripped the glass in her pocket. If Armand did something inappropriate, she would clock him on the forehead with it to slow his movement and dash off.

"You know, you deserve to know, Tolbert . . ." His eyes were the color of a dried oak leaf. ". . . liked men."

She opened her mouth, reaching for words, feigning mild surprise. Armand thought they were lovers even though Alain was gay? "Oh uh, yes. Thank you for mentioning it. We were never very serious. I always suspected that was the reason."

He gave a sympathetic nod.

She shook his hand, then while holding the glass against her soaked thigh, went down the stairs, her sandals clacking quickly, in time with the rhythm of her fast heart.

INSIDE LE SANCTUAIRE, a suffocating warmth enveloped her. With its lavender walls and gold sconces and white-washed furniture jammed with plants, lotions, linens, and tools, the shop felt like an attractive, claustrophobic sauna. Minh was on a step ladder, fiddling with the air conditioning unit. At hearing a droning voice, Renia spun around, her eyes shifting from the hedge shears to the toothed shovels to the wrought iron decor with their pointed spears, fearing Armand had followed her. A singer chanted on the stereo. Tabla drums beat, a whip cracked in rhythm. The New Age music felt too ritualistic and punishing so she hit pause and inserted Mozart's String Quartets.

As the chirpy violins skated into the air, Renia asked, "No success?" Earlier that morning, they'd called three repairmen. All were *en vacances*.

"Well, I adjusted this doo-dad with the screwdriver, which is attached to the mechanism, and it worked for twenty seconds before shutting off and starting again and I thought, wow, these are complicated. No wonder the contractor charges so much to repair them, and no wonder my parents replaced theirs when it broke, and still, it's a fascinating piece of machinery."

Renia had known Minh talked a lot when she'd hired

her. Her chattiness engaged customers, but at the moment, Renia longed for silence.

A woman in a satin sundress wandered in, a Gucci purse on her bronzed arm. When she realized she would bake inside the shop, she avoided eye contact and walked swiftly out.

This was the fifth time this week a customer had left because of the heat. Between the noise of fixing the air conditioning and the lack of air conditioning, the shop would go broke.

Renia let go a defeated breath. "I'll be in the atrium." She went to the back of the shop and through the door, then closed it. A fan, clipped to the window ledge, blew in warm air. She yearned for a cool breeze, for a peaceful, composed moment. With a careful hand, she removed the aperitif glass. It had a curve of water left. Her skirt—knee-length and cotton, decorated with tiny daisies—was marked with a wet stain the size of a grapefruit. Her coat pocket too. She hung the coat on the wall rack and left her skirt as it was, then sat on the stool, eyeing the crispy flowers.

Stupid plant. She wanted to curl a hand over the dead blooms and squeeze, wanted to rip apart the Violet Smoke branch by branch. It was like a misbehaving child she'd inherited, one that couldn't be sent away nor changed for the better. Her only choice was to manage it and thus far she hadn't done that very well. She tossed the flowers in the trimmings basket, chiding herself for being so careless.

The door opened and Minh swooped in.

Minh was all modern rustic: physically petite at twenty-one but bold with an orange wrap-around dress and macramé sandals that wound to her knees, a pounded silver necklace, rings on her thumbs. A wooden brooch shaped like a tiger. Her face, always at ease and almost always sporting a smile, morphed to disappointment when she noticed Renia's thigh. "Your clothes."

Renia examined the stain, stuggling with what to say. "Oh, yes. Accident. At a . . . drinking fountain."

"Are you okay?"

"Yes. What is it?"

"Madame Palomer called."

"Does she know?"

"Definitely."

She imagined François keying through Alain's phone for contacts, calling their friends and colleagues, sharing the awful news. And when he called Madame, she'd have verbally burst forth in shock, probably rambled in despair. And now she summoned Renia, for what? To share the news? To vent? That Renia may have played a part in the death of her "dear Alain" . . . she moaned, then slouched forward. "Yes, I suppose she would."

"She wants to see you."

"Did you tell her I know?"

"Yes. She still wants to see you."

"Okay. I'll visit her on Monday." On Sundays, Palomer went to mass and "rested."

"She can't on Monday. She's going to the hairdresser."

Oh, right. Mondays were hairdresser days. "When does she want to see me?"

"Tuesday afternoon."

Afternoon because she took the dog to the groomer in the morning.

"Oh," Minh said, "by the way . . ."

"Yes?"

"That customer from last weekend, the woman with the baby? That baby was so cute, such curly hair. Well, that woman returned the botanical sketches."

Renia had spent six hours drawing those sketches. "Returned?"

"Yes. She had a big explanation about it clashing with her furniture, but I didn't argue because I thought it best to be upbeat even though we did lose one hundred euros on it."

Renia waved a hand, then cupped her forehead. "Okay, I'll record it."

"And that landscape designer, the one with the blue streaks in her hair? She didn't buy the iron urns. I tried to talk her into it, even offered her a discount, but she wouldn't budge."

That was a four-hundred euro sale, lost.

The bell jingled. They glanced toward the doorway. A customer. Minh left to greet her.

Renia closed the atrium door. She scrutinized the counter where old seed packets lay, shriveled at the corners from once being wet. With a plastic price tag, she gathered the basalt pebbles left from topdressing ferns. Business had been glacial. In August, everyone was at the beach and not thinking of gardening. Tourists sometimes visited but they, with the burden of flying with luggage, usually bought smaller, inexpensive items. The shop's bank account had been draining, the monthly statements clearly showed it, and Palomer only worsened the situation. Years ago, after she'd gained Alain's account, she'd stopped contributing to the shop's overall income from her at-home flower arranging. Now she often dipped into it for personal expenses. Alain's hefty orders had always replenished the depletion but with him gone, Renia wondered how long she could justify Minh's part-time employment. How long could she justify her own? That hearty income would now disappear, and she might be forced to give up what she'd worked for her entire life.

Relax. You have to be resourceful.

But how?

The scent of Minh's cinnamon tea floated in the air, reminding Renia of Christmas time. Frigid cold. Kraków. Frozen streets, the snow, the oppressive gray sky. Frowning faces tucked into scarves. The ominous call of church bells. Her father's growling voice as he reminded everyone they'd be late for mass. She remembered how, for the last few years, she and Estera had grown poinsettias and amaryllis to sell at church bazaars. They'd start the plants atop the heater of their bedroom window, nursing them until they were fully grown.

One day last December, after selling at a bazaar, they went on what Estera called *a memory call*. They'd carried cardboard boxes of plants through the crunching snow, opening Tata's creaky hatchback, and settling them in. Estera wrapped the plants' foliage with the tablecloth they'd used for their display, a plaid cloth perfumed with cinnamon.

They drove to a suburb of brick houses with quaint courtyards. On those streets, there were no pecked garbage bags or rusted cars. Estera parked before a two-story house decorated with fir boughs and twinkling lights. When she shut off the engine, Renia felt the cold air bite her nose. "I'm worried about leaving the plants. They'll die from the chill."

"They'll be fine," Estera said.

Renia eyed them behind the back seat. The red bracts were supple and perky. "They won't last an hour. It's twenty degrees out."

"Don't worry, we'll be quick."

They went to the front door and knocked. The neighborhood was quiet and serene, no revving engines, no one calling out. Renia suspected she knew what a "memory call" was but hoped to be wrong.

A woman in her mid-fifties opened the door. Streaks of gray in wiry black hair. The smell of ham and mustard. She wore a long sweater with a colorful folk print on the front. She had a broad face, light make up. When she saw Estera, she smiled and kissed her on the forehead. "Ah, my savior! Come in."

The sitting room had tufted brown furniture covered with knitted throws and tall bookcases lined with books and pottery. Stacks of newspapers. A framed print over the sofa showed two dogs, one black, one white wearing mirrored sunglasses. The black dog stared straight at the camera, its mouth open as if smiling; the white one stared off in the distance, its mouth closed.

Estera introduced Pani Anna Markowska. Markowska giggled at Renia as her eyes shifted between the sisters. "Twins! Yes, you have that special life bond forever."

Renia nodded. That was true. They often made similar decisions about situations and yet they were different.

"So, my dear," Markowska said, rubbing her hands. "Did you bring me my treat?"

Estera pulled a waxed paper bag from her pocket, sealed with tape, and presented it on her palm with a smile. Inside lay a Violet Smoke flower, its purple cup velvety, its light pinkish stem wrapped in a wet napkin.

"Wonderful."

"Now, we can only do a memory trim," Estera said, "not a complete pruning. Just remove a few branches of history here and there."

Renia stared at the ceiling, scratching her arms. Her skin itched. Estera was about to carry through on this ridiculous task. She was really about to do it.

"Yes, yes, of course," Markowska said. She took a

folded wad from her sweater pocket, counted eight 20 złoty bills and pressed them in Estera's palm. Her face glowed with adoration.

"Thank you," Estera said. "I'm grateful."

"No." Markowska touched Estera's cheek. "I'm grateful, my dear. Me. But don't leave the flower, it won't last. And I want to be happy for as long as possible."

"Well, okay, but you said the hospital calls to remind him about the chemotherapy."

"Yes, but I'll have forgotten for at least one beautiful week. And I won't recall Bartek's devilish behavior." Her expression darkened. "That boy's debt will be his undoing."

Markowska went to the sofa and tossed off her shoes. She reclined like a patient, tossing a fringed throw over her lap. "I'm ready," she said. "The list is on the table."

Renia paced with arms folded. She leaned against the wall, chewed her lip. How could Estera take money for it? She knew so little about how it worked. What chemicals, the dangers . . .

Estera sat in a chair beside the sofa. She set Markowska's paper, a slip that looked like a grocery list, on her lap and took out two surgical masks from her coat pocket.

In a discreet tone to Estera, Renia said, "Are you sure you want to do this?"

"Oh, yes, I'm sure," Markowska said loudly. "I've never been more certain."

Estera grinned and shrugged at Renia as if to say *Isn't she adorable? Isn't she sweet?* She put on the surgical mask. Her emerald eyes relaxed and filled with confidence.

In a foiled reluctance, Renia took the other mask and hooked the bands over her ears with an embarrassed snap. Estera had swiped them from their mother's medical stash. Mama would not approve.

"Listen closely," Estera said. She opened the bag and pulled out the flower, handed it to Markowska. Markowska, her eyes bright, stuck her nose in the flower and inhaled a full breath. She blinked several times, slightly frowning at the powerful scent.

Renia pressed the mask against her face. Faintly, she caught the smell of burnt apricots.

Estera read from the list. "Your husband doesn't have cancer. He's a touch sick but he'll be fine."

Markowska's face deflated into calmness.

"And Bartek is not in debt. He doesn't do drugs," Estera said. "His creditors do not visit his apartment. He never had a car anyway. And he won't be homeless."

"No," Markowska said. Her eyes blinked in a slow tic. She stared into nothingness.

"Bartek, even though he's lost sight in his eye, he's fine. It doesn't depress him."

Markowska's mouth drooped. Her folded hands slid apart. Her eyelids closed.

Estera's voice soothed in a tender tone. "And Liza didn't die, because you never had a cat."

Markowska's head dropped to the side. Her chest rose and fell, her breathing, audible.

Estera put the flower in the bag, pressing the tape tightly on the seam. "I'm not sure if she heard that last one."

"Finished?" Renia said.

Estera slid the bag in her pocket, monitoring Markowska. The woman rested in a peaceful sleep. "Yes, I think so."

Renia shot up and marched out the door. Outside, she got in the car and waited in the freezing air, folding her coat over her stomach. In the back, the poinsettia leaves sagged. She regretted not asking Estera for the keys to run the heater. Soon, a lamp illuminated in the house and Estera came out, gently guiding the door shut.

They drove out of the suburb and onto the highway. Beside the road, crushed beer cans and flattened bags lay in ditches. They passed a clump of blackened trees, burnt from a brush fire. In the distance, a factory billowed white smoke. Soon, they veered onto the off ramp and into a neighborhood of tall cement towers. Renia suppressed the words she wanted to say. Instead, she said, "Is this the first time you've done it?"

Estera's eyes stayed on the road. "Sort of."

"What do you mean?"

Estera wiped her nose, gripping the steering wheel. "I may have visited Pani Markowska before."

"How many times?"

"Not sure."

"Not sure?"

"No," she said.

Renia shifted in her seat. She couldn't help herself. "This isn't a proper way to earn money."

"Proper? You sound like Tata."

Renia swallowed her annoyance.

They came to a red light. An elderly couple with a small dog yanked at its leash. The dog resisted. The man slapped the dog's back. The dog cowered.

"I hate this place," Renia said.

They were quiet.

"Well," Estera said, "we certainly can't move without money."

"We can make money in a . . . more resourceful way."

"Oh yeah? How? I can't even find a second job."

The light changed. Estera drove off.

They were silent.

"If I sell more flowers," Estera said in a lighter voice. "I could make a few thousand."

They passed a sleek sports car on cinderblocks, the tires removed, a side window smashed.

"More? You shouldn't sell any." Renia's breath fluttered. The tall buildings with their vertical windows, like exaggeratedly open eyes, watched them. The two of them, in their late twenties, still lived with their parents in one of those dismal apartments on the thirteenth floor, with a hallway that smelled of mildew and stewed onions, made her heart shrivel.

Estera threw up a hand, hit the steering wheel. The car swerved. "So, should we stay? We've been talking about this since we were fifteen. And you said the system here doesn't care about the environment or women or helping people make a better life."

Renia imagined the letters Uncle Feliks had sent them over the years. Magazine clippings about French scientists and architecture. Photos of him and Aunt Nanette by the Seine. In a café. At the Sacré-Coeur dome. His young face with windblown hair, proudly content. He was right; the best of everything happened in Paris. She wanted to leave, she did, but she wasn't sure what Estera was doing was worth the risk. Irritated at not knowing the solution, she sat still and said nothing.

Estera slowed into the parking lot. Their neighbor, an old squat woman wearing a babushka, limped past the car carrying bags of groceries, vodka bottles clanking. She was the grandmother of their schoolmate Sylwia Kozłowska. When she noticed the twins, she nodded, her mouth closed like cracked cement.

"We're working so hard," Estera said, "we barely stay awake at dinner."

Renia's face warmed, her stomach cramped. They

would never leave. They'd been saving for years, but something always came up, something interrupting the flow of money. Once, Estera was mugged on the tram. Mama's car broke last month. They had to repair the electricity in the bathroom. An exterminator had come in October. She breathed out the lump of sadness in her throat as Estera shut off the car. It knocked to a halt.

"Hey," Estera said.

Renia fiddled with the door handle. It had to be jiggled, then fully lifted to open.

"Hey." She slipped her hand into Renia's. "*Renka*, don't worry. We'll get to Paris. We'll find good work there, jobs that make us happy. We'll see the great art and hear the symphony and eat the delicious food." She squeezed her fingers. "Look, I can see you reading about your favorite, what's his name, Delacroix, in a café. Like this . . ." Estera mimicked a contemplative, nodding face, tapped a finger on her chin.

Renia smiled.

"Right? So, leave the money to me. I'll make it happen."

CHAPTER THREE

On Tuesday afternoon, Renia walked her bike out of her apartment building foyer, dreading the visit in Montparnasse. She knew Palomer was devastated at Alain's death but what her boss might do in response worried her even more: close the shop and take a three-month vacation; buy a new car; repurpose the shop as a clothing boutique—all of which she'd done in the past when distraught. She pushed off on the straight-handled black cruiser and headed for the Rue de Rennes. As she rode under the sun, she felt a spirited rush. The cruiser, with its nicked paint and cracked handlebar cover, rattled at bumps harder than she liked but it served well for shopping and deliveries. When she'd seen it for sale at the Clignancourt market, she'd bought it right away, remembering a childhood bike her father had found in an alley and had fixed up. She used to ride to the park where she'd collect clover blossoms and watch ducks swim. Now, the black cruiser gave her that same sense of freedom, as if every nook and alley of Paris were hers to discover.

Madame Palomer lived in a Beaux-Arts building on the

Rue Liancourt with winged cherubs and baroque railings. Iron boxes of magenta petunias, blue lobelia, and white alyssum lined the windows of the third-floor apartment, perfectly watered, perfectly trimmed. Renia rang the bell, re-banding her hair in a ponytail, straightening her blouse, smoothing her capri pants. The first time she'd come to this apartment had been last January. After interviewing her at a café, Palomer brought her to the apartment to sign paperwork before asking that she go directly to the shop. The rapid hire had been illegal but was small compared to the questionable inconveniences Renia had experienced since.

Palomer stuck a head out the window and called Renia's name, her voice cutting the air like a broken clarinet. Her hair, dyed a classic chestnut color, was curled and sprayed in the ways of a 1950s actress. It sparked Renia's memory of a poster for the film "French Cancan," which she'd once seen in a store window. "You have to use the stairs, dear, the elevator's broken."

Renia tapped up, swiping flies that zoomed in from the open landing windows, and knocked on the door.

"Come in," she called.

The apartment was Madame Palomer without apology. Curtains and furniture in Provençal colors of yellow and sea blue blasted cheer into the room. Paintings of still-lifes and framed pencil sketches covered the walls like a funhouse of jagged puzzles. Antique tables and book cases elbowed each other for floor space. Renia had always liked the ceramic figurines of children feeding deer and reading books and blushing with love though there were two dozen too many. Wire birdcages hung like empty prisons, devoid of birds or candles. Most greenery came from the cut flowers in vases on the dining table. The scent of freesia mingled with tangy hot camembert. Renia wanted to crack a window but the humidity outside would make the air more stagnant, so she didn't, instead giving Palomer the obligatory *bises* before sitting in the torn velvet chair across from her boss's polished rocker.

"That ridiculous elevator's been broken for five weeks," Palomer said, "and Lord knows when the repairman will get the part to fix it." She waved a Spanish fan at her neck. "Would you like some cold water, dear?"

"No, I'm fine."

"Oh good. I'm too tired to make it anyway."

Valentina Palomer was a plump lady in her early sixties, sporting wrinkles only around the eyes and mouth. She wore a silk blouse with tan slacks; a diamond wedding ring sparkled on her left hand though her husband, twenty years older than she, had passed away seven years earlier. Her feet, soft and healthy, sat in kitten-heeled sandals. That her toenails were perfectly manicured, as were her hands, always impressed Renia. Though Madame claimed to be too weak in the ankles to perform the tasks of managing a plant shop, she had little trouble maintaining her impeccable appearance.

"Renia, Renia, this is such a dark time," she said. Her blue eyes were covered by giant, black-rimmed sunglasses, donned, Renia suspected, because she'd been weeping. Their roundness burst against the scarlet wiggle of her mouth. "Alain, my Alain, our dear Alain is gone." She sat back and looked at the window as if there were a view to be seen in the closed drapes. Her profile loosely resembled Catherine Deneuve with a flatter nose. "I don't know why he did it. He was upset, of course. We all become upset, aching in the heart as it were from time to time, but . . . for him, a beautiful young man to do this." Her voice faded. She swallowed hard, fingers resting against her pinched lips.

"Yes, it's a tragedy," Renia said. "He was a good friend." When she said that, she believed it, though a memory came of Alain last spring when he'd unexpectedly stopped by her apartment and talked too much about an auction he was planning before asking her how she was feeling. She'd battled a severe cold and their conversation left her disappointed at how self-involved he could be. Now, she scolded herself for remembering the flaws of the dead.

"Of course, now what will I do with all of this fresh inventory? We're going to lose a fortune." She pointed at the small room off the kitchen that was her work area. A wooden table sat with vase after vase of lilies, dahlias, baby's breath, fern fronds, roses. On the table, rolls of wire and wrapping paper lay scattered.

"Do you know his customer?" Renia said. "Perhaps, we could still serve the account."

"I may have it," she said. "But I don't know where it is." She glanced at the hall. "Maybe in the bedroom. I can't look now, dear. I'll look later." She sighed, which almost sounded like a scoff. "Oh, beloved Alain. He was a wonderful friend and a loyal customer."

"Yes, he was."

Palomer waved the fan at her neck, its tiny griffin bounced up and down as if flying in the sky. "I'd hoped his death would be deemed an accident, that's what it seemed like to me, but we won't know until the autopsy."

The autopsy. Yes, an autopsy. That word bothered Renia. It had to be obvious to the police that he'd committed suicide. "Why are they doing an autopsy?"

"Oh, they must. They must. He didn't leave a note. It's required."

"Ah, yes," Renia said. "Did you hear about his death from François?"

François and Alain, three years in love, then out, over and over.

She nodded. "He's devastated, of course. Just devastated," her face stiffened, "then again, considering how he left Alain for that, that other man, was horrible. Horrible. A slap in the face."

"Yes," Renia said. "He must feel guilty about that."

Palomer leaned forward. "What he feels is the guilt of a murderer and rightly so."

Renia flinched. She kept her voice reassuring. "Well, he didn't murder Alain."

"In here, he did." She pointed to her heart. "In here, he was cast away for a younger prop and François now, only too late, realizes his mistake. Only too late. He's already broken it off with the other man."

"Isn't his name Mosi?"

"Well, I, for one, am glad of it," she said. "I don't know how François ever thought he could enjoy his lifestyle on a substitute cellist's money. A few jobs per week and teaching ten-year-old brats won't buy him a Rolex now." She shrugged. "Of course, maybe the new boyfriend is rich, I don't know."

Renia searched the floor for the miniature mutt that often roamed at her feet. Focusing on the incidental would soothe her boss. "Is Julo at the groomer?"

"Yes. And now Alain's family will come in from Orléans."

Alain had mentioned his parents once to Renia but not in detail. Orléans was only two hours away, and yet they didn't seem to visit their son often. "His parents live nearby?"

"Yes, and a sister. I don't know what his father does for a living, but he called me, wanted to know if I wanted any of Alain's things to sell at the shop. Can you believe his insensitivity?"

"Oh." Renia weighed whether it was rude to give away your loved one's things to sell. "Did you tell him you weren't interested?"

"No, not at all. I'll take whatever he wants to donate. I mean, after all, we're experiencing a crisis here, Renia. We won't have Alain's account anymore. Seven wonderful years, gone. We need to act. That's why I wanted you to come. You need to create a plan."

"A plan?"

"Yes, a financial plan that outlines how Le Sanctuaire will stay solvent."

Renia wanted to remind her that a plan was premature. They had enough money to buy inventory for Christmas, to pay the utility bills. The budget was tight, but they could get through it. If they were careful, they could keep Minh on through Christmas. They didn't need to panic, but Renia wouldn't dare remind her she was panicking.

"Anyway," Palomer said, "when Alain's father comes to town, go to his apartment and see what's there. I'll make a list of what would be useful. I can't go. I'm scheduled to go to Normandy for the weekend."

Again? Palomer drained the emergency cash in the safe whenever she went on weekend trips, which meant Renia paid for supplies with her own money. That would cripple the décor budget for Christmas. The worst times were when her boss withdrew money from the main bank account without warning, leaving Renia no time to plan. She stiffened, as if this would send Palomer a wordless protest.

"*D'accord*, I'll go to Alain's apartment," Renia said. She had done this kind of sorting once before when her grandmother passed away. In that case, there had only been a box of jewelry, a closet's worth of clothes, and nine pieces of furniture. Still, she and her cousins had bickered over a supposed piece of Christ's shroud that was preserved in a locket from the late 1800s. Renia wanted to keep it. Estera gave it to their cousins.

She imagined sorting through Alain's personal items. Being inside the apartment had been heartbreaking enough. Now, she'd sort through furniture, books, clothes, even old junk in storage. Her eyes settled on the Aubusson rug beneath her feet, the swirls of acanthus leaves wove into a vine pattern that seemed to have no end. Alain's innocent life ended too soon. He didn't deserve a short life, but maybe he had wanted it. And perhaps thanks to Renia's flowers, he'd gotten it.

Fatigue weighed on her shoulders. Her mouth sagged.

Palomer set a hand on Renia's forearm. Its clamminess woke her.

"Alain would have wanted us to have his things." Her voice softened. "I knew him for nine years, Renia, before he became an event planner, when he was still trying to scrape by as a violinist. I know he would have wanted us to take his things."

She nodded. Heaved in a breath. "When will the autopsy results be ready?"

Palomer sat back and fanned herself. "I don't know, who knows . . ."

Alain's death had been a suicide or an accident. Renia wondered whether the toxicology report would reveal an unknown chemical in his bloodstream. And whether that chemical could be traced to a flower. The idea that her flower . . . she felt hot, too hot.

"Also, I was thinking," Palomer said, "maybe you should keep the shop open an extra hour in the evenings. Maybe it will attract people as they commute home."

An extra hour? Renia's face hardened with resentment. "There isn't a lot of foot traffic in the evenings."

"Yes, but we have a crisis here. We must make up the income."

Renia suspected she wouldn't be paid for the extra hour she'd work every day. What a mess. A financial mess. A personal mess. A loss. She leaned forward, feeling like sludge. She thought she heard her boss say, "Consider it," but she wasn't sure. She stood up, mentioned getting back, and said goodbye. She saw herself out, slinking down the stairs.

Outside, she footed up her kickstand and pushed off on the bike. She pedaled fast, away from Palomer, away from the hidden shame she felt at not being true to herself in Palomer's presence. The sky, with its low, thickening clouds, darkened. She caught the smell of hot ink from a nearby print shop. Inside its office, the lights buzzed in a bright white; an older woman in a pants-suit sorted papers. A phone rang. Bland carpeting. A plant on a windowsill. It all took her back to another time in Kraków, a year ago, when she hadn't been true to herself either.

Last September, Renia had found a second job. The hospital where Mama worked hired her. They needed someone to file records and organize forms. Renia's duties included separating release forms, tearing off carbon copies and setting one paper to the right, one to the left, again and again. A blur of lines, names, numbers, the smell of ink. One day, at three o'clock, Renia had finished her work early. She was bored. Employees took breaks to smoke outside, so she taped an "Open in Ten Minutes" sign to the top half of the door and closed it.

On the windowsill, a snake plant grew. Its vertical leaves looked like giant, thick-leaved grass. The contrast of the tall leaves with the octagon-shaped container was interesting, so she took out her sketch pad and drew it. It was a brief glimpse into the moment of a plant, there at that time of day. When she wasn't working with plants, she loved to sketch them, just for fun. She smiled, admiring how each one was different, had its unique characteristics, bloomed to attract different pollinators, and stretched their leaves to photosynthesize. What she loved most though was how plants had a secret life of their own, a secret communication through their roots and scents. This was why she never tired of them. They gave her a wonderland to live inside where time stood still.

"Renia."

Mama. Mama had opened the top half of the door and was at the counter. She wore her white uniform, a delicate gold cross at her neck. Her hair, the color of driftwood, was curled and sprayed. She had the same large green eyes and roundish face as her daughters, but she was pudgy and short. Beside her stood four nurses and a doctor. The nurses seemed disappointed to see her sketching. The doctor, his face dour, checked his watch.

Renia's blood rushed. She rolled back from the desk, willing her hands not to shake.

Mama was everyone's friend at the hospital and everyone knew Renia was her daughter. "These are files from this morning," she said. She didn't say "they need to be refiled," or "I need you to take care of it right away," or any other instruction. She opened her eyes wide and nodded to let her know she wanted it done promptly. Her colleagues watched in silence.

One of the workers, Eva, who was no one's friend at the hospital, glanced at Renia's sketch. "Keeping busy?"

Renia took the files and said in a promising tone, "I'll have these done soon."

"Good," Eva said, "because the health of children is our top priority."

The colleagues glared as they walked off.

In a tight voice, Mama whispered, "Put away the pencils."

After Mama left, Renia sat at the desk, the stack of files on her lap. If she lowered her knee, the files would slip and fall into a spread of test results and doctor's notes and receipts on the floor. She wanted to dump them, dump them by abruptly standing up and stomping out.

Regret washed over her. She hadn't been fired, but she'd embarrassed her mother. Mama was so respected at the hospital that on her birthday, her boss brought in a cake, iced with the number of years she'd worked there: twenty-three. He didn't do that for other staff. Still, separating receipts was such a chore. And the sick children, always sick children, were everywhere. Sometimes she wondered if there were any healthy children in Kraków. She scolded herself; she should have been happy to help, she should have had her mother's attitude. They were all God's children, all in need of God's love.

Her eyes settled on the chip in a coffee mug. The truth was she didn't want to see thin children with bluish skin shuffle along the corridors. She didn't want to interact with their worried-to-death mothers, the smell of antiseptic and ammonia, or the sound of toddlers wailing in pain from exam rooms. She thought of one girl, hospitalized over a month for what Renia knew not, who walked in a permanently rickety way, one leg seemingly shorter than the other. And boys, young at eleven or twelve, appeared every few weeks with black eyes and knife cuts. Yes, there were plenty of kids in and out in a flash: for stitches, a cough, a broken arm. But others weren't. The really sick ones, who were bald and pale, were the ones that appeared in her mind again and again, on the tram, on the street, and worst of all, in her dreams at night.

The light overhead blinked, the tube buzzed. She snapped out of her thoughts. She had an urge to put the files away, hoping Eva would return to see her working in a flurry, witnessing her dedication and efficiency, but all she could manage to do was put the sketch book in her bag and zip it shut.

RENIA RODE her bike into the Rue Sereine, grateful for her job and for her apartment above Le Sanctuaire. Palomer rented it to her for a reduced rate. She was grateful that she could live in St. Germain-des-Prés itself. A neighborhood with creativity and class, a place where a person like her belonged. So, she forgave silly old Palomer and nasty Eva and hopped off the bike. She walked it down the sidewalk, forcing herself to feel grateful for her life in Paris, even if Estera wasn't with her.

The street's activity cheered her. It bustled with noise. Well-dressed diners with expensive haircuts and gold jewelry sat at tables on the bistro terrace, chatting and eating, while waiters carried trays of steaming food and chilled bottles. Some shops were open late, their interiors flooded in warm light. It was now the first day of September and residents had returned from *vacances* while tourists hadn't yet left. The street was in the midst of one last summer party and she was a small part of it.

As Renia maneuvered around a group of teenagers at the crêperie, she spotted a man standing outside Le Sanctuaire. He was stocky, of medium height, and wore a brown trilby with an argyle shirt. Dark hair, almost black, flayed out from under his hat. His face was angular, his jaw square. Smoke billowed up from his mouth. When the smoke cleared, Renia stopped. It was he. That *śmieć*. He was in Paris. He examined each woman that passed, head to toe, smiling at the ones in short dresses. As he leaned against the window, the sole of his boot sat against the wall as if he was about to push off and tackle someone, ready for a fight, or a joke, as his mood dictated.

Renia blinked. She drifted closer, then stopped. Tingles ran up her neck. He did say he had business contacts in Paris, but that he would find her here was unbelievable. Her breath quickened. Her heart beat fast. She yanked her bike around.

She ran alongside it before hopping on and churning the pedals hard, steering around the corner and out of view. The good news was he hadn't seen her—at least she didn't think so. But she couldn't go home. She thought of where to go as the world kept turning around her—cars, people, lights, chatter.

What to do . . . What time did the last train to Valenton leave? And how much cash did she have? She had no coat and the air was cooling. She rode down the Boulevard Raspail before curving into the Boulevard du Montparnasse, nearly colliding with a car making a left turn before checking over her shoulder. She expected to see him, walking the way she knew he did, with a thumb in his pocket, sauntering like his presence was a gift, but all she saw were a row of street lights, illuminating a way that went back, or forward.

CHAPTER FOUR

Later that night, Renia rode down a dark road along an open field. The black sky enveloped the flat countryside and a waxing moon lit her way. When she saw the industrial greenhouses in the distance, their gray frames rising from the ground, she nodded in relief. She'd remembered the correct turns. She coasted past the sign that read "La Pépinière des Racines" and into the dirt driveway, careful to watch for rocks and potholes. Even in the last days of summer, deep puddles dotted the ground. The tractor tires had dug rivets in the dirt before the sprinklers watered. She gripped the handlebars tightly, steering around hazards, the bike's light offering a white oval of visibility before her. It spot-lit clusters of wood pallets and stacked plastic trays. She passed greenhouse after greenhouse, surprised by two new ones she hadn't seen before. The air was autumn-cool. It chilled her arms. Just as she wished for warmth, she saw the house lamp glowing by the door.

At the stone cottage, she leaned the bike against the chopping stump with a louder clang than she intended, prompting Maya to bark. A shadow drifted to the window. She went to the stoop, about to knock, when the door opened. Uncle Feliks appeared.

His expression was flat, as if he'd been expecting her, even at ten o'clock at night. He had a narrow nose and almond eyes and a silver mustache that spread neatly over his thin mouth with a wisp of gray hair at the top and sides. It was the twin face of her father.

"I tried to call from the train," she said. The journey to Valenton had taken two hours.

"I was in House 8. The watering system's broken."

Maya, a German Shepherd mutt, trotted up and banged her tail against Renia's thigh.

She pet the dog's head, her legs aching, her fatigued mind not ready for a verbal fight. She waited to be invited in. "Are you busy?"

"Do you want a job?"

Again with that. He couldn't forgive her for leaving.

Then, like a grower whose diseased crop had fulfilled its promise of failing, he said, "Come in."

He was dressed in slacks and sweater vest and the heavy socks he wore with his boots, which meant he'd indeed been out to a greenhouse. They went into the small kitchen furnished with a Formica table and ancient appliances. It smelled sour, of fish and lemon. A few pots hung from a rack above the stove. A soapy pan lay in the sink. Scissors and twine and mail were piled on the butcher block island. A metal tray with two dozen small pots sat on the counter. Beside the tray was a plate filled with sand-colored pellets and a newspaper holding dried spinach plants. The sound of TV news rose from the sitting room. Ever since Aunt Nanette had left, he lived as if he had no one to answer to, mostly because he didn't.

He took a few spinach seeds and dropped them in pots, continuing the work she'd interrupted.

"So?" he said. His face was stern. "Another boy problem?" He referred to a man she'd dated in June who she'd thought she might be in love with. She realized she was wrong when she discovered he was avoiding his classes at law school and drinking beer every morning with friends. Feeling lost and yearning for family, she'd come to Valenton to mourn the breakup, which he'd promptly scolded her for. "Never trust men who don't make money with their hands," he'd said.

"No, not a boy problem."

He dropped two seeds in the pot, then poked them with a Popsicle stick before covering them with soil. "Business problem?"

"No."

"What then?"

She thought of what she'd seen at Le Sanctuaire. The threat that awaited. She could go one of two ways: tell the truth and risk him panicking, or create a story that might spawn a lecture. She opted for something in between, a truth but not the troublesome one in Paris.

"I'm . . . lonely."

He gave a slight purse of the lips as if he didn't have time for loneliness. Not when at sixty-seven, he'd run a nursery in the country for thirty-four years. Loneliness wasn't for a man whose sole love was plants. The silence of nature came in at a close second.

"You're lonely because you live in a city," he said.

I'm lonely because the one person who understands me is in Poland.

"Constant noise everywhere, traffic, loud engines, and trucks." He waved a hand. "The city's for visiting, not living. You can't escape it. And people only do by retreating to their little snuff boxes until the night passes and they must survive it all over again."

She waited for him to talk about the factories outside of Kraków. That was his specialty, which would inevitably lead to talk of her father and the "silly notion" that Feliks owed Feodor money. A twelve-year debt grudge had prevented them from speaking, a grudge whose origins Renia hardly knew and didn't care to remember.

"When you've had enough," he said, "you can come back. My house isn't too small. The office fits a bed just fine. There's a closet. I have plenty of room." He was resuming an argument they had had last December. "I need a manager I can trust."

"Paweł is efficient."

"But not with the books. Not accounting. Too careless. Besides, he can hardly speak French even after five years. He's okay with the plants and customers, but I could use a blood relative, someone who's invested in the future to help me care for this place. We're growing. And I'm getting older." He examined a darker seed before setting it aside.

"You're not old."

"I didn't say I was old. I said, I'm getting older."

He'd never admit to the very thing that kept Palomer going: his mortality. Renia noticed the kitchen towel at her elbow on the sink. Aunt Nanette had knitted it some twenty years ago. She had been that person for him. Not only did she work the nursery counter, she knitted and sewed and canned and cleaned. Most of all, she vacuumed. Renia would not be the person to help care for Les Racines because he insisted she always do things his way, which was probably why Aunt Nanette left. Plus, Renia didn't want to live in the country. "I'll think about it," she said, which was what she always said.

He poked more seeds in the soil. Maya approached,

her tail wagging. He eyed her with a hard suspicion. The dog sat, her brown eyes alert. He put his stick down to pet her head, then took a dog biscuit from a tin and tossed it in the air.

Maya caught it with a snap, trotted away to chew.

Renia rubbed her eyes, her body feeling like gum. "Can I spend the night?"

"I'll clear the bed."

She knew the single bed in the office held stacks and stacks of file folders. Every sale he'd ever made. They needed to be sorted and stored in a proper cabinet. He, of course, had never bought a cabinet because that meant driving to an office supply store in a city.

"I'll help you," she said.

As they tucked a fresh sheet around the mattress, she imagined that *śmieć* waiting outside the shop. He'd wait for what, another hour? He could be viciously persistent when he wanted to be. But ultimately he'd slink back to wherever he was staying for the night, which may have been nowhere for all she knew. He may have wanted to sleep at her place. She shivered. The idea of him inside her apartment . . .

Tonight, she'd avoid that, but what about tomorrow? If she were lucky, he'd be too hungover to return, though he hadn't seemed drunk. She put the case on the pillow and sat down to take off her shoes. Uncle Feliks grunted a goodnight and closed the door. Tomorrow was Wednesday. Minh would open the store. She wondered if, while she was in the country, she should buy a weapon. But as she went through the choices of pepper spray, a knife, a gun, which she didn't know where to buy or how to use, a heavy drowsiness overcame her. She lay down on that lumpy, musty bed, rolled over into the blanket, and fell asleep.

. . .

THE NEXT MORNING, she woke to blasting sun in her eyes. The house was empty and quiet. In the kitchen, the tray of pots and spinach were gone. In its place was a ceramic bowl filled with ripe tomatoes, their scent meaty. She took a croissant from the breadbox, put a pad of butter on, and nibbled, noticing Maya trotting around outside. She slipped on her shoes and followed the dog as she galloped toward the greenhouses. The damp air was warming. The smell of sweet tobacco rose over the smell of dry earthy peat. Bees swerved from flower to flower. A perfect September day. Estera would've loved it. She liked the country, the fresh air, the natural life all around. Renia imagined Estera watering tomatoes with a hose, a content smile on her face.

At House 8, she came into rows of bamboo and grass plants. Black pots held short grasses that poked up like tufts of messy hair. Then knee-high Dwarf Whitestripe stood at attention before giving way to bamboo with pointed leaves like little blades. At the back, dozens of ten-foot-tall bamboo plants darkened the air as if creating an Asian forest.

A sprinkler system, attached to metal girders, hung in a low framework above Renia's head. It had a long track that spanned the length of the house with a bulky, black engine box at its center. The box was attached to a strong metal pipe that ran the width of the house, which held some twenty sprinkler emitters that faced downward. From wires attached at the ceiling, two thick hoses hung in undulating loops like giant snakes. Whenever the system crawled forward to spray plants, the hose unfurled and flattened. Clicked over and over. The engine hummed in an ominous buzz.

What an outdated robot. As she slogged down the narrow aisle, foot over foot, she called for Uncle Feliks.

The black box with its sprinkler arms lunged forward.

Woah. Renia ducked, the engine box grazing her hair. It stopped, the hoses swinging. Clicking and humming noises rang out, a buzzing, then silence.

"Uncle Feliks?"

In the corner, bamboo rustled.

"*Allô?*" she called.

"*Zut.*"

The engine box clicked once and shot forward again. Renia flinched.

The suspended hose bumped her shoulder. "Are you in here?"

His voice was curt. "Yes, yes, I'm here . . . damn thing. It's on the fritz again. Every time I use the remote, it blasts forward. I'll have to call a mechanic." He emerged from the bamboo, taking out a screwdriver from his overalls pocket, then went to the engine box and removed the case. Renia held out her hand for the screws.

After a minute, he said, "Your phone rang early this morning."

"Oh. I must have left it in the kitchen."

"It was that silly raccoon," he said. "Palomer."

"Did you talk to her?"

He scoffed. "If I answered, she would never let me hang up."

She opened her mouth to tease him about how Madame had once mentioned he was handsome, but stopped. He wouldn't be impressed.

She wanted to ask why, if he despised Palomer so much, he had introduced her and Renia, but she could predict his answer: "You wanted experience managing a business, but this business of growing plants in the clean air wasn't good enough. You wanted to be in Paris. So I gave you an opportunity to meet an employer in Paris."

He fiddled with a wire. "She called three times."

"She's concerned because a client of ours died and his account was large." She watched him take apart the engine's innards. "We don't have a means to make up the income."

"What you do," he said, "is find different kinds of customers."

Renia thought of Anna Markowska and Estera and all that had come afterward. "But what if those different customers aren't the kind of customers you want?"

"Well, sometimes in business, you must do what you have to do to make money, not what is ideal. If you don't, you will fail. It's simple."

She bristled at his lack of empathy. Feliks spoke from a successful businessman's point of view. Les Racines Nursery had rarely struggled for customers. Five years ago, a large wholesaler went out of business and he'd been forced to expand. Now, he supplied the major plant retailers in Paris and a few smaller shops like Le Sanctuaire with perennials and shrubs. But he didn't view himself as well off, only luckily in-the-black for decades. Once, she'd asked him to lend her money. He lectured her on how suffering built character. Instead of reminding him how comfortable, if modestly, he'd often been, she thought it best to be quiet and help him put his engine back together.

LATER, that afternoon, Feliks drove Renia and her bike to the train station. Instead of saying goodbye, he handed her a cloth bag filled with tomatoes and peppers and garlic. "Make a stew," he said and drove off. She boarded the train and settled in to a window seat. As she inventoried the vegetables, she noticed a group of teenagers walk by on the platform. A whiff of marijuana rose through the window, reminding her of what she was returning to, how she couldn't avoid *him*. A tight panic filled her chest. She dialed Estera's number, wondering if Estera knew he was in Paris. At the voice message, she explained the situation and asked Estera to call her, then hung up.

As the train rolled out of the station, it left the teenagers behind. She thought about when Estera started slipping away. Last year, after Renia's acceptance letter to the School of Economics arrived, she'd quit her job at Biały Manor. Whether Estera resented that, she never knew. She only knew that, as months went by, Estera spent more time in the evenings on her own, maybe selling the flower to customers like Anna Markowska, maybe with friends, maybe both. What Renia did know was how quickly Estera got sucked into his vortex.

In Kraków, one night after class, Renia waited for Estera in Planty Park. It was a cool, misty night, about eight o'clock. The park's path was ominous in the last light of dusk. Tree branches zig-zagged against the cadmium sky. The shrubs humped forward like sleeping beasts. A student carrying a stack of books passed, then a young couple. A dense hedge of yews obscured her view around the corner from where the odor of marijuana floated.

Soon, she saw the orange glow of a cigarette. Five young men. They wore brown leather jackets and chunky athletic shoes. They laughed in harsh staccatos, scanning the park as if ready for a confrontation. One had a sharp gait. One threw punches at the air. One had hollow eyes and stringy hair. He carried a portable stereo that played heavy metal music. A voice sang in a low rhythm, *"Searching . . . seek and destroy."*

Gang of losers. But they engulfed the sidewalk and would encounter her soon. She considered backing onto the grass. That made her look weak and put her in the shadows. She hardened her expression, pressed her elbow against her purse, and walked on.

As they passed, all five examined her as if she were on display for their consideration. "*Hej, dziewczyna,*" one said. "*Co robisz?*" He offered her a drag from his joint. She wanted to say, "Drop off a cliff," but didn't.

She took out her phone and dialed Estera. "I'm in the Planty. I'm getting hassled. Where are you?"

"I'm nearby, I'll see you in a minute."

One of the men jumped onto a bench and imitated a soccer kick.

Renia flinched.

They argued about strategy.

She headed for a lamp and stood beneath it.

The men bumped each other around, joking about "buttholes" and "asses."

She folded her arms and stared in the opposite direction.

A roar sounded. Hands grabbed her shoulders. She stumbled, heart pounding. She saw a face, a woman, Estera.

She exhaled. "What was that for?"

Estera laughed. "Your face was complete panic."

She yanked her arms away.

"I was playing around," Estera said.

"I know. It was . . . " she swallowed, feeling choked up, too ashamed to say she'd been frightened by the men.

Estera cupped Renia's hands in hers. "Hey, I'm sorry, I shouldn't have done that."

She nodded. She'd thought the men would drag her into the bushes.

"Are you okay?"

Renia nodded. "I'm fine."

"Listen, I have an idea to cheer you up," Estera said.

Renia smelled gin on her breath.

"Let's go to The Tomb."

"The Tomb," Renia said. "Tonight? It's Wednesday."

Estera smiled a coy smile, her face taut with a secret. "I met a guy and I want you to meet him."

"At The Tomb?"

"He works there."

Estera's face was flush, red and warm. Her eyelids drooped, her shoulders bobbed.

"How drunk are you?" Renia said.

"Me? How dare you!" she said. "Well, a little."

"I don't want to go to a loud nightclub," Renia said. "I was hoping we could eat and catch up. It's been three weeks since we spent time together."

"Well, you're the one with a night class."

Renia felt grateful to be in a prestigious business school. She was about to complete the degree she should have had as an undergraduate, instead of art history, which had never been useful for getting a job. At least Estera's horti-culture degree got her steady work.

"Come," Estera said. "We'll talk on the way there. I made some money and I want to celebrate."

Renia didn't want to celebrate how she'd made the money. "You need to work tomorrow. And I have class."

"Look, let's go for one drink, then we'll eat. I want you to meet this guy. He's insane. Has endless friends. And I really like him."

Renia checked the bench for the men. It was empty. In the distance along the path, a white bike light shown in the blackness. "I don't know," Renia said.

"He's working the door, which means we'll get in for free."

That didn't sweeten the deal. "You're dating a bouncer?"

The bike light broadened as it neared, blinding Renia.

"He's amazing," Estera said, not noticing the light, "funny, and crazy, and very cute."

Now, riding her bike from the Gare du Nord through the Latin Quarter, Renia didn't think of him as "cute." Cute was what a puppy was, cute was how an innocent child posed for a picture. He was no puppy and no innocent child. She coasted up the Rue Sereine to Le Sanctuaire, disappointed that he'd sought Renia out and Estera hadn't, but forced herself not to dwell on it. As she locked her bike to a sign post, Minh came out to water plants on the terrace. Renia quizzed her on how business had gone that day. Minh explained how it began slowly but picked up after lunch, then slowed again until an elderly lady came in and bought a rubber tree for seventy-five euros. Nothing out of the ordinary.

Renia asked about male customers. Minh said none had visited. Relieved at the news, Renia offered to water the plants so Minh could leave early and fetch her mother from the medical clinic. Later that evening, after she'd worked the extra hour as Palomer wanted, she rolled the tiered shelves into the store, watching for him. No sign. She checked up and down the street as she carried in the bistro table and chairs, wondering if she had been mistaken. She had expected to see that tan hat, those motorcycle boots. She knew that someday he might fulfill his promise but hadn't expected her parents to reveal where she worked, let alone speak to him. They'd broken their promise. As she mentally scolded Mama and Tata, she stopped and told herself to relax, to rethink this, and most importantly, plan what to do when she saw him again.

CHAPTER FIVE

On Sunday morning, Minh came to Renia's apartment to brainstorm a financial plan for Le Sanctuaire. The two drank tea by the window, discussing musical performances, horticulture classes, and free croissants to attract customers. Ultimately, those ideas necessitated money. They debated whether to contact François and pursue obtaining a list of Alain's old clients, but wondered if that seemed too brazen. In the end, they decided the business could stay afloat if they could reign in Madame Palomer's spending habits. Getting through to her was the trick. In the end, Renia promised to speak to her.

After Minh left to open the store, Renia changed into formal clothes for Alain's funeral. As she searched for her pearl earrings, she noticed Alain everywhere: in the oval mirror he'd combed his hair in once, in a ticket to the Moreau museum they'd visited, and in a rusty étagère he'd lent her money to buy. The étagère was her favorite piece of furniture. She sat in the east chair every morning so she could look at the objects she'd most recently added to her collection.

It was tall with a twisted iron framework, topped with a fleur-de-lys. On the upper shelf was a tiny, paper maché Eiffel Tower she'd made as a teenager. Below it, a Chinese tea tin Uncle Feliks had given her from his junk closet. It had gold-lined windows where inside, lovers kissed. She hid her spending money in the tin, which this week had a mere thirty euros. On the lowest shelf were her French language books, the basic textbooks from college in Poland and the more advanced from her class last spring. Scattered throughout were shop plants she'd nursed back to health: two devil's ivy, a fern, small philodendron, maroon bego-nia. The étagère was a reminder of her new vital life in Paris, though now that Alain was gone, she didn't feel very vital.

As she cleared her and Minh's dishes, she remembered how she and Alain had found her table beside a garbage bin. He'd helped carry it home, the two giggling. After-ward, he brought over rickety chairs and a fringed lamp for it. Sometimes they would drink wine there and gossip about neighbors or talk about his and François's relation-ship. Once, over coffee, she told him how she'd fallen at the Kraków train platform on the day she'd left for Paris. Her clothes and toiletries had scattered. She'd scraped a knee. A man called her a *dumb clutzy girl*. Alain's brows wrinkled, that warm hand not letting go as he reassured her that she lived in Paris now and would never experience that again. It was in the past. A past, unfortunately, that he had joined.

THE FUNERAL WAS HELD at Saint Joseph's cathedral in the 17th *arrondissement*, not far from the upscale leafy neighbor-hood of Monceau where François lived. It felt strange to ride her bike in a fancy black dress, so she took the métro. As she emerged from the station, a downpour began, and she hurried inside to search the pews for François. She wanted to say goodbye to Alain but she also wanted to learn what had happened, whether it was suicide or an accident. She ached at the idea of François knowing about the flower, and even more so at the idea of it killing Alain.

Near the altar, four string musicians began a melancholy song, signaling the start of the service so instead of searching, she slid into a seat on the side aisle. The church's nave, decorated with enormous flower arrangements, hefty candles, and framed photos of Alain, felt sadly final. The room smelled of incense. It seemed every client Alain had ever had was there: couples whose weddings he'd planned, symphony employees, people from non-profit organizations. François sat in the first row with people that looked like Alain's parents and sister, a trio she'd once seen in a family photo atop his fireplace. After the violinists played, a priest spoke. He outlined Alain's talent as an organizer of high-profile events and involvement in three local charities. "He gave in heart and action," he said. How a man regarded so highly in his professional circle had been friends with the young woman at the plant shop, Renia didn't know. He'd never cared about her age or reputation. They'd just clicked from the beginning, like easy friends.

Below the altar, a closed casket sat draped with an iridescent net of tiny birds. The closed casket worried her. Did it mean his body had been too injured for display? His sister approached the podium and spoke of their mischievous friendship as children. Later, François spoke of Alain's design talent. At telling a story of his charitable work with a *Côte d'Ivoire* family one Christmas, François wept and declared Alain the most generous man he'd ever known. Though he mentioned "human fallibility" and "depression," he didn't mention their troubled relationship or Alain's bitter unrequited end.

After the ceremony, a crowd of people consoled the Tolbert family outside the cathedral. François stood beside them. He was short, dark-eyed, and wore a pressed black suit and charcoal tie. He exchanged warm *bises* with elderly ladies in hats and hugged young gentlemen couples in suits. Now was her chance to speak with him. Despite her efforts to squeeze forward, Renia dropped back in the mass of bodies. She inched along while people funneled into the daylight. Finally near the door, she waved, but rain suddenly dropped in a thick sheet and people scattered. A few young men maneuvered in front of her, carrying giant baskets of flowers. Flowers, Renia knew, Palomer had arranged and sent through a delivery service to the church. She'd told Renia by phone she'd miss the memorial as she needed to stay an extra day in Normandy.

As the last few people hurried away, Renia arrived at the door's threshold where the priest and altar boys stood. The priest awkwardly shook her hand as car doors slammed and the gleaming hearse veered into a procession.

She sighed in frustration. Everyone had left.

Two police officers were in the street, beside their scooters, one directing traffic, one talking on an intercom. She set the hood up on her raincoat and tapped down the steps, eyeing the second officer. Tall, thin, boyish. It was Kateb, she was sure of it. He had those skinny legs and skinny arms. He wore a chunky, stiff helmet, which hid his face. She wondered if he were there to take note of who had come to the service and who hadn't.

Renia called out.

He clicked off his intercom, looked around.

She waved. "I'm . . . I'm Mademoiselle Baranczka,"

she said, "from the plant shop?"

Whether he registered her identity or not was unclear. His face remained neutral.

She made her voice soft, innocent. "I wanted to ask if you if an autopsy had been conducted. I understand there was no note. I'm concerned Alain's death might have happened because . . . of some other event." Of course, that wasn't true, but in setting that idea up, perhaps he'd negate it. Then, at least she'd know whether Alain had taken his own life.

In a flat retort, he said, "The autopsy report hasn't come back, but when it does, I can't talk about it. His parents can, but I can't."

"I understand," she said, her voice laced with disappointment. His parents had just driven away. She forced her face into a sympathetic half-smile. "But, can you tell me, I saw blood . . . a lot of blood, coming from his apartment and I need to know, did he cut himself?"

"I can't talk about it."

"Was it, do you think a suicide? It's important for me to know. I was a close friend."

Kateb's leg bounced in a nervous tick. "You didn't tell me that before. How close?"

"Well," she hesitated, noticed a dandelion growing from a crack in the sidewalk. *Be honest.* "As close as a business person can be to another business person. I mean, we used to have dinner occasionally. I sold him flowers and plants every few weeks."

He wiped his nose with a quick finger. "So not involved in an intimate way."

"Oh no. Alain—" She stopped. She wasn't sure if she should mention that he was gay and had zero interest in her.

"Yes. Okay," he said.

"Please," she said. "I was wondering, was his mind altered, maybe . . . from drugs or alcohol?"

She could've been setting herself up for questioning but took a chance. If a chemical did show in Alain's blood, no one could trace where it came from. At least she didn't think so. The Violet Smoke was a never-before-seen hybrid. And she'd removed the flowers from the apartment. Of course, photos may have been taken. But no one had seen Alain take the flowers from Le Sanctuaire and she doubted he'd told François—though it was possible.

"Why? Do you think he had a drug problem?" Kateb said. "Did you sell him drugs?"

Drugs? Goodness, no. She wouldn't call it drugs, but what would she call it? "No, no. I mean when you saw him, could you tell whether he accidentally was cut, or did it look more self-inflicted?"

Kateb glanced around. "I can't tell you that. I'm not going to tell you that he may have hit his head because I don't know." He paused and stared at her an extra second too long.

She nodded.

"I have to go," he said.

The last car, François's, was down the street, idling at a stop light.

"Can I call you to check in?" Renia asked.

Kateb threw a leg over his scooter. "Why do you want to do that?"

"Because, because, I can't bear to be . . . " she stopped from saying, *prosecuted and sent back to Poland,* and instead expressed another true feeling: "I can't bear to think he suffered before he died."

LATER, at Le Sanctuaire, Minh stood on the terrace with a

customer, talking about how to winterize a 'Dangerous Beauty' dahlia. Damp and chilled from the earlier rain, Renia mumbled "I'm not here" as she passed and went in the atrium. She closed the door, shook out her coat before hanging it on the hook, and sat down, letting go a listless breath. Outside the bank of windows, the neglected courtyard lay in shadowed silence. On the eastern side, a few dead weeds leaned toward a thistle that had grown between the cobbles. The thistle's flower had already faded to a white tuft, ready to throw a hundred seeds to the wind and bring about more prickly problems. On the western side, a brief row of unclipped boxwood sagged beside a broken bench someone had set out years before, a resting place where no one rested.

Renia imagined the forensic doctors discovering an herbal relative of a narcotic in Alain's bloodstream. He'd been addicted to natural medicines, popping supplements for the slightest ailment or prevention trend. After fearing the police would discover a toxic chemical in his blood and link it to the flower, she felt a dreadful finality in her heart. Alain was dead. Her fault or not, she'd never see him again. There would be no more shopping excursions, no more morning chats in the shop, no more dinners in the Latin Quarter, her smiling as he teased about which passing scruffy student should be her boyfriend. To her surprise, the depression had won. He'd started ordering arrangements by email, stopped texting her, gave one-word answers when she asked how he was. He'd hole up in his apartment for days, in his bathrobe, unshaven, hair unwashed. When she'd stop by to bring him leftover flowers, he was blank faced, unmoved by the gesture. Now, he was a body in a coffin, and she . . . alive and helpless, a vine struggling to survive in sudden shade.

Through the door, Minh's voice popped in animated

exclamations. A man's voice answered. They laughed. The shop had grown busy.

She considered leaving to help but stayed to think. She had to figure out a next step. What she *could* do until she learned the autopsy results. From her bag, she dug out her phone and dialed François's number to get Alain's parents' number but remembered they were all at the memorial luncheon. A luncheon she hadn't been invited to and couldn't have stomached anyway. She hit the End button and tossed the phone on the counter. It landed with a thud in a scattering of dirt. A puff of dry grit billowed up.

The door opened. Minh poked her head in. "Sorry to bother you. Can we order 'Black Ghost' tulips from Poland?"

Renia shrugged. "Of course." Many retailers ordered tulips from Poland.

The door closed. She teased apart a nearby clump of dried moss, thinking about the one task she could do. The one task she'd wanted Estera to do a year-and-a-half ago. Renia had vowed to do it again last week but hadn't carried through. Contact a botanist, a plant breeder. An expert that could determine how dangerous the Violet Smoke was. To find that out would not only ease her conscience but would honor Alain. But where to find one? She got up and opened the door, marching into the store. "Minh, is there a horticulture school in the Parisian university system?"

There he was.

She swallowed her shock, stifling any hint of surprise in her face.

He leaned against the counter, arms folded casually like he belonged there. Zbigniew. Zbigniew Wójcik. Zbiggy. Silly name. Even sillier person if he wasn't so dangerous.

Her heart sank.

He was as oddly good-looking as she remembered: strong nose, close-set eyes, blocky chin. His mouth was a brief line that looked like a knife. He smiled in a sly pinch, as if he'd been waiting for her to stumble into him. In broken French, he said, "So *Pani* Baranczka isn't so busy. Hey, Polish girl, I didn't know you owned this place."

"I don't."

She wanted to ask what he was doing in Paris and how he'd found her, but she didn't. She glanced at Minh, who was thankfully oblivious of the problem. She stood behind the counter with a pen and pad, smiling at the long list of plants on the receipt.

"This gentleman would like to buy plants," Minh said. She tapped the pen against a credit card in excitement. It was a big sale, she must have thought, a sale that could save them for the month. "He asked about you, said you two were old friends, but I thought it best we settle up first."

"Yeah," he said, "your assistant's been really helpful. You know how it is when you need a special plant but like, can't find just the right one." With a self-satisfied smile, he rested his hand on a cart with an odd collection of ferns, geraniums, hostas, the last of the tender fuchsias. The most expensive plants were 'Ozawa' alliums whose drooping flowers impressed plant collectors. Desert succulents too. Unusual choices. None of which made sense for end-of-season planting. They had been randomly chosen, as if to kill time, as if he'd been waiting.

In a controlled voice, she said, "Minh, why don't you take a ten-minute break? I'll help this gentleman."

Her smile withered. "Well . . . alright, but I've got the list written up. The total cost is here. All you have to do is run this through." She waved the card around as if to say, "Here's our ticket to solvency," and laid it on the counter.

"I'll make sure to do that," Renia said. She took the list and waited as Minh left, staring him down. She wanted him to know she wasn't intimidated, wasn't disturbed even though the fact that he'd found her in Paris rattled her to her toes. His eyes were a washed out brown, not pathetic like Monsieur Armand's, nor pronounced like Kateb's, nor even unintentionally aggressive like Uncle Feliks's. Just forgettable, the color of a thin muddy pond.

After the door clicked shut, Renia ripped the list in half. In Polish she said, "What do you want?"

"Are you surprised to see me?"

"Is anyone surprised to see a spider? Yes, but not in a good way."

She reached far over the counter and slid up the dimmer switch, brightening the lights to the highest setting. She wanted all passersby on the sidewalk to see them clearly.

"I thought we were friends, Renia."

She watched him like a mother watches a child who's standing on the back of a sofa, ready to slip and crash into a glass lamp.

Friends? What a joke. "Were we ever friends?"

"This is a really nice place, where you work now."

He scanned the room, taking an inventory.

She tracked his eyes as they landed on each object: large fountain with a statue (too heavy to steal), dozens of plants in the windows (not worth stealing), tables of soaps and lotions and books (perhaps worth stealing for personal use), and earrings on a rack (definitely worth stealing). At least he hadn't noticed the two stereo speakers in the corners.

"Why are you here, Zbiggy?"

"What do you mean? I came to see you, Polish girl." He

spoke as if she should be excited by his thoughtfulness, as if she should be impressed with the shimmery suit coat he wore and his clean trimmed nails. He tipped his hat back, in an almost challenging way, so that Renia had to notice his square forehead and angular face—a face that said, *I'm here. Deal with it.*

"And why did you come to see me?" Her voice was as dead as dead was, even though her heart thumped. How had he found her?

"Because you called us, right?"

"I never called you."

"But you called your sister."

She willed herself to stay silent. He couldn't know she'd called. Then again . . . but Estera had no idea where she was.

"Your sister and I want your help. Since you screwed her over, and me, it's only fair you help us." His tone was casual, but she heard the anger beneath. He roamed around, scanning the lacy button plants and thin-leaved lettuce in the windows, eyeing the delicate life on the tables outside. He tapped a restless hand on the cart. She half-expected him to bat an arm at everything and send dirt and pots flying. "Don't you feel terrible about what you did to your sister?"

Renia thought about the last time she'd seen her. What Renia had done was end a toxic situation. Yes, she had regrets. After all, Estera wasn't with her in Paris, but she'd had no options. And her choice had worked, at least until now. "No, I don't."

"Well, maybe you should."

She wanted to say *Don't tell me what to feel* and *Get the hell out of my store*, but she swallowed her thoughts. His rage was wilder than hers.

"Hey, anyway, let bygones be bygones, right?" he said.

"If by saving my sister's life, you mean bygones, then yes."

"I'm here to give you a chance to make it up to us," he said. "And I know you want to."

"Make it up to *us*?"

"Yeah, me and your sister."

She bristled. He was lying, lying to get at her. But she wouldn't bite.

"Renia, do you know how sometimes you say something and wish you could take it back? You wish the person who heard it had never heard it?"

What a ridiculous question. How rich when a man who'd not only said horrible things but done horrible things expressed fake regret. But she knew this wasn't about regret. "No."

"Or you remember something you wish you hadn't?"

Unconsciously, she stepped back, bumping the counter. "No."

"Well, a lot of people do, Renia." His eyes examined her from top to bottom. "A lot of people do—even in pretty Paris."

She stiffened.

"The market for that is great here," he said. "People will pay even more money than in Poland to forget what they don't want to remember."

Her mouth tasted sour. "You've wasted your time coming." She set a hand on the counter, touched a sticky patch of an unknown substance. "I don't have it."

He came toward her, a look of surprised confusion on his face. "You don't?"

She shook her head and held his stare. If she didn't, she knew she might glance at the atrium. The door was open. It would be all over. She breathed out slowly and steadily.

"See Renia," he said, "Estera told me you have the plant."

Hearing her sister's name spoken aloud by this creep, after such a long stretch of time, felt sacrilegious.

"No, she didn't."

"How do you think I found you?"

She imagined Estera speaking to Zbiggy about her. She wouldn't have. Estera wouldn't give Renia the dignity of her mental energy. Then again, Renia hadn't spoken to Mama in a few weeks, so things may have changed. He *had* appeared a mere four days after she'd called Estera. "I don't believe it."

"It's true. Estera and I are back together."

That was a punch. The idea made her nauseated.

"Yeah, and she wants me to sell the Violet Smoke flowers."

Had he always known the plant's name? It sounded pornographic coming from his lips. She wanted to spit on his shoes, on his motorcycle boots with their pointed steel toes. "I chopped it up before I left," she said. That lie was a risk, but she bet he couldn't confirm it.

He blinked in a bitter smile. "Look, I'll lay it out for you, Renia. I'm staying in Paris a while."

"Where? Under a bridge?"

"I'm crashing at my cousin's."

"Then why isn't Estera with you?"

"You know she can't travel."

Another lie? Not sure. The bottom line was he was in Le Sanctuaire, where she worked, and could come back anytime.

"My cousin, he owns a bar in the 18th. And he has customers who want your little plant. Good money. One hundred euros a piece. Are you going to turn down good money?" His attention went to the atrium. "This is a fancy shop you work in, must be a nice lifestyle. But Paris is an expensive place to live, isn't it?" He touched a glossy design book, tapped a silver necklace on a stand. It had a mother-of-pearl pendant. "All the nice clothes and nice jewelry a poor girl from Poland has to afford."

Her fingers trembled. She folded her arms to still them.

He spun the rack of earrings on the counter. "Hey, I recognize that. Amber from the Baltic Sea. That's like, so precious. How do you keep all these precious gems safe?"

A slap to his face would've felt great. Knock the dumb hipster hat off his head. But she knew she'd lose a physical battle. She raced to think of what might intimidate him. The credit card. The name on it was Charles Arsenault. She grabbed the card and went to the shop door. "You know, I wonder what the police will think when they learn a man tried to fraudulently use Charles Arsenault's credit card."

He blinked, wandered to the door, trailing a finger through the fountain's bubbling water. The goddess with her urn, a calm face tilted, seemed to track his finger. "I see you need more time to think about it."

She opened the door, happy that he was closer to it but unhappy because he was closer to her body. "Leave. Now."

"There's money in it for both you and me—and Estera. She lost her job you know."

He pulled out a Gauloises cigarette and stuck it between his teeth. The harsh smell of tobacco hit her nose. She chewed her lip. It might be true that Estera had lost her job. She'd been badly hurt. But more likely she was—

The smell of tobacco reminded her of Kawa Tomasza. That scummy diner. Last September. Early morning. Scraped paint on the walls. Broken floor tiles. Stains on the chair cushions. She'd found Estera slumped in a booth, sipping coffee, in a stained blouse and her sequin skirt. The odor of cigarettes rose from her streaked hair like smoke from a chimney.

"And why didn't he take you two home?" Renia said. She stood over the chipped table. A wrecked plate of half-eaten fried eggs and chomped toast lay before Estera. An ashtray jammed with cigarette butts.

Estera sipped black coffee. "He had to work."

"Work? I thought he worked nights."

She flinched. "Quieter, Renia. I'm battling a killer headache." She closed her eyes, her lips wrinkled. "He had . . . other work to do."

"Where is she? I have to be at the hospital by nine."

"Shhh. Not so loud, Renia. There." She threw a thumb over her shoulder. In the next booth, a young girl in a tight dress with dyed auburn hair, slouched to the side, earrings spread across her cheeks as she slept. Their neighbor, Sylwia Kozłowska.

"Let's get her home," Renia said, "and get you cleaned up before Mama notices you were out all night."

She gulped her coffee. "They already know. I told Tata I'm moving out. He threatened to lock me out."

"Moving? Where, to France?"

She puffed a smile. "No. In with Zbig."

Renia set her hands on her hips, her stomach churning. "I know he's fun, Estera, but he won't be fun anymore when you live together. Now, let's go."

Estera called to the waiter and set two bills under her cup, then helped Renia lift Sylwia out of the booth. As they hooked the girl's arms around their necks and walked her drowsy body to the door, Estera said, "Actually, I think living with Zbig will be more fun. His apartment is near the club and he's got a cool roommate who's loaded. Yuri pays for everything."

Renia struggled under the stumbling body of Sylwia.

"And what does he do, steal cars?"

"What?" Estera frowned. "No. Does it matter where he gets his money from?"

As Renia swung open the exit door and they emerged into the bright chaotic city, she said, "Yes, I think it does matter where his money comes from."

As RENIA OPENED the door of Le Sanctuaire, fresh air and bright, cloudy daylight filled the room. The zooming sounds of mid-day traffic echoed. People hurried along the sidewalk carrying purses and briefcases, talking on phones. Across the street, Vida Nova's terrace bustled. Two couples, in suits and dresses, ate a late lunch. Their delicate laughter rang out. The waiter uncorked a bottle of wine and displayed the label for the closest gentleman. A refined *bossa nova* played with sensuous singing. On the sidewalk, the travel agent next door, Justine, a woman of a certain age in a sleek blue skirt and jacket, waved as she got in her glossy Jaguar. Renia forced herself to smile and wave back. Sophisticated Parisians never dealt with slimes like Zbiggy.

A gardenia scent floated in, clearing Renia's mind. Zbiggy hadn't seen Estera. They weren't back together, no way. With a firm resolve, she said, "Goodbye, Zbigniew."

"Think about it, Polish girl. I'll be in touch."

After he left, Renia shut the door and locked it. She cut up the credit card and tossed it in the trash, then fetched a rag and spray and wiped the sticky residue from the counter. Soon, Minh returned, knocking on the window. As Renia unlocked the door, Minh noticed the cart, still filled with plants. "What happened?"

"Oh. He changed his mind, couldn't find the plant he really wanted. We'll need to re-shelve those and put everything back in order."

CHAPTER SIX

The next morning, after her panic subsided, Renia's curiosity grew. She wondered if Mama had indeed told Estera that Renia had gone to Paris. That she worked in Saint-Germain. They'd agreed she wouldn't, though Mama had never been satisfied with that agreement. After Renia unlocked the shop and switched on the *Ouvert* sign, she dialed the Kraków apartment. No answer. She left a message asking Mama if Zbiggy had contacted her and hung up. The idea of Estera reuniting with him seemed laughable, then again, slightly possible.

She phoned Estera.

When the voicemail clicked on, she left a message. "Hey. I know we may never speak again, and I'm willing to accept that, but Zbiggy came to where I work today and told me you've lost your job. Is that true? I need to know, Steri. I need to know whether I should help him or not. He said you need money. Do you need money? Please call me back."

Afterward, she shut and locked the atrium door and got out the crow bar to pry out the panel. *Don't be a fool. He won't help her.* Through the tiny Wardian Case windows, she examined the Violet Smoke. The five blooms from the cluster Alain had clipped had expired. To their left on a lower branch, another cluster grew. She debated whether to cut and toss them away. It was wrong to leave them just in case. Still, they were already magenta, a lovely beam of color, like a small gift in her day. So, she let them be.

Before she'd encountered Zbiggy, Renia had intended on calling the horticulture university. While online the previous night, she'd found the phone number for Edogogo Bankole, *Directeur de l'horticulture* at HortPolytech. But now, staring at her note with the number, she hesitated to dial. It was a risk to let an outsider know about the Violet Smoke.

She opened the vent to air out the greenhouse, then held her breath and hurried out to push the wall panel back in place. She wrote a list of inventory to buy for Christmas. She opened her laptop, dented at the corner and taped at one edge, and checked the Le Sanctuaire bank account. Yes, the deposit she'd made on Friday had registered: six hundred euros. But to her surprise, the account was short three hundred euros. A withdrawal had been made on Saturday. Palomer. *Merde.* How to convince her to stop dipping into the account?

With a frustrated stillness, she sat a moment. Palomer might change if Renia spoke to her about it, but Renia couldn't do it. She'd promised Minh she would but then imagined Palomer's appalled face, the awkward conversation. Being accused of insulting a long-established business woman. Even losing her job. Her breath quivered. Too frightening. Well, who *could* she speak to? What could she change? She grabbed her phone and punched in Director Bankole's number.

His phone rang three times. As she was about to hit End, he answered. His voice was deep, masculine, tinged with an African accent. Maybe West Africa, she wasn't sure. She explained she managed a shop in Paris and had a plant she needed assistance identifying. It wasn't hers but a friend's, she said, and it seemed to possess a special scent that she, nor anyone else, had encountered before.

In a slow cadence, he said, "And what is your name?"

Instead of answering, she said, "May I show you the plant?" She sounded artificial, as if her voice were another person's voice, and panicked. She ended the call, shaking her head. Bad idea.

Outside the atrium windows, a robin landed on a broken branch in the boxwood, trying to balance before it launched into flight.

Guilt squeezed her stomach. She exhaled a long breath. *You're not guilty of a crime. You didn't kill Alain.* She wondered if Kateb would monitor her calls. But why would he? Alain had appeared to commit suicide. And a plant shop manager calling a professor was not unusual. She could be seeking botanical information, which she actually was doing.

She hit Redial.

When he answered, she said, "Professor Bankole?"

"Yes."

"I'm sorry, we were cut off. My name is Renia Baranczka. As I said, I'm having trouble identifying a plant. I hope you can help me. I'll pay you for your time."

He didn't hesitate nor did he seem eager. His voice was low and steady. "Is it possible to bring the plant to the university?"

"I'm afraid not. It grows in a small glasshouse. It's difficult to transport."

"Hmm, I understand."

Silence.

"I suggest you inquire about your specimen at a local nursery," he said.

"Nursery?"

"Yes. I'm certain you can take a cutting to a retailer and they will help you identify your plant."

"But I am a retailer. And it's not only the identification, it's . . . " She couldn't say more without incriminating herself.

"Though I'm sure this plant has much value to you," he said, "we at the university must use our time to focus on research. I find that what's rare to one person is quite common to another. A professional, for instance, a plant buyer who knows botanical classification, I'm sure, can assist you."

Renia fisted her hand. "I am a professional buyer. I manage a plant shop. I know botanical classification, at least for European flora. I assure you this is an unusual plant. It needs a researcher's attention."

His voice was brittle. "Mademoiselle, you are requesting a doctor's call regarding a plant that's most likely a variation on a mass-produced, supermarket ornament."

Her body warmed. "Sir, I assure you, if you examine this plant, you'll discover that this is no 'supermarket ornament.'" Her neck grew hot. "I urge you to visit so that you can verify this in person."

"I'm sorry, I'm very busy at the moment."

"I'm willing to pay you for your time."

Silence. "I don't have my calendar with me, but I urge you to check with a large nursery first."

"I urge you to visit so you can apologize to me in person. Goodbye."

Her heart raced. The damned thing may have killed her friend, and some haughty professor accused her of ignorance. She tapped a finger on the counter, ruminating on his snobbery, then got up, remembering the more pressing work she had to do. In the store, the peels from an orange she'd eaten earlier sat on the counter. Its crisp citrus scent launched images of her father, a flickering TV. The window behind, a blinking antenna tower. The sound of the fridge slamming. Lamp light. A knitting basket. Crucifix on the wall. Renia took off her boots in the entry-way, hearing the neutral voice of a journalist.

Tata sat in his chair, dozing, the remote control about to slip from his hand. On the television, a TVP3 reporter stood with a microphone in a kitchen, talking about the trend of burning potpourri to freshen air. "Many believe simmering the leaves and petals of flowers is safe," he said. "But the plants release toxins in the air, creating hazards for both pets and humans."

Orange peels and rose petals simmered in a pot of water on a stove. Steam rose. A young woman bounced a baby in her arms. "I like the way it smells," she said. "Inhaling the scent makes me happy."

Renia thought of the Violet Smoke. She'd seen Estera come out of Pan Górski's orchid house that day, a guilty smile on her face. Renia went to the bedroom, closed the door, and called her. When she answered, she told her she didn't think Anna Markowska or Sylwia or Zbiggy's friends should inhale the flower. Its scent could be harmful.

"Don't be silly, it's natural. It smells like an apricot," Estera said.

"A burnt one."

"Well, Anna Markowska wasn't poisoned, was she? In fact, I'm seeing her on Saturday. And Tata wasn't poisoned, was he? He's perfectly fine."

A few months earlier, a plane had crashed in Russia. All of the passengers died. They were on their way to the

Katyn Massacre Memorial. Tata saw the aftermath on the news. The plane had emerged from the fog too low. It skimmed into trees, then rolled as the pilots lost control and flew upside down before ramming into the ground. Blasted apart. Bodies thrown. Luggage strewn. President Kaczyński, dead. His wife, dead. With the hull in the woods and the nose in the open, the plane blew smoke in the air, mixing with fog up to a white sky. The runway, a flat open expanse of concrete, sat waiting with its small lights aglow, meters away from the plane. At the sight of it, Tata had cried out.

"Poland, once again, attacked by the Russians," he'd said. He'd stormed around, insisting Putin had orchestrated the crash, ordered Kaczynski and the other families murdered That they, the Baranczki family, had a distant relation to the late admiral, Czernicki, prolonged her father's outrage.

For days, he watched newscast after newscast, growing more distraught. He'd bellow about politics at dinner and argue with Mama before bed. At first, she reasoned with him but after several days, she couldn't take it and argued that even if Putin had planned it, they could do nothing about it. One evening, as he watched more coverage on television, Estera set the flower on the piano beside his chair. He fell asleep instantly, slept eight hours. After he woke, he didn't speak of the incident. It wasn't until Mama, days later, reminded him that he regained the memory. But by then, he only vaguely remembered the incident and wasn't as upset.

"Yes," Renia said, "but exactly what happened to Tata's mind? You don't know. I saw a report on the news. It said burning flowers in water releases toxins."

Estera snapped with a proud annoyance. "I don't burn the flower. I don't do anything to it. It's all natural."

"Yes, well, tar is natural."

"This isn't tar, Renia."

"But what do you really know about it?"

"I know it can help prune your memories," Estera said. "And I'm helping people trim off what they don't want."

How quaint. To Renia, Estera stayed out late with friends more often than helped people but she set that opinion aside. "You said the smell gave you a headache."

"Not after you wake up. In fact, people tell me they feel better than before."

"But it's like alcohol or radiation, it could have long-term effects we don't know about."

Estera's voice strengthened. "Renia, I'm not hurting anyone. I'm helping."

Then why don't you tell Mama about it?

"This plant has changed my life," Estera said, "and other lives—for the better. You're the only one who's not supportive."

THE NEXT DAY, Renia regretted how she'd ended her call with Director Bankole. If she wished to honor Alain's memory, she needed to learn more about the Violet Smoke. So, on Wednesday, she called Bankole and apologized. She described the plant in more detail, cataloging its unique botanical characteristics: a hybridized cultivar, a branching structure on a traditionally basal plant, profusion of hairs on the stems, flowers that resembled African violets but were larger. Bankole listened with neutral responses. It sounded intriguing, he said, but he normally did not make identification outings. If she could send a photo, he'd consider her invitation. She made no promises and thanked him.

On Friday, Renia added autumn plants to Le Sanctuaire's terrace while bringing the last summer stock indoors. The 'Heaven's Chance' hydrangea had declined into sagging branches and wilted leaves. Over the summer, it had grown in a robust burst, producing large blossoms, but the flowers' red color had faded and the plant's roots had overgrown the pot. It was strangling itself. She took it to the atrium, laid it on its side, and gently teased out the sickly thing, pulling tenderly at its brown roots and detangling. In helping a living being, one that couldn't talk or cry but only survive in its own quiet world, she felt whole.

Afterward, she set the plant in a larger pot and dressed it with soil. She watered, waited for the spongy earth to drain, and watered again, smelling the wet loam. In a few hours, the plant's leaves would no longer sag. They would hold themselves straight outward, green platforms ready to soak in the light and make food. That's how the hydrangea would let her know it appreciated her effort and that's how she'd feel successful.

A knock on the door sounded from the other room. She went in the store as Professor Bankole entered. He was tall, bald, an African-Frenchman, with large slim hands. He wore a button-down dress shirt, long sleeves despite the heat, and khaki slacks. Dress shoes tied with shoestrings of white and green colors. He wore no hat and beads of sweat floated on his chocolate-colored forehead. His eyes seemed confident and serene.

Renia went to shake his hand. "Thank you for fitting me in your schedule. I'm happy to pay you a fee."

"It's nothing," he said. "No fee required. Your photo raised my curiosity."

Yes, the slightly blurry portrait she hadn't been happy to send but did out of necessity.

Renia locked the shop door and flipped off the *Ouvert* sign before leading him to the atrium, passing a small concrete statue of a dragon. It perched atop the armoire, its wings spread, mouth open, eyes fierce, about to breathe fire. Once they were inside the atrium, she closed the door. He watched her, a shadow passing over his face when she made sure to turn the lock and slide the bolt. She noticed his concerned look and said, "It's best that no one interrupts us."

She dug around under the counter and found two gas masks. Minh knew of the Violet Smoke but not of its special trait, she only knew that when a person inhaled the scent, they got a headache. So, Renia kept two masks for when she and Minh removed the greenhouse to water the plant. "Do you think this will fit?"

His large body overtook the small space and yet his wide eyes betrayed his worry. "Is this a harmful situation?"

"No, it's not. Well . . . no."

His lips were pursed, his brown eyes focused on her next move. She plopped the masks on the counter. "I should start from the beginning. This plant, it produces a strong odor. Some find it painful. It can . . . can . . . " she stopped herself from confessing too much. "I'll tell you more after you see it. You may know it and what it does." She held out the mask. "Please."

He stared at it, then took it and loosened the strap, set it over his face, transforming himself into a goggled astronaut. Renia slipped her mask on and took the crowbar from the high ledge. Bankole stepped back and she smiled, trying to soothe his uncertainty. With a confident slap, she stuck the bar in the seam between the panel and stone wall, yanked, and cranked it free.

As she dragged it aside, Bankole said, "I see you've done this before. May I help?"

She forgot to answer, and instead leaned the panel

against the door, making sure it wouldn't waver and fall forward.

As they approached the Violet Smoke, Renia noticed Bankole's eyes. Mesmerized. She felt a tiny sense of pride as she flipped the window vent shut and set both hands on the Wardian Case to lift it. He took one end and they carefully set it on the floor.

"This is it," she said. It had three blossoms. In a hidden tier of foliage, another four buds had grown.

Bankole crouched. "Fascinating." He rubbed his ear in thought. "It has the leaves and inflorescences of *Saintpaulia* but I've never seen a trunk as woody and branched as this. Where did you discover it?"

"I didn't. My sister and I worked on an estate where the owner was an amateur breeder. He crossed this with another plant, but he couldn't remember what."

"*Alors*, a homemade hybrid." From his front pocket, he took out a pair of clean cotton gloves and put them on, gently lifted the leaf to examine its underside. "The branch structure reminds me of *Crassula ovata*, but the leaf formation is uniquely *Saintpaulia*." After examining the twisting branches, he said, "Not truly *Crassula*, but a vague resemblance."

"A Jade plant?"

He nodded, pulled a miniature ruler from his pocket, and crawled below the shrub to measure the space between leaf nodes. "The internodes are one centimeter at best. And here," he counted each leaf node from the plant's main trunk through to the highest branch, then double checked his work by counting other branch leaf nodes. "My estimation is that this plant is twenty-two years old."

The turgid, upward-facing leaves made the Violet Smoke seem newly born to Renia.

"How much water does it prefer?" he said.

"It likes to dry out for long periods but when I water it, I water two times in two days. It seems to bloom more when I do that."

"Ah yes, like a monsoon in the desert."

"Yes, but it also likes moist air, like a tropical." She was about to ask if he'd ever seen blooms on African violets as large as these when he interrupted her thought.

"And have you had any incidence of Botrytis?" he said.

"The disease?"

"Yes, you would see yellow edges or spots."

"No, I often take off the glasshouse for air circulation."

"*Alors*," he said. "This is most exciting." He took out his phone and tapped the camera icon.

Renia's hand touched his. "You already have a photo."

Through the gray goggles, his eyes blinked slowly. "But that is a distant, overall portrait. If I could photograph the leaf structure and inflorescences, it would be most helpful."

She considered it. A quick identification would be ideal, but not worth the risk. "I'm sorry, I'm not comfortable with a lot of photos circulating."

He opened his mouth, closed it. He set the phone in his back pocket and stood erect. "That limits me to local colleagues."

She preserved her determined expression.

After a few seconds, as if he'd become suddenly aware of his mask, he said, "Ms. Baranczka, what do you know about the toxicity of this plant?"

His body filled the entire space between them. She shrank back, felt the damp air of the store's stone wall. "Nothing. That's why you're here."

"Then it will mean little to you if I remove this mask." He reached a hand for the bottom, but she came forward.

"No, you shouldn't."

"Ms. Baranczka," he said. He pronounced her name

with a musicality she hadn't encountered before. She imagined him singing in a men's choir. "Why am I wearing a mask when standing beside this plant? Why do you hide it behind a false wall?"

She looked from his mask to the plant, back again. *Stay with the story or trust him?* "As I said, its scent gives people headaches."

"Why not clip the flowers?"

"I do. I mean, I have. But I need to let it bloom as it likes. Otherwise it wilts from stress."

He folded his arms. "And how severe are these headaches?"

"Well, not very, they're slight, but it has made some people faint." If she told another person about the secret, another person may be an accomplice. *Relax, it didn't kill Alain. Okay, maybe it did. But he doesn't know that.* This man didn't know about Pan Górski, he didn't know what happened to Estera, he didn't know about Zbiggy, and he certainly didn't know about Alain. Nor did he need to.

"That's not fully true," she said. "A person doesn't exactly faint, they fall asleep. Before they fall asleep, they can get a slight pain in their forehead." She didn't want to sound as if she knew too much about it, had too much experience with it, so she added, "It seems so anyway."

His face locked on hers, his eyes shifted to the floor as if he'd been exposed to secret information. "How long have you had it?"

The truth, or lie? She weighed her options. "About nine months."

"And why haven't you contacted a botanist prior to today?"

Because Alain hadn't died.

"I wanted to but . . . I've . . . I'm new to Paris. I've been establishing my career, my life here, learning the language. I've been very busy."

He seemed to accept that answer. "And how long do the flowers bloom?"

"Once cut? Or on the plant?"

"Eh, both."

"On the plant, several days, when cut, about two days."

"Interesting."

She wondered if she should mention putting the stems in water prolonged the bloom time, but that may have been obvious.

He circled the plant. "You won't reconsider more photos? Or allow me to take a cutting? It would be helpful to examine its vascular system and meristematic tissue."

Her breath jittered. A photo, a cutting? She wanted the interview to finish. He didn't recognize the Violet Smoke, so she wanted him gone. "No, no cuttings. And no more photos, please. I prefer . . . discretion. This is unusual, and it's back here so as not to alarm anyone."

"Alright. I think I've seen enough."

Renia stirred to lift the glasshouse but Bankole picked up the case first and set it over the plant.

She opened an atrium window to air out the space. A cool breeze blew in.

Bankole leaned on the counter, both hands pushing against it as if he were sorting out ideas. After a moment, he said, "You've shown me a truly unique specimen. I've never seen anything like it."

Her hope plummeted. "Never?"

"I'd like to consult at least one other colleague. He will need to study it in person if no other photos are allowed."

She debated what to do. Another stranger equaled more risk.

He frowned. "Mademoiselle Baranczka, are you inter-ested in propagating and selling this plant? Do you want to be first in the market with it?"

"No, no, of course not." She took off her mask. "It's just . . . I know it's unusual and I don't want to cause a stir."

"Is it yours?"

She bit her lip. *Kind of?* "Yes."

Bankole nodded, took off his mask. "I will be discreet, and you have my confidence, but I'd like my colleague to see it. He's worked for several years in plant hybridization."

"Alright," she said. "But how is he at discretion? I mean, I wouldn't want a botanist getting hold of this and using it to forward their own reputation." That was a lie. She wanted to emphasize secrecy.

Bankole flashed a bitter smile. "Excuse me, Mademoi-selle, but we botanists are hardly a cabal of people with nefarious, impulsive intentions. We are scientists seeking the truth."

"Of course."

As Bankole helped position the wall panel back in place, he said, "I will pass along your information to him today."

His reassuring voice alarmed her. She imagined her name, her phone number, the shop name and address on a note circulating around the university. She would gain a word-of-mouth reputation as the woman with the unusual plant.

"No, I'd rather call him," she said.

"But it's no trouble," Bankole said.

"I'd like to . . ." she couldn't think of another excuse, so she said, "I need to be respectful of my boss."

His eyebrows lifted.

"I want to make sure I talk to your colleague during non-business hours."

"Ah, yes, of course. I will write his information down for you. It is Professor Andre Damazy. He's extremely experienced at solving botanical puzzles."

"Great," she said. She handed him a pad of paper. But as he wrote down the phone number, she worried that solving this puzzle would break her life further into pieces.

CHAPTER SEVEN

The basement in Alain's building was as eerie and low-ceilinged as the Paris catacombs: cool, humid, void of light. It reminded Renia of the first time she'd seen a skull. She was a teenager, on a tour of the catacombs with Uncle Feliks and Aunt Nanette. It had smelled of dry dust. Thousands of stacked bones laid in silent darkness, making her shiver at the idea of her own bones inside a coat of flesh. Now, since neither Alain's father nor François could meet her that day, she'd been left with Armand as a guide. In faded dress pants and a sweat-stained shirt, he steered the flashlight beam toward the storage room. Renia shadowed him closely, smelling his musky neck. They stooped as they skimmed the shelves, Renia trembling with the idea of a rat scurrying by. In that damp claustrophobic hole, she was not only anxious to sort through Alain's things but felt guilty at feeling anxious to get out of there.

Thankfully there were no bones. Not even a plastic skull. Instead, everything one needed to throw a party was boxed up and labeled with neat letters by Alain's hand:

Weddings, Performances, Baby Shower, Birthdays, Retire-
ment, Funerals, Private. Spider webs hung in a ghoulish
joke from the tub that said Funerals, but the candles and
tablecloths inside were tidily folded and arranged. There
were loose clusters of cleaning supplies, signs, fake flowers,
plastic glasses. On the floor in the corner was a child's slide
and ping-pong paddles. A new carpet shampooer. But
nothing Renia could sell. It was a dismal result. She'd
hoped for an antique vase or rare imported statue.

She skidded aside a short stack of storage tubs in the
corner, searching for decorative concrete or a balcony
grate, when she spotted a burlap bag hanging from a hook
in the wall. She opened it and stuck a hand in, fishing
around for the bulbs she predicted would be inside.

Armand directed light in the bag.

She smelled a hot sharp odor from his breath as she
pulled out two paper bags marked, "Lilium Nepalese 'Far
and Away.'"

Each bag held a half-dozen bulbs that resembled arti-
chokes. They were clean and spiky, hard with health and
able to sprout. Their earthy smell reminded her of Alain's
joyful face last June at a wedding. The bride had wanted
living lilies and at the last minute, Alain had ordered fifty
plants from Renia. After Uncle Feliks and another grower
delivered the flowers, she'd used Palomer's car to take them
to a banquet hall in Boulogne-Billancourt. When Alain saw
her carrying in boxes of pink 'Stargazer' lilies in ribboned
pots, he hugged her and said, "No one else comes through
like you do."

Now in the dim basement holding these rare bulbs,
Renia felt an ache in her stomach, yearned to experience
that compliment once more. "Lilies were his favorite."

"Here," Armand said. He handed her two index cards

from the bag, each with a faded photo from a plant catalog called *Reach for the Stars*.

"He must have been saving these for a special occasion." When she realized that special occasion may have been his and François's own wedding, her heart sank. Alain didn't even get the opportunity to have them displayed at his memorial. "I'll take these," she said, yearning to nurture them into healthy, beautiful flowers, "it's the least I can do."

EVERY OTHER TUESDAY, Uncle Feliks delivered his perennial orders to his Parisian buyers. In addition to seasonal plants, he sometimes brought Renia crafts or canned food for consignment from nearby farmers. Today he was bringing dried corn and pumpkins. It was September 15th and she needed autumn decor for the terrace. Right now, a measly row of mums in mahogany pots sat atop a hay bundle. Inside, along the window she'd hung a tacky string of apple lights. They were sloppily painted and too bright but had to do until she could afford more sophisticated lighting.

As she watched for Uncle Feliks's van, her phone rang. It was her mother. In Polish, Mama said, "Did I hear you say that the mean moron is in Paris?"

The mean moron? "Oh. Yes. I don't know how he knew where I was."

The sound of sizzling rose in the background. Renia guessed she was frying *kaszanka*. And behind the sizzling, music: Tata practicing, banging out a Chopin étude on the old piano.

"Well, I didn't tell him," Mama said.

"Did Tata?"

"What?" Her voice popped. "No, of course not. He won't even get up to answer the phone."

From the background, Tata's voice shouted.

In a resentful clip, Mama said to him, "When was the last time you got off that chair to answer the phone?"

More mumbling. As they bickered, Renia went to a nearby display table and repositioned a toppled bar of soap atop a small pyramid of soaps. She didn't miss her parents' bickering, didn't miss Tata's dour opinions, the lamp with the burn stain on the shade. His patched sweater. His frustration with every Polish politician. And Mama took him to task for the slightest words.

Renia raised her voice. "Mama, it doesn't matter. How did Zbiggy know I was here?"

To Tata, Mama said, "Estera's moron has found Renia."

In the background, Tata said, "How?"

"She does not know."

"Mama," Renia said, "did Estera tell him?"

"No, of course not. She hasn't seen him in months."

"Are you sure?"

"Of course I'm sure."

Renia closed her eyes, gathered courage. "Is she there now?"

"No," Mama said. "She is at Biały Manor. She sleeps there."

"At Biały Manor? Sleeping where?"

"In the room of the caretaker. He is off somewhere, I don't know the details."

"I thought she lost her job."

"What? No. I don't know this."

"How do you know she hasn't talked to Zbiggy?"

"She no longer has a phone!" Mama said everything as if Renia should already know.

"She doesn't?"

"No, I had to take it from her. She has no money to pay the bill. And she started talking nonsense about leaving Kraków. I told her to pray for clarity and God would answer."

"How long ago was this?"

To Tata, she said, "What?"

He mumbled inaudible words.

"Does she have it or not?" Mama said to him.

Mumbling.

"She may have the phone, your father left it for her. What did you say, Renka?"

"How long ago did you take away her phone?"

"Weeks ago. She was in a strange fit about traveling to America, anywhere but here, she said. She talked about 'a plan' or 'the plan.' It made no sense. She was tired. She had been working many hours."

Estera getting into a fit. That was hardly new, yet Mama spoke about it as if it were.

Outside the shop window, a Mercedes pulled up.

Renia's heart dropped: Madame Palomer.

"Will you ask her if she talked to Zbiggy?"

"I don't think she has, she knows she cannot."

"But will you ask her?"

In the shop, the fountain's dribbling stream seemed to grow louder. The goddess poured water into the pool in a deafening trickle. "I have to go," Renia said. "My boss is here."

"Yes, yes, we will ask." To Tata, Mama said, "What do you mean she will be another week?"

The car door opened. Palomer's hand with its painted burgundy nails gripped the roof.

"I have to go," Renia said.

"Yes, yes, go."

As she ended the call, she heard her parents arguing. Debating how long Estera would be gone, she guessed. She wondered why they never talked nicely unless Renia or Estera were in the room. Then, they often disagreed about facts and events. Being with one wasn't bad, being with both, trying.

She yanked down the apple lights. With no time to unplug, she kicked the glowing heap behind the curtain.

Palomer got out of the car with a hefty cardboard box.

Renia went outside, feeling a sudden sense of loneliness. "Sorry, I was on the phone."

Palomer handed her the box. Its flaps were folded and taped over a mound of merchandise. "Oh, thank you, dear. Take this for me, please."

Renia held the shop door open with her back as Palomer squeezed through.

"I've been on my feet for too long," the older woman said. She scooted sideways behind the counter with a spangled purse and plopped on the stool. "My foot has been at me. It won't give me a break." Palomer had worked as a nurse in the Medical Corps during the Algerian War. A faulty gurney had fallen on her leg. Since the injury, she'd had chronic pain in her foot. Renia had always respected her for her service, but at Palomer's wish, rarely mentioned it. Her boss had had too much regret at not saving a young soldier who'd been her patient that day.

Renia forced her voice to sound airy. "So, what did you bring us?"

"These are the shoes I was telling you about."

Palomer preferred to sell clothing in winter. It was what she had done successfully years ago when she'd managed the store alone as a gift shop. Renia, who tracked the buying trends of city dwellers, had learned recent buyers preferred rare plants and gardening accessories. Though customers sometimes came to Le Sanctuaire for gifts, they almost never bought clothing or shoes. There were too many specialty boutiques in Saint-Germain-des-Prés for that. And Le Sanctuaire touted itself as a store of the natural. Shoes were a far cry from straw hats and hemp aprons.

Renia opened the box and took out the shoes. There was an assortment of fancy flats and leather boots and dress shoes with gold chains or buckles. All garish. A pair of glossy high heels with bows at the toe seemed used, their inner soles showing cracks and wear.

She was about to ask whether the shoes were second-hand when Palomer said, "*Et donc*, these are very in demand. These boots as well . . . look, this is you, isn't it?" She fished out a copper boot with fringe tassels and glittery buckles, the kind of boot Polish teenagers wore.

"Yes. Not my size though." Luckily, that was the truth.

"Ah. Well, better to make a few euros off them anyway."

Renia's face reddened. If she put the shoes on display, their wealthier customers who wore authentic diamonds and bought expensive unique plants would snicker and leave the store. She didn't know how to say this without insult, so she said nothing.

Palomer got up and limped to the oak armoire in the corner. "What have you in the cabinet nowadays?"

Renia kept the drawers open with a display of garden-themed scarves and linens. She'd folded the scarves so they overlapped, showing the beadwork and patterns in each. In the lower drawers were cotton dish towels and tablecloths.

Palomer pulled open the upper drawer and removed a

handful of scarves. "Let's display these on a rack and put the shoes in the drawer."

"But I'm not sure we have one free."

She pawed out the rest of the linens, throwing a few placemats over her arm, determined. "We need this cleaned out," she said to herself. When what Renia had said sunk in, Palomer paused. "We have three racks. Shouldn't one be available?"

"Yes, but the ponchos and hats have one, the aprons another, and the third's broken."

Her face crunched. "How did that happen?"

"A customer. It's a long story, she didn't mean to, but a customer tipped one over." She thought of the mother holding a toddler who'd reached out and grabbed a scarf printed with elephants, bending the metal rack irreparably. Renia never forgot the horrified expression on the woman's face. She was a Muslim who couldn't have been more than twenty years old. She'd struggled, while holding the child, to put the rack upright and set the scarves back. Renia had told her accidents happened and she didn't expect her to pay for it. After the woman left with her crying child, Renia had reconfigured the armoire to include the scarves and put the rack in a closet, intending to repair it, which after an involved attempt she'd been unable to do.

"What will I do with these scarves?" Palomer said. "We must display scarves, they're one of our biggest sellers in autumn."

This was true. Of course, Renia couldn't suggest leaving the shoes out of the display, so she instead put on her most sedate voice. "Here." She took the scarves. "I'll create a pretty display."

She went to the empty cardboard box, about to set them in, when she realized the bottom had wrinkled papers and a grease stain. "I have a small empty drawer in back. I can paint it with fleur-de-lys and set it atop the dresser."

"Well . . ." Madame said, unconvinced, then "oh, my foot," and limped to the stool.

For the next hour, Palomer sat behind the counter, greeting customers and offering advice on what Renia should pull from the displays and what she should order more of. Renia wrote down her ideas on a notepad though by the end she wanted to throw it at the wall. Palomer suggested Renia remove the dried hydrangeas that a neighborhood customer liked and replace them with ceramic figurines. She wanted Renia to remove water from the fountain so it would dribble in a louder, more pronounced way and pointed out brown mold on the bowl's bottom though Renia could see none. Renia's only reassurance was that Palomer wouldn't be in the store for ten days after this latest visit. She would leave soon for a "buying" trip to Athens where her half-brother and his wife lived.

Finally, at three o'clock, the older woman said, "I must get to the 8th. I'll leave things in your capable hands while I'm in Greece." She took her purse and put on her sunglasses, shuffled toward the door. "Oh, one more thing, my dear."

Renia swallowed. "Yes?"

"I'm afraid with business so slow, I'll need to collect full rent on the apartment upstairs. I know it will be difficult for you, but perhaps you can dip into your savings for a while, until we get back on our feet."

Her heart dropped. Her monthly wage was already the amount of the full rent: 1600 euros. That didn't include all of the bills, plus food or clothes, or a life.

"I know you're disappointed, dear. I'm sorry, but you and Minh couldn't come up with a financial plan and so we have no extra income."

Renia trembled. "Well, we're still working on it. It's . . . we need to spend money to make money."

"If you can't make the rent, perhaps you can live with Monsieur Baranczka for a few months. I do need to rent it to a tenant who can pay full price."

His name is Baranczki. And commute from Valenton? From countryville? Close to two hours, every day? Where there was nothing to do except sit with an old grump who liked to lecture as he cracked walnuts by the fire?

Renia opened her mouth. The reduced rate was what allowed her to be a part of St. Germain-des-Prés. "Oh, I . . . I wish . . . " She stifled her despair, searched for the gratitude she felt at Palomer allowing her to keep the Violet Smoke, a plant her boss only knew as a high-maintenance exotic.

"I know, I'm sorry, it's terrible to do," Palomer said. "But we don't have the revenue anymore. Now that summer is finished, and Alain's gone, I need that revenue to keep the lights on."

Palomer needed the revenue for her monthly trips to Normandy, or Provence, or Greece. She needed the money to convince herself she was still as wealthy as she'd been when her husband was alive. Renia swallowed words of resentment.

"You mentioned new income ideas that demand money up front. What are they?" Palomer said.

"Well . . ." Renia cleared her throat. In a frantic rush, she searched her mind for an out, "Minh and I were talking about a variety. One idea was to throw a party for customers on our mailing list. Maybe a cocktail party but make it a craft show with jewelry and gifts."

Palomer shook her head, "No, out of the question. The liquor permit would kill the budget. In fact, I'm surprised at you for thinking in such cavalier terms." Her sharp look was a warning. "Oh, and Minh, yes, I must think about that. I don't know whether we can keep her on. Maybe that's the solution. Maybe we should let her go."

"Let her go? She only works two days a week." Renia's voice came out like a siren. She paused, smiled an easy smile, a smile that said she didn't disagree even though her spirit was crushed.

Palomer softened her expression. "Look, my dear, the reality is our beloved Alain is gone and so is his lucrative account. François tells me he might sell Alain's business so until we know more, I need the full rent. It's either that or let the Japanese girl go."

She wanted to correct her and say, "She's Vietnamese," but she didn't. She didn't want to be fired. Nor did she want Minh to be fired. Minh needed that income for her mother's experimental therapy. The fact that Palomer did the flower arranging at her home and had an entirely separate ledger for that was not lost on Renia. Yes, Alain had ordered flowers, which Renia then ordered from growers, sometimes Uncle Feliks, and sold for a tidy profit. But Palomer's arranging labor was revenue that she kept for herself. If Palomer would only stop withdrawing money, they might stay afloat. Renia opened her mouth to mention it, but when she noticed her boss's folded arms and the keys dangling from her manicured hands, the sleek Mercedes key, the tiny key to the money box, and the shop's antique key, she closed her mouth and said nothing.

"We'll talk when I return from Athens, dear. But now I need to take a bit extra from the safe. My hair stylist has raised her rates."

Of course. Renia sulked. The day was falling apart. It was all falling apart. Despite her best efforts, her dream of belonging to this cultured city was dying. As if reading her mind, Palomer, with a regretful expression, patted her shoulder. Renia caught the scent of her mint gum. She heard Uncle Feliks's words about Paris: "The ladies are fresh and neat and the gentlemen are strong and rich."

Palomer's bracelet, a distinguished gold chain, delicate with a small opal at the center, glinted on her wrist. In her high heels, cream slacks, and caramel colored jacket, her presence was tall and stately with squared shoulders and head held high.

"The ladies are sophisticated," Uncle Feliks had said. "They know how to dress well." This was years ago, talking by phone. Renia was twelve years old. "The center of Kraków is not like the foolish building your father chose for you." The Baranczki family lived on the perimeter, in a Soviet high rise, built in tall blocks of concrete, one of five with a broken playground at the foot and a nearby highway. Uncle Feliks said old Kraków had ornate architecture and soaring statues and French-style windows. There were dignified clock towers and a giant castle. It was historic and beautiful, like Paris.

And so, one week in autumn, she and Estera decided to go to the old town. Estera had said, "We deserve to see the noble places too." That helped Renia be brave. They would go on a Saturday morning, when Mama was at work and Tata at their aunt's. But Estera caught a fever, and at her urging, Renia went alone, supplied with only seventeen złoty and a hand-drawn map Estera had made from a book.

Renia accidentally boarded a tram heading east instead of west. Estera had mislabeled a street name. She found herself in a neighborhood of graffiti and boarded buildings. When she got off the tram, she saw a church steeple, and thinking it an ancient landmark, headed to it before asking a gentleman for directions. He, with a huge mustache and frayed wool coat, scolded her for bothering him and told her to "scurry back" from where she came. He smelled of vodka. Renia trudged on, hoping to recognize a street name. The sun lowered. Sirens blared. A woman in bright red lipstick and a low-cut sweater leered at her. She cracked mint gum between her teeth. She was not fresh or neat. Renia marched on, passing a series of sooty store fronts until, exhausted and frightened, she found a phone booth at a gas station and called her mother. A half-hour later, Tata's car idled before her, the exhaust fuming up her nose. As she got in, he scolded her for "being stupid" and thinking that venturing some place new wouldn't end in danger and failure. Afterward, she wasn't sure what hurt more, the burning of her embarrassed face or the burning of her swatted rear end.

Now, in Le Sanctuaire, with a loose heart and quiet voice, Renia stepped back to allow Madame Palomer to approach the safe. "I understand."

"I'll give you until I get back from Greece to figure out a solution for the rent," Palomer said. She smiled an endearing smile, the smile of an established woman who didn't need to apologize. Estera would have hated her. As she rolled through the combination, opened the safe, took out the money box, and used the tiny key to unlock it and count out two-hundred euros, she said, "Maybe you and Minh can find a place together."

A university student, Minh lived with her parents, two brothers, one of their wives, and a grandmother in a three-bedroom apartment. She slept on a lumpy fold-out sofa. She *couldn't* move out because she didn't have the money. She *wouldn't* move out because her mother was too ill to be left alone at home.

Palomer maneuvered around the counter. "Feel free to leave a bit early tonight, my dear. That is, if business is slow." At the door, she said, "*A bientôt*" and with a weak yank, tossed it closed. She limped around the Mercedes and unlocked it. A small truck slowed to a halt as she got in the car. After she started it, she fiddled with her phone a minute, then revved the engine and zoomed away, leaving Renia to stand alone beside the fountain, the goddess and her urn jiggling from the rumbling street.

CHAPTER EIGHT

L ater, after the work day was done, Renia dragged herself upstairs and stood idly in her apartment, surveying everything with a troubled heart. It had all been enough for Palomer when she'd lived there in her twenties, and it was more than enough for Renia now. In fact, it reflected all that she cherished about Paris. She ran her fingers over the circular leaf emblem on the marble fireplace, smiling at how the government protected the city's historic architecture, then wandered to the kitchen and opened the lace curtains. Oftentimes in summer, scents of warm chocolate and roasting lamb blew in the window, reminding her how she could eat whatever cuisine she liked at any time. Once, she and Alain had drank sangria at a tapas bar, then eaten Kung Pao chicken for dinner, then nibbled on Moroccan ghriba for dessert. A glimpse of the university showed where scientists created new advancements, reminding her she'd planned on finishing her business degree.

In her tiny bedroom, she opened the antique armoire, touching a dress whose style had come to the boutiques a mere few weeks after it had appeared in a haute couture show. She'd painted the walls a smoky scarlet before hanging a gold mirror, inspired by the Maison Souquet lobby. Beside the mirror, her sketch of a Delacroix painting meant studying the great masters' originals was only a short walk away. She sat on the bed, remembering falling asleep one night to the sweet lullaby of a neighbor practicing jazz saxophone, and realized how every morning, when she emerged into the Rue Sereine, she saw her most favorite trait of all: the peaceful variety of people.

Now, it was all in jeopardy. She went back to the living room and up to the étagère, opened the tea tin, and counted the bills. She had one-hundred sixty euros saved. Not enough to supplement her income to the roughly 1900 euros she would need. She had a modest bank account, but what sat in there was less than what her bills added up to. She'd have to take on another job. She knew how to manage medical accounts, but the thought of a sterile clinic made her sick. A day job was out of the question, unless she worked on Sundays, part of Wednesday, evenings—her official free time—but who would hire her for one and a half days?

She knew the answer. And she didn't like it. Uncle Feliks. She could work a day and a half, maybe another half-day. Still, his pay wouldn't add up to more than three-hundred euros a week—not enough of the six-hundred euros difference. She went to the window and looked at the street. At Vida Nova, two men and a woman sat on the terrace with steaming drinks, a stack of books on the table. In large letters, one spine said, "Marval," another, "Vian." The woman creased a magazine folio and handed it to one of the men who read it, then gestured argumentatively. She laughed. He kissed her neck. These people weren't faced with any dilemmas. They were simply young and smart and liked to discuss books and art. Random Parisians with whom she longed to be friends.

She made herself a cup of strong coffee, resentment rising to her mind as the warm liquid went down her throat. Why should she live in dismal Poland? A country where her mother and father worked their entire lives and barely made ends meet? Where every night people ate boiled cabbage and slimy pierogi? Where the government wanted to drag women back into the 1950s and big businesses polluted without consequence? Was it wrong to pursue a better life? She hadn't only escaped to a safer place, she'd built a home here. A home that didn't include Estera, but some day might. Zbiggy didn't deserve Renia's cooperation, certainly not. But if his connections could save the shop and her new life in Paris, why not take advantage of them?

For one reason: Zbiggy was Zbiggy. As the coffee's bitter odor rose to her nose, she thought of the day Estera had moved in with him. How they'd hauled her possessions up three flights of stairs again and again. The chunks of clothes on hangers. Renia had helped her carry the clothes through a hallway that smelled of burnt coffee and motor oil. She'd been suspicious of a boyfriend who'd invited his girlfriend to move in after two months, but Estera was lost in his world.

As they hoofed up the stairs, Renia said, "Is he at the apartment?"

"No, he's out."

"Is he at work?"

Estera said nothing at first. The chrome trim on the stairwell railing reflected their similar faces, stretching Estera's sideways.

Her voice was quiet and softly casual. "No, he lost his job."

"At The Tomb?"

"It wasn't his fault."

"Isn't this the second job he's lost since you've known him?" Renia said.

"This boss was an asshole. They'll take him back later."

On the landing, an old twin mattress littered with stains lay bowed in the corner. A nearby doormat smelled like cat urine. "Are you sure you want to stay here?"

"It's fine for now. We'll get a better place soon."

"Does he still have a roommate?"

She blinked, staring at the floor, shook her head.

"So . . . is he looking for a job?"

"Yes, but there's not much out there."

"You work six days a week." As a gardener, for pennies.

"You just don't like him because his mother is Russian."

She didn't mind that his mother was Russian, Tata minded—any older person who remembered World War II and life under the Soviets minded—but she didn't. She couldn't convince Estera of that though.

They came to the apartment. The area around the door's lock was scratched and chipped as if someone had stabbed a screwdriver at it. Estera set the clothes on the railing while she looked for the key in her pockets. At catching sight of Renia's face, she said, "Don't worry, my sweet plant keeps us afloat."

"Do you still sell to Anna Markowska?"

"No, her husband recovered from his illness. Her son went to jail though. We sell to a lot of customers in Chorzów."

"Chorzów?" Renia imagined the smokestacks on the city's outskirts. "Aren't there mobsters there?"

"No, no. Well, maybe, I don't know."

"You're selling flowers to gangsters?"

"I don't ask questions."

"Why not? It's your plant."

Estera took in a slow breath, stared at her boots. They were black, zip up, high heel boots. "He got mad at me when I asked." She frowned, searched her purse for the key.

"Moving in together may not be a good idea," Renia said.

Estera's face tightened. She brushed at her bangs so they lay more fully over her forehead. Three weeks ago, Estera had changed her hair and got bangs for the first time since they were children, appearing less like Renia's twin. "Look, Renia," her voice brimmed with sour resentment, "life's short. And no one's giving me money for nothing."

"Why did he get mad at you? You have a right to know what he's doing with your plant."

"I don't know, he just blew his top. He's different when he drinks." She found the key and put it in the lock. Her face softened with a smile. "But he's a teddy bear when he's sober."

HERE IN PARIS, Renia believed Estera was right. Life was short and no one was giving away money. In fact, the opposite. But for Renia to work with Zbiggy . . . that "mean moron," she had to be careful. What had ultimately happened to Estera, and the possibility of another person falling as she had, ripped at her conscience. She needed to find out what chemicals the Violet Smoke produced. In the meantime, she could make the money she needed. And she could keep her distance. She'd sell to Zbiggy and he'd turn around and sell to petty thieves and scumbags who used it to cheat each other's memories. There was little harm in that. It wasn't for her to judge anyway. On her phone, she scrolled to his number, then set it down and crossed her arms. Should she wait? She couldn't afford to wait. She only had two weeks to come up with six-hundred euros.

She dialed, promising herself to sell the flowers only once until she found another job or a cheap apartment, whichever came first. Through the window, she watched the sidewalk, empty save for the yellow leaves that skittered by. Estera would love how the wind made them dance in circles around the pretty street lamp.

"What?" A voice answered in curt Polish.

Renia took a breath, centered herself. "Hello, Zbigniew. This is your old friend."

Outside at Vida Nova, a group of young people streamed out of the restaurant. One man with a tidy haircut and pressed wool coat looked toward her window, clicking the remote of his Volvo. When their eyes met, he smiled, as if about to wave her down to join them. He got in the car while a man in a fedora, jeans, and boots traipsed by. He finished a cigarette and tossed it on the sidewalk. Behind him, a mother with her gold hair in a ponytail, held the hand of a girl as they disappeared in its billow of smoke.

"What?" Zbiggy said again.

"It's your friend from the shop. I'm calling about the . . . scarves you wanted for your mother."

"I didn't order any scarves."

Renia closed her eyes. "I'm sure you did. You came and visited me in my shop last week?"

A pause. "Oh, okay, great. I'm glad you have what I need."

"Yes, I do." Renia backed away from the window and into the darkness of the apartment's interior. "I have three scarves to sell you." She doubted a police officer was listening to her calls, but they may have been listening to his. "The price is one-hundred twenty euros for each scarf."

He laughed. "Sorry, I can't pay that much. You have to lower your price."

"Really?" she said. "I sold a scarf last month for one-hundred fifty. I'm giving you a deal because you're an old friend. I don't need your business. I sell a lot of these scarves to other customers. These scarves are made of fine material."

Silence.

"I'd like to buy as many as you have." His words were warm, his tone sinister.

"Great, three scarves then. If you meet me at the square Boucicaut this Friday at noon, I'll have them wrapped and ready."

"Okay."

"And please, from now on, old friend, I prefer to do business face-to-face, rather than by phone. It's often possible that our connection will be lost."

On Friday, Renia went into Le Sanctuaire early. If she worked quickly, she could cut the flowers before Minh arrived for work. She put on her mask, pried open the panel, and lifted the Wardian Case off the Violet Smoke. It seemed to have grown in the last week. Its twisted branches had elongated so that a few more buds were forming amidst the leaves. In some ways, the plant looked like a lanky teenager dancing, bending its arms this way and that. Goofy and homely. Yet it did have an unconventional beauty. She clipped three flowers and set the stems in water vials, then taped the bag shut so no air could escape. As she inspected the velvety petals, so pure and complete, she felt a wave of shame. The plant didn't deserve this. Nor did anyone who inhaled its gas. She swallowed her doubt and stood up straight. *The blossoms will expire anyway. It's not your place to worry about the outcome. You're offering a service, nothing more.*

Her phone rang.

Professor Bankole.

Quickly she opened the window so she could take off her mask. When she felt the breeze on her face, she answered.

"Mademoiselle Baranczka," he said, "I have informed Professor Damazy about your plant."

She leaned against the stone wall. Ugh.

"He happened to be in my office after I returned the other day. However, I let him know that you will contact him during your non-work hours."

"Did he tell anyone else about the plant?

"Eh, I'm uncertain. I did emphasize discretion."

She cringed, wanted to kick the table.

"Professor Damazy is very interested in examining the plant. He thinks he may have seen it once in the mountains of Kenya. He wanted me to let you know that he's available to visit this afternoon at a time of your convenience."

She looked around for her calendar, forgetting what day it was. The bag of flowers on the table reminded her.

"No, that's not good," she said. "Please tell him I'll call with other dates. Today . . ." Oh, today, no, not today. "I have an errand to take care of."

After she hung up, she secured the false wall and sat down. It was only morning, yet she felt exhausted with guilt. She needed Alain, needed to know if all of this was the right thing to do. She remembered him sitting on the counter, right where her arm rested, last July, with the window open. The smell of a rose floated in. He had smiled knowingly. What had spawned the smirk she couldn't recall. It had been Bastille Day. Trumpets and drums played in a distant square. They'd gone shopping at the Mouffetard market. Talked. Alain had a sharp, "I like you but don't mess with me" approach to life. Now, she yearned for his snappy wisdom.

In the shop, low music wafted through the door. Soothing keyboards, floaty vocals. Minh was in. How much of the conversation had she heard? The atrium door had been closed but . . . And where to put the bagged flowers? She decided to leave them in her raincoat pocket, knowing she'd wear it today. She straightened her blouse and hair, then opened the door and went in the store, ready to act as if whoever she'd been speaking with wasn't important.

Minh sang a word of hello. She cleaned the windows with a natural cleaner that gave off a lemon scent. Every time Renia smelled a lemon, she thought of Minh. Happy Minh. Always hopeful. She was the type of person who would make a joke and then laugh, or make a mistake and then laugh, or read an article and laugh. Sometimes Renia believed she was better suited to work in a pub or restaurant rather than a retail shop purposed to calm the mind and entice customers into buying rare forty euro begonias.

Still, that friendly personality sold merchandise. She related to French people better than Renia. She had been born in Paris and had more of the sophisticated breezy ease with which French women conducted themselves. That Renia had no inclination to laugh or even smile at most points of the day bothered her only in that she saw it as a small failure of character rather than an outward emblem of her feelings. In her heart, she was thrilled to work at a job that combined her horticulture and business skills. She just didn't feel compelled to let the world know it.

"So, your friend, the one from Poland, stopped in," Minh said. "Byggy, or Ziggie, I can't recall his name right now but he's that cute guy with the hat."

Surprised, Renia said, "He did? So early? I'm supposed to . . ."

"He said he can't make your lunch date."

That was probably a lie.

"He said he'll meet you tonight at nine o'clock at this address. At least, that's what I think he said. His French isn't great."

Minh handed her a green Le Sanctuaire business card. On the back was a scribbled address: *Bar Misha, 80 Rue Riquet, 18th.*

"He said he was sorry," Minh said.

Renia tapped the card on her hand in a frustrated rhythm. The 18th arrondissement was not the safest neighborhood in Paris. "Alright."

"So," Minh said, "does this guy know about the violet?"

"Why? Did you hear my call?"

"No, not at all."

Minh was under the impression that Renia was taking care of the Violet Smoke for her sister who was traveling. But she also knew Renia was sometimes in the atrium with the door closed when it didn't need to be.

"It's that," Minh said, "that guy is . . . I get a strange vibration from him."

Renia rubbed her forehead, debated what to say. "Yes, that guy, that guy is . . ." *a loser, a criminal, a liar, a cheat, an addict?* What should she say? "That guy is my sister's ex-boyfriend."

The shine left Minh's eyes. "Oh."

Through the windows, leaves from the street trees fluttered down and hid the sidewalk.

"Does he want that African violet tree? Like was it his once?" Minh said. "Isn't it your sister's?"

Renia forced herself to smile. "Yes, it's hers and only hers. Don't worry about him, but I wouldn't mention where we keep it."

"Oh, I won't," she said. She searched Renia's eyes. "Wait, is he dangerous?"

Of course he is. She looked at Minh straight on and said, "No. He wasn't the best boyfriend to Estera but he's a good enough guy."

Her dark brown eyes were filled with worry.

"Is your mom visiting later?" Renia said.

Minh nodded.

"Good, I look forward to seeing her." She almost said, "I miss having a mom at home to talk to," but caught herself, not wanting to dive into the complicated situation.

The door bell jingled. Minh greeted the customer.

Renia took the cleaning fluid and cloth and put them away in the atrium. As she closed the storage closet, she thought of Minh's mother, in a wheelchair, cared for around the clock by a nurse. Minh had once explained her illness but Renia couldn't recall the name of it. She couldn't even recall Minh's mother's name, she only remembered that she breathed through a ventilator. A petite lady with wavy black hair and chunky glasses. She was able to speak though and get a joke. She had a kind, modest spirit. Once in a while she gave Minh lemongrass plants to sell for extra cash. She'd come to Paris as a girl in the 1950s, an immigrant like Renia, now with a daughter who was in some ways more French than Vietnamese.

Once, Minh's mother had taught Renia a few words in Vietnamese. The words for "plant" and "tree" and "water" and "sky." Renia could only recall the words for "twin sisters." *Chị em sinh đôi*. In French, it was *soeurs jumelles*. In Polish, it was *bliźniaczki*. How many times had she heard that last word? On impulse, she took out her phone and keyed the number for the apartment in Poland. *No, not now.* Would she really get sympathy from Mama for a choice she had been against? Instead, she dialed Estera's number. It rang. Three rings, four. The ringing stopped as if someone answered but no greeting came. She heard a breath. Renia started to speak. An "eh" escaped her mouth. She wanted to say, "Estera, is that you? Estera, are you okay? Estera, Zbiggy's here, is he supposed to be? Please call me, please talk to me," but she didn't want to dampen the warm flare of hope she had at Estera changing her mind. So once again, she said nothing and hung up.

CHAPTER NINE

That night, Renia rode her bike to the Marx Dormoy neighborhood. She avoided the métro after dark since subway workers went home and thugs came out. She couldn't run fast enough to escape "streeters" as Mama called them, but she could on a bike. At a few minutes before nine, she found Misha Bar at the corner of the Rue Riquet and Rue Pajol, its red awning covered in gray soot. As she locked her bike to a post, she felt like the awning looked: worn and desperate. She made sure to securely lock her tire and frame to a sign post covered in scratches and dents whose sign's bold letters read *Interdit*.

The bar's door, a hunk of black wood, sat closed. It had no window but a sloppily painted white skull and crossbones. She hesitated. It faced a corner where intermittent traffic roared by before flying onto the bridge over train tracks. No one was about. Across the street, a boarded-up store held onto a faded sign that said *Alimentation*. As she debated whether to unlock her bike and ride away, she saw a rat scurry by and slip in a sewer cover hole. Inside was safer.

The bar was a rectangular room that stretched deep into the building with a counter on the right and tables on the left. Red walls, black chairs. Two men in sweatshirts and jackets sat at the back, nursing short glasses of vodka. The air smelled like cigarettes though no one was smoking. The bartender, a muscular man in a sleeveless shirt with complex tattoos on his forearms, took a long look at Renia. He had a tuft of short black hair, head shaved at the sides. Five silver rings laddered up his ears. He slid off his stool and sauntered over, without a greeting, and gave her a glance up and down.

"Wine," she said.

His mouth slightly loosened. "White or red." His voice was gruff, like gravel scraped from the bottom of a metal drum.

"White."

On a TV behind the bar, Ukraine played Estonia. A crowd roared every few minutes over a Russian commentator's play-by-play. The men in the back watched the match animatedly, throwing up their hands, pointing at the screen, moaning at fouls. One had buzzed hair, gelled so it seemed like white spikes on his head. The other had a large scar from his nostril to his cheek. After the bartender set down her wine, he went to the opposite end, hunched over a Cyrillic newspaper, and slowly flipped the pages.

Renia shifted in her seat, remembering her first day of school. The rough boys, the towering teacher. Estera immediately ran off to play with the rough boys, bouncing a ball hard at them. Renia slinked to the edge of the courtyard and cried. Now, with that sense of worry at her throat, she sat utterly still. She monitored the men, forcing her face to stay blank.

She cursorily watched the TV until nine o'clock when a group of people entered. Three men and one woman.

They spoke Russian and sat at a table along the wall. The woman, with black hair that matched a black vinyl skirt, went to the bartender and ordered three vodkas and one beer. Soon, harsh staccato guitar blared from the stereo. Renia pulled out her phone and checked for messages. None. She promised herself not to wait past nine-thirty.

The phone rang.

"I'm on my way," Zbiggy said. "I ended work late."

"Work?"

"Yeah, don't leave. I'll be there in like, fifteen minutes."

Did he really have a job? Renia set her phone face down on the bar, careful to hide the photo of a rose outside the Musée de la Vie Romantique, which at the moment seemed wimpy. She sipped the last of her wine. Her stomach growled.

The bartender came over.

"Do you serve food?" she said.

He shook his head.

"One more."

When the wine was set before her, she didn't touch it. Instead she put a bill on the table. As the bartender took it, she said, "Are you Zbiggy's cousin?"

He blinked in a frown. "What?"

"Zbigniew?"

His brows crinkled.

"Zbeeg-nyev. Do you know him?" She was careful not to smile.

His eyes were hollow. "No. No one."

Another cluster of people entered. Drums and guitar blasted. Meanwhile, she waited, not sipping the wine, longing for nuts or olives, anything. At nine forty-five, she picked up her phone, about to call, when the door opened. Zbiggy stumbled in, opened his arms, and smiled.

"Hey, Renia." He leaned in to kiss her cheeks. She endured his pecks in a rigid hold. He smelled of whiskey.

"Where were you?" she said. "Let's get this over with."

"I have a job just like you." His mouth was jiggling in a faint smile. "You're not the only lowly Pole employed in Paris, Renia."

"Where's your cousin?"

Zbiggy leaned forward to search the bar. It was filled with people. The bartender made drinks at the far end. "I don't know. I think that's . . . what's his name? That's . . ."

"I waited almost an hour."

"Oh, sorry. I had to help a friend after work."

Right. "Yes, I'm sure you were 'helping.'"

"Yeah, for Yuri. So what?"

"The plan was to meet at nine," she said.

His frown solidified. The hard lines that framed his mouth appeared. With that and a high forehead, he seemed like a general who'd committed war atrocities. "Listen, I'm making you rich Polish girl, don't forget it."

"Where's the money?"

"Come," he pinched her shoulder hard and led her in a rough yank along the bar. "I'll show you."

Glad that she hadn't brought a purse and had buttoned up her raincoat, she stumbled along. In the hallway by the bathroom, he faced her. With a small bulb in a cracked fixture overhead, the area was dim, his face a fuzzy gold outline.

"Let go of me," she said.

He pinched her shoulder.

"Let go."

"Where are the flowers?"

"Let me go and I'll show you."

He loosened his grip. She took the waxed paper bag

from her pocket and showed it to him before slipping it back in. "Where's the money?"

He handed her four folded bills. Three hundred notes and three twenty notes. She held them to the grimy light to check authenticity.

He laughed in a low huff. "They're real." A man headed toward them. "They're real," he said in a stronger snap.

She checked the third against the light.

As the man neared, Zbiggy slapped her arm down. The man passed, glanced at Zbiggy, and disappeared in the bathroom.

She folded the bills and stuck them in her coat's breast pocket, gave him the package.

"You didn't get them from me," she said.

"But I did, my little polka, and I've got a couple more people interested in your cute flowers."

He smiled a lazy smile. His eyes blinked in a slow tick. During the second they were closed, he seemed like he might fall against the wall and pass out. Renia spun around and scurried away, slipping through the crush of people. The smell of cigarettes, sour breath, and body odor enveloped her, urging her along. She had actually done it. She had done what she'd vowed to never do again, and with a petty criminal. Her heart sagged. She felt like a wet rag in a dirty puddle.

As she squeezed through, avoiding the faces jammed around her, she locked eyes with a random woman drinking a stemless flute of vodka. She wore thick eyeliner, reminding Renia of a girl she'd once seen in Poland. Big sprayed hair, the smell of sharp perfume. Who was she? The string of white light bulbs behind the bar jiggled her memory. She threw open the door, the rumble of voices following her into the street, reminding her of the rumble of voices she'd heard in a shopping mall in Kraków.

She and Estera, roaming under a string of decorative lights. The shushing of a tumbling fountain. Escalators. They chatted about how to wash an expensive sweater Estera had just purchased when Estera stopped. Her face froze. She grabbed Renia's wrist. Her eyes changed from animated joy to locked attention. Near the bathroom hallway, a young woman in a short dress and high heels leaned against a wall, speaking with a hefty man in a wrinkled suit. Her brown hair was teased and sprayed, highlighted with blonde streaks as if to attract attention. She had full, frosty lips. Her long earrings jangled as she spoke. The hefty man slipped a folded clump of bills in her hand and she discreetly handed him a small package.

"That's Maria," Estera said.

"Maria who?"

"Maria Kozłowska, Sylwia's little cousin."

Renia studied the girl. With such sculpted hair and defined eyes and showy cleavage, she looked like a woman. "I thought Maria was only fifteen."

"She is."

They approached the hallway. While her customer scuttled away, Maria retreated to the hallway's dead end. Renia peered in. In the murky corner, Maria counted a wad of bills. The smell of sharp perfume hovered in the air.

"She's become a drug dealer," Estera said.

"Are you sure?"

"Look, here comes another guy."

A skinny man in a long overcoat went in the hallway. After a moment, he emerged, tucking a similar package into his pocket.

"This is the third time I've seen her dressed like that," Estera said, "standing by the restrooms, selling packages."

Renia was about to say, "Maybe she's shopping," but knew she wasn't. Maria had become one of those destitute teenagers who sold drugs. She thought of Maria's parents, and the one time Renia had seen their apartment. Instead of a couch, they had two easy chairs and a rumpled blanket on the floor where her brother slept. Her father smelled of hair gel and beer. They often watched TV in the dark. "We should talk to her. Let's wait until she comes back."

"No, let her be," Estera said. "We don't know her life. Her parents may be in trouble."

"But she doesn't have to do this."

"You don't know what happened. Maybe her father lost his job. Maybe her mother's ill."

To Estera's left, a dragon tree grew in a chrome container. The plant's leaves were littered with brown spots and split at the tips. Renia felt a creeping sense of doom. "But she's ruining her life. She'll go deeper into a dark world." She marched toward the restrooms, intending to intervene.

Estera snagged her arm. "Hey, don't." Her face was crumpled, her eyes accusing. "This may be exactly what she needs to do. It might be temporary, or it might be part of a larger plan. Either way, it's not up to us."

"She doesn't have a plan," Renia said, "And besides, no plan is worth lowering yourself to . . . that."

In Paris, Renia paced in the barren night outside the Misha Bar. She couldn't shake Maria's face from her mind. Her innocent blue eyes were outlined in black to seem mature and streetwise, but the joyful spark had been snuffed out. Her expression had been tough and vigilant, as if only concerned with her customer or who might arrest her. Renia had felt that way a few minutes ago. She cringed.

At her bike, she set her hands on the bars, tried to stand up straight but couldn't. She sucked in air. It was cold but not fresh or rewarding. Almost condemning. It smelled of an odd faint chemical. She felt soiled. A passing freight train vibrated the sidewalk as if agreeing, the noise growing until it roared.

After the train passed, she looked up and down the street. One car was parked nearby, its dashboard alarm light blinking red. Far down, two men walked in her direction. Their gray sweatshirt hoods hid their faces, their hands in pockets, silently moving together as if programmed robots. She hurried to stick the small key in the lock on her bike, her fingers trembling. She hoped Zbiggy wouldn't come out to argue about the price or quality of the flowers. She freed the bike from the post and as she rolled it off the curb, she noticed the rear tire was flat.

"*Merde.*" Her head pounded from hunger. She searched around. The men neared at a steady clip. They watched her. She checked her pocket for her phone. Call a cab or take the métro. She'd made three-hundred sixty euros. She'd spend forty getting back to Saint-Germain, or more. And waiting for a cab would be . . . she tapped the map app and punched in "Marx Dormoy, métro station," then took the handlebars and ran alongside the bike, hearing one of the men whistle, maybe mocking maybe not, like a siren sounding from an ambulance.

CHAPTER TEN

On Saturday morning, Renia woke with a hangover. Her head ached more from regret than alcohol. In the bathroom, she examined the puffy, tired woman in the mirror, resolving to get her life together. She brushed her teeth with extra toothpaste, then took a long hot shower and brushed her hair free of knots. She washed dishes and dusted and laundered her clothes. Even shined her shoes. Afterward, she trudged with her bike to the Marais and dropped it off at a repair shop before heading to the *Préfecture de Police*.

There would be no more flower sales. Successful people in Paris worked at legal jobs, did honest work to earn money, and so would she. As she went inside the police station, she reviewed her utility bills on her phone. The main bundle was up to date, but the electricity was late. She hadn't paid it in two months and had accrued a late charge of sixty euros. If she could sell a few more botanical sketches, she could make another one-hundred euros—although she'd have to account for the shop's consignment cut, which would leave her short again.

Inside the police station, she waited at the counter. A dozen uniformed officers sat at desks typing and talking on phones. The French flag hung on the wall. Beside it, a framed photo of Sarkozy emanated wit and intelligence. It rattled her. Sarkozy wasn't an angel, but he was the president. Official. The man all good, law-abiding citizens answered to. As she stared at his fine haircut and expensive suit, her early morning resolve to make wholesome choices crumbled. She wasn't Parisian. Zbiggy was right; she was just a lowly Polish girl.

She wondered if Officer Kateb had monitored her calls. If he'd followed her last night. She'd made the appointment a few days earlier, after she'd spoken with Director Bankole and before she'd decided to work with Zbiggy. Now, she kneaded her hands as a female officer neared and asked why she was there. She started to answer but lost her voice. She cleared her throat. "I have an appointment with Officer Kateb."

The woman motioned to a wooden bench along the wall. Renia sat, her stomach hurting with a pang of shame. The fluorescent lights burned with white heat. The traffic outside beeped and zoomed too loudly. She searched through images of houseplants on her phone, trying to lose herself in the leaves, the exotic flowers, thinking if she could find a rare plant to sketch, she could dazzle the shop's customers and make honest money.

Soon, Kateb came out and greeted her. He was in a light blue shirt with a tie, navy pants, a thick belt of gadgets, and a baton.

Renia stood, waiting for him to lead her to his desk but he didn't move, a hand on his walkie-talkie.

In an awkward start, she said, "Do you still have time for a meeting?"

"Yes." His face was neutral, his eyes neutral.

"I wondered whether the autopsy results had come back."

"Yes, they've been completed." A red shaving scar bobbed on his neck as he spoke.

She waited.

He said nothing.

"And did they? What did they find in Alain's blood?" she said. *After all, I'm an innocent friend who wants to know how my friend died.*

"I can't divulge details."

Now both hands were on his belt. A small gun in a holster hugged his leg.

"Can you tell me the . . ." she searched her mind for the term, "the cause of death?"

"No."

"Not even that?"

"No," he said. His voice was blank. "Sorry."

"Will it become public later?"

"Maybe," he said. "I advise you to call the deceased's parents. If you're curious about cause of death, they can tell you. They have a copy of the report."

"Oh." Renia thought of Alain's parents. Catherine and . . .? What was his father's name? She couldn't remember. But his father would be Tolbert. "His mother's name is Catherine Tolbert, is that correct?"

"I can't tell you that."

"I think his mother's name is Catherine." His father's name was Christian, or Christophe, maybe.

Kateb was silent.

"Do they live in Orléans?"

"I don't remember, but if I did, I can't tell you, I have to protect their privacy."

"Was an obituary published?"

"I don't know if an obituary was published. That's a family matter."

He glanced at his watch, rocked back on his heels. His face had the smoothness of youth. Sections of his cheeks hadn't sprouted hair yet.

She thanked him and left. As she went downstairs, she sucked in air. Hot tears formed in her eyes. This guy wasn't on her side. Kateb wanted nothing to do with her. And why should he? For all he knew, she may have helped drive Alain to kill himself.

Who *was* on her side?

Quietly, she said, "No." She wouldn't collapse, she wouldn't. Instead, she headed to Le Sanctuaire, searching her mind for Alain's parents' names. She recalled a birthday card addressed to him on his desk. Their names were Catherine and Christian Tolbert. She was sure of it. She got out her phone and called François.

"I'm happy to hear your voice," he said, "but I don't have time to chat. Their names are Catherine and Celian Tolbert. I'll text you her number. Let's get together for lunch. I'd like to know how you've been."

She wiped her eyes, her breath calming. She remembered Alain, last month at Le Sanctuaire, in the atrium, rearranging flowers in one of Palomer's bouquets—a bouquet he was about to take to the symphony for a soloist's performance. The soloist, a violinist, was an old friend of François's. "My mother wanted me to be a violinist," he'd said. "Instead, I became an organizer." He smiled and sorted cut flowers into three piles. "You know how I like to organize everything."

She did know. That's why they'd been friends: they both appreciated control. As she cut through Place Saint Sulpice, she thought it odd to know that particular fact about two people she'd never met. Alain's opinion of his parents wasn't negative, though she knew they hadn't approved of his move to Paris. He'd told her, as he'd deducted baby's breath and added more fully bloomed roses to the bouquet, that they thought he'd spent too much money and chased after status by moving to Paris. Of course, Renia didn't know the whole history. Families, including her own, were like multi-colored lines in a child's abstract drawing: jumbled, inter-secting, and making only a nebulous, highly imperfect picture of togetherness. Alain's parents had raised him. They knew a more intimate, more vulnerable side Renia had never known, and now unfortunately never would.

When she arrived at the shop, she flipped on the *Ouvert* sign as her phone dinged. She lay the phone on the counter, eyeing François's text with the number. Would they welcome a friend of Alain's they'd never met? A random young woman with a Polish accent? She smoothed her hair, checked her nails for dirt, then straightened a display of snips and scissors and other cutting tools. Would they think her needy and ridiculous? She gathered her breath and dialed Catherine. She blurted a request to meet for her own closure. Alain was a close friend, her first friend in Paris, she explained, and it would help her grief. Without hesitation, Catherine said her husband was sched-uled to be in Paris for business the following week and that she could join him for a day to meet Renia. Renia ended the call, relieved at the woman's warmth.

ON TUESDAY, she locked the shop and rode her bike to meet Madame Palomer in Montparnasse. She would have transferred the rent money online, but Palomer didn't trust the online system. So Renia met her at the Carroll Café, lunch time being the only window Palomer had available. Inside the café, the walls were decorated with a Belle Époque mural of Alice in Wonderland. The Mad Hatter loomed over the back wall, his hands raised, reciting his poem beside a clock with a broken face. To his right, the Queen of Hearts, dressed in vibrant cherry robes and glaring at a skinny flamingo, floated above Palomer. She was seated at a private booth in the corner. With her powder blue jacket and strawberry blonde hair, Madame blended in as if she too were a character. On the table, her phone quietly played Berlioz's "Symphonie Fantastique."

They exchanged *bises*. Palomer's face was ruddy as if she had gotten too much sun. She wore her sunglasses and light pink lipstick that matched her manicured nails. She had returned from Greece early, claiming the sunny weather hadn't agreed with her, but Renia thought it more likely that she'd gotten into a spat with her sister-in-law, who this past spring she'd called, "a foul-mouthed, short-tempered snake."

"Who is at the shop?" Palomer said. "Minh?"

Renia sat down, reluctant to mention she'd closed it for an hour. Nine months ago, Palomer had encouraged her to close at lunchtime, but lately she'd been emailing about exact work hours and sales numbers.

"Yes, Minh's there." She took the rent envelope from her purse and laid it on the table.

"Oh, wonderful. Thank you, dear, for preparing it early and coming in person."

"It was no problem."

"And I'm so relieved you'll stay. I can't imagine interviewing potential tenants in the state I'm in."

"Are you ill?"

"Well, the migraines!"

"Ah, yes."

"They flare up whenever they like. I can't schedule anything anymore."

They chatted about Palomer's trip. She told Renia how a con artist had removed a gold necklace from her neck as she napped on the beach though, fortunately, it was returned later by a boy who claimed to have "found" it. As Palomer finished the story, a waiter came to take her order, which Renia politely declined despite her gurgling stomach.

"Leaving so soon?" Palomer said. "At least have a coffee."

"I have to get back to the shop." The truth was she had no money for lunch. She'd used that week's lunch money toward Minh's paycheck. Lunch would be stale baguette and butter later.

"Yes, of course. And I have to call the clinic. This pain in my foot has gotten worse but I'm going to a specialist in a few weeks to see what he can do. He'll probably do nothing, but I'll give it a try anyway."

Renia was about to wish her good luck when Palomer said, "In fact, on the way home from the specialist, I'll save you a trip to Montparnasse and stop by the store to collect November's rent."

"November's? It's not even October."

"Well, yes, but my appointment's on October 28th, that's almost November 1st anyway."

"Yes, three days from November." Renia needed those three days. She imagined the tea tin on the étagère, its gold interior reflecting nothing.

"This way, you don't have to ride your bicycle here and catch a cold. In fact, I don't know why you don't take the métro, dear. We have the best subway system in the world."

She was about to say, "I know" and "I ride because you live equidistant from three stations," and "I can't afford the few euros for the damn subway," but instead said, "Yes, next time I will. Good luck with your appointment." Renia gave her *bises*, catching the rosy perfume on Palomer's neck. She stifled a frown and said, "I hope they can help you."

RENIA LEFT THE CAFÉ, maneuvering around a woman in an apron polishing the restaurant's wooden doors, catching the odor of furniture wax. The same wax used to clean the desks at the School of Economics. Strong. A sour smell with a touch of lemon. The shined oak, the polished floor. She remembered the small amphitheater, the dim lights. Her class, Interpersonal Communications. The room was a half-circle with counters ascending in concentric rings. A scattering of students listening, taking notes. At the front, a mammoth projection screen glowed. On it was a drawing of a person speaking to a listener with folded arms, then below, a listener covering his ears, and below that, a listener covering his face. The professor, in a dry recitation, lectured on the value of unlocking communication.

She sat at a counter halfway down the stairs by the aisle, writing notes on paper.

A loud thud echoed. Students looked around. The professor paused. Above at the room's entrance, a woman dragging a suitcase had angled in and was jerking the door, so it shut with a boom. The professor resumed his lecture. The woman shielded her eyes as if the ceiling lights were too bright.

Her hair had shifted awkwardly out of a messy barrette at the back, greasy and uncombed as if she'd run a marathon or gone on a drunken bender. She had on a dirty coat that was unbuttoned. Her jeans were ripped at the knees, but not in a purposefully fashionable way, and her boots were covered with splashes of mud. If she hadn't had such a new suitcase, Renia would have guessed she was homeless.

Estera.

In a panic, she hurried up the stairs, and viciously whispered, "What are you doing here?"

"I need to talk to you."

A few students turned.

"Wait for me outside," Renia said.

"No, I can't. I have to leave."

"Wait for me. I can't miss class."

"But I have to leave."

Her purse was under her seat. In a spring, she hustled and grabbed it, leaving her books and bag. She yanked Estera by the upper arm and escorted her out the door.

The hallway, carpeted and quiet, was empty. In the brighter light, Estera's face showed two bloodshot eyes, as if she hadn't slept all night.

In a thoughtless blurt, Renia said, "What happened to you?"

Estera shrugged. "I was up late."

That was obvious. "Why?"

Estera brushed her bangs so they lay spread over her forehead. She lifted her chin. "I'm leaving Zbiggy."

"Leaving him?"

"Yes."

Renia knew they'd been arguing, but at seeing her face, her clothes, her hair, she realized things were worse than she thought.

"I'm going to Paris," Estera said.

"What? With what money?"

"I have enough for a train ticket, a hotel for a few nights." She took Renia's hands to hold in hers. They were hot, sweaty, like she'd been running a fever. "Come with me."

"Come with you? I have class. I can't go anywhere." Renia doubted Estera had enough money to stay in Paris. And that wasn't part of the plan. "This isn't the right time."

"But it's never been the right time." The look in her eyes was desperate, a desperation Renia hadn't seen since Estera had dented Tata's car years ago. Renia thought of Biały Manor. She hadn't worked there since August and now felt regret that she hadn't been watching over her sister closely enough. "Estera, did you lose your job? Did you lose it?"

Estera chewed her lips. They were dry and chapped. She ignored the question. "Do you have any money?"

"No. I mean yes, but did you lose your job?" Renia asked again.

"I didn't get fired but Pan Górski's mad at me."

Estera's hair had earlier been curled with an iron. Now, it hung in limp chunky strands. "Well, if you've been hungover like this and missing work, I can see why. It's Monday for God's sake."

"Can you drive me to the train station?"

"No, but I'll drive you to Biały Manor."

"I can't stay in Kraków."

"Why?"

Her face flushed red. "Because if I do, I have to help him, and I don't want to anymore."

"Help who?"

Estera's eyes shifted downward.

Renia understood. Estera wanted to escape—with the Violet Smoke. She didn't want to sell the flowers. Why Zbiggy needed to sell the flowers was the real problem.

"He uses the money to party, doesn't he?" Renia said. "What is he using? Please don't say heroin."

"No, not at all. He likes . . ."

"He's a pothead."

"No!" Estera glared.

Cocaine. Renia couldn't say the word. It would wound her. "Oh God, Estera, he's exactly like the last two men you dated."

"No, he's not." She bristled. "He can't help it, he likes to have fun. We like to have fun together. But I told him he'd taken it too far and he had to stop, and we got into a fight and that's when . . ." Her face crumpled. She sobbed into her knuckles. "I have to leave him, Renia. I have to. Otherwise, I have no self-respect."

Renia opened her arms and Estera fell into them. Her hair, despite not being washed, was silky in her hands.

When Estera calmed down, Renia said, "Listen, let's get something to eat. Some soup, something warm. You'll feel better. I'll lend you a couple hundred if you still need it. But let's wait to go to Paris. We can do it soon. Maybe next month, if we do it together."

Estera wiped her face. "Really?"

"Yes."

"You're right," Estera said. "Let's make a vow: never go alone."

"No, never."

"You're my best friend, Renia, my best."

"I know, you're mine too, Steri." She wrapped her arm around her shoulders. They felt bony. "Let me get my books and I'll call Jan at the estate. I'll tell him you've been sick."

She wiped her eyes with a sleeve. "No, no. I'll go, later. Pan Górski will understand. Jan won't, but Górski will. And I'll work things out with Zbiggy tonight."

Renia paused. "Are you sure?"

"It's fine. I don't want to leave anyway. He feels awful about the whole thing. This morning he cried because he'd been so harsh. You should see those sad eyes in the mornings. He's such a teddy bear."

"Estera, you just said he spends too much money."

"Well," her voice was high, as if she couldn't explain the change of heart, the change back to forgiveness. "I love him Renia, and our life isn't that bad. My little Violet Smoke does bring in eight-hundred a month for us. I only wish he didn't pressure me to grow more flowers. And I wish he didn't go to Chorzów and sell to Russians. Otherwise, we get along okay. He loves me, Renia, he really does."

"Wait. Russians?"

"Oh, oops." She weakly smiled. "Yeah. They're a bit scary, especially that guy Vlad, but they're nice enough. They're quiet. The best thing though is they keep us in business."

CHAPTER ELEVEN

That Friday, Renia left the shop to Minh and rode her bike to Les Invalides. When she entered the Hotel Charles Floquet, she found Catherine and Celian Tolbert in the lobby, a small classic lounge with navy walls and brass mirrors. It smelled of warm croissants. The couple sat on leather arm chairs, Catherine reading a magazine, Celian staring at a painting above the fireplace. She saw Alain's brown eyes in his mother, his knowing expression, his long fingers. His father, dressed in khaki slacks with a sweater tied at the neck, was reserved. Neither smiled at their introductions nor looked away. When Renia suggested they have tea in the nearby café, they both declined in shy voices.

An awkward silence hung until Renia realized that, since she'd suggested the meeting, she better say something. She thanked them, which they brushed off. She offered condolences and talked about what a good friend Alain had been, which enlivened their spirits. They asked how Alain and Renia had met, whether he had seemed happy in Paris. Renia, predicting they knew Alain's mood swings, tried to sound positive. "He loved his job very much."

"When was the last time you saw him?" Catherine asked.

Renia thought about those last weeks in August, after a huge wedding that had drained him. She thought of not the last day, that Tuesday at Le Sanctuaire when he'd been humorously bitter, but the Thursday before. How he'd holed up in his apartment, had only ordered food out, and hadn't cared whether she visited. "I saw him in August." She'd brought him a bouquet of leftover bluebeard, cosmos, and hibiscus. He cared little, waving toward the kitchen for her to set it down.

When she was inside, he had asked her about the Violet Smoke. At first, he said he wanted to try it again, try anything to get out of his depressive hole, but then he changed his mind and told her to forget it. She agreed it was best he recover without it. Then he disagreed. Their polite exchange escalated into an argument. He paced, said he did want the flower. He pleaded with her in an angry snipe. When she had given him the flower the first time in July, he'd forgotten François had had an affair but later remembered when François accidentally referred to it. So, she refused.

"He was feeling okay, a little sad," Renia said to Catherine. She remembered him threatening to kill himself, then laughing, saying he was too much of a coward to kill himself. He'd wanted to escape into another life. "Open a time portal and jump through," he'd said.

"He might have been ill," Renia said, "with a cold."

They nodded, their expressions taut with pain.

She imagined Alain's blood dripping down the building. The booming sounds of the tympani and trombones. That dramatic concerto No. 2. "All of Rachmaninoff's turmoil and sadness went into it," he'd said. He'd left the world in a very Alain way. The question was, was it by accident or intentional?

Cautiously, she inched forward on her chair. "I was curious. Do you know if the autopsy report showed any . . . medicine in his bloodstream?"

"We wondered about that too," Celian said. "But no. Not even his anti-depressant medication, which may have been part of the problem."

"So, there were no medicines or unusual chemicals in his blood?"

"Which chemical?"

"Oh, I don't know. Any chemical."

"If you mean drugs, like, what is it?" he said. "Ecstasy? Then, no. Nothing like that. Some alcohol but not an excessive amount."

"Wait," Catherine said. "Yes, there was something unusual. Didn't the examiner say they found a relaxant in his blood? It was some kind of natural sleep aid."

Celian clicked his tongue, thinking. "Yes, the examiner did mention it. A natural supplement, like Valerian Root. But the only obvious drug was alcohol."

Renia nodded, wondering if the Violet Smoke was a botanical relative of Valerian Root. She pictured Alain on the floor, a lifeless body, his arm cut. "So . . . I'm sorry," she stopped, feeling her throat constrict.

Catherine patted her forearm.

"Did the examiner determine his death was an accident?" Renia said.

She thought either parent would say "yes," or "no," or "it was a psychotic episode brought on by a strange scent," but instead Celian declared, "We'll never know."

Renia blinked. "What?"

"He said he did deem it an 'accident', but he really couldn't determine whether it was or not."

"He cut his wrist on a broken piece of glass," Catherine said. "From his desk."

"Then he hit his head hard on the balcony railing," Celian said. "Bled to death. Whether he cut himself before he passed out or stumbled and cut himself, we don't know. The examiner thought he may have tripped and tried to catch himself with the table edge, which then broke and sliced his wrist. The wrist cut did not seem clean, it was a gash. So as soon as he hit his head, he could have blacked out . . ." Celian sighed, "unable to rouse himself and attend to the wound."

Renia's stomach tightened. Alain must have felt alone and frantic. Not knowing whether he'd inhaled the flower and fallen asleep ate at her. She would never know. And that reality sank in her mind like heavy silt.

Stupid plant. That day when she was at the bank, he'd removed the panel in the atrium and found it. She condemned herself for letting him know about it and condemned him for going against her warnings. Forgetting where she was, she said, "Oh, why did he do it?"

Their stunned faces brought her back to the hotel. Did they think she knew he killed himself? "I'm sorry, I mean . . . I don't know if he did it to end his life. He probably didn't. He was mostly a happy person. Very happy." That was a light lie but they seemed to need reassurance.

With a soft, wavering voice, Catherine said, "He was our joy. We didn't want him to live in Paris, but he refused. He loved Paris. You couldn't talk him out of leaving the city."

Renia thought about how she and Alain would never shop at the flea market or visit a museum or share dinner again. She hung her head.

"I'm glad he had a good friend," Catherine said. "He mentioned you from time to time. Said you were as sharp as a lightning strike."

"He said that? 'A lightning strike?'"

She nodded. Her eyes lit with the memory of her son's eloquence. "He said you had revived Le Sanctuaire. He thought it was tired and considered closing his account until you came. He said you had created one of the most interesting shops in Paris. That there was always some unique plant or handmade lotion to find. And according to him, it was the talk of Saint-Germain."

Renia exhaled a smile. The residents of Saint-Germain were talking about her? She'd thought he'd always viewed Le Sanctuaire as a necessary but practical evil. And that he was doing her a favor by being her friend. She sat back. The painting above the fireplace showed a soldier riding a horse. The horse, a brown stallion with a leather bit in its mouth, the whites of its eyes clear and bold, reared back about to plunge forward on a mission. Whether the soldier's contorted face displayed lust for battle or worry at his impending death was a matter of interpretation. "Thank you for letting me know," she said, "it helps me go on."

DURING THE NEXT SEVERAL DAYS, Renia focused on bringing in more income to Le Sanctuaire. Now that she knew people actually liked the shop, she felt more committed to keeping it afloat. She drew four new sketches of trees and put them in cheap frames she found at a charity shop. With Minh, she built a display of hay, blue corn, pumpkins, and purple cabbage on the terrace. Uncle Feliks brought three potted dwarf apple trees with red fruit to sell on consignment. She offered free croissants and hot cider to anyone who signed up for the store's email list. Though she and Minh debated about having a Cocktails and Crafts party, they decided against it, knowing Palomer would not approve of the initial cost. Instead, they decided Renia would offer a weekly "How to Draw Plants" class in the atrium.

Though there was a brief uptick in business, a turbulent spell of weather chilled Paris through two weekends. In the early evenings, pedestrians hurried home to avoid the wind. Ironically, the few customers who visited mentioned stopping in simply to warm up. One day, a young woman came in, in need of a pair of rubber boots in an unusually large size. Renia special ordered them. After they arrived and Renia made reminder calls, the customer never returned. Lastly, only two people signed up for her drawing class, forcing her to cancel it.

Meanwhile, Zbiggy called. She ignored the message.

The final blow happened one morning when Renia went downstairs to get her mail. The electricity bill was stamped with a Final Notice warning. Her service would be shut off in three days. Seeing the boxy red letters on the bill made her panic. She couldn't live without heat or lights. She went upstairs, paced in a worn circle as her pride deteriorated.

There was no other way. She gave in and called Zbiggy.

His voice mail clicked on. A simple "Yo!" and a beep. She hung up, wanting to tell him she would not meet him in a shady bar again, would not wait more than fifteen minutes, would not let him jerk her around. Her finger hovered over his number, tempted to redial and leave a message on his voicemail, when the phone rang.

"Saw your number, Polish girl. Let's make some money."

What does that mean? Was he taking a cut? "I'm not doing what I did last time."

"I know, I know. I won't be late again."

She laid out the terms for future transactions. Meet at the square Boucicaut. Never come to Le Sanctuaire again. Ring her twice by phone and she would call him back. Arrive on time.

"Yes, yes," he said. "We can do all of that. Last time I got busy. Don't worry, this time I won't. In fact, this next deal is even better. This guy I know, he saw what the—your merchandise—can do. He's rich. But he likes women, you know? And his wife, she's a problem. And he's got other problems too he'd like to take care of. You know what I mean? Your scarves could take care of them."

A philanderer. "So, this guy wants his wife to forget an affair?"

"Well . . . it's more complicated than that but kind of. Listen, he's rolling in it. Wants five flowers—I mean scarves. He'll pay."

"Then meet me at the square Boucicaut tomorrow evening."

"Is tomorrow Wednesday? See that's a problem. I can't make it Wednesday."

Renia's voice fell flat. She promised herself she'd control the situation. "Really? You've got to be kidding."

"And this rich friend, he can't make it either."

"But you haven't spoken to him yet."

"Yeah, but I know he can't by tomorrow. And I'm working."

"Do you truly have a job?"

"Yes, working for my friend. But listen, our boss will meet you. He wants to meet you anyway."

"That sounds worse."

"No, no. He's a cool guy, he's like part owner of that bar, where we, you know, had a drink."

He didn't want to mention the Misha Bar by name, or his "friend" or his friend's "boss."

"Whatever. If we meet, we need to meet tomorrow."

"I'll let him know," he said. "Pick out five nice scarves for him, *mała polka*."

ON WEDNESDAY, as evening fell, Renia entered the square Boucicaut. She felt glad because she wasn't in Marx Dormoy, but worried that no one else was in the park. The sun set. Its faint glow dipped behind the trees and the shadows stretched together. She waited on a bench beside an exotic monkey puzzle tree, her leg bouncing as she tried to distract herself by counting its scaly branches. Soon, a lone family—father, mother and child—strolled through with briefcases and backpacks. They shared blond hair and pale, innocent faces. The father spoke warmly to the boy, pecking his head with kisses, reciting a poem. Renia couldn't recall if her own father had ever read a poem. He certainly had never kissed her head. The air dampened, the wind bit every time it blew. She buttoned her overcoat, checked her watch: ten minutes after six. The park closed at sundown. She debated whether a city worker, soon to come and lock the gate, would help or hinder what was about to happen.

Five minutes later, a man emerged from the foliage on the less used western path. He wore a thigh-length leather jacket and jeans. He was broad and tall with a muscular neck and thick hands. He had a sagging mouth, a high bony forehead and thinning hair the color of wheat. As he advanced, he scanned the square, especially the bushes. He wore a gold ring with an ebony gem on his right hand and a gold chain at his neck that glinted in the park's lights.

Renia took a few steps toward him, then paused, wanting to stay in the open and off shady paths.

He walked with a casual, confident gait, his hands away from his hips. His expression had a slightly tense smirk as if he expected someone to pop out of the shrubs and jump him.

As he approached, she addressed him with a code name. "Monsieur Fleur?"

He nodded with a wink, passed her, and went into the shaded path.

She scanned the park. No one was about.

"I prefer to stay in the open," she said.

He turned around. He was a full head taller than she. He smelled like fried onions. "Come under trees, it's better this way."

"I prefer it here."

He rubbed her shoulder. "Of course you do. But come."

"I won't. It's getting dark."

His mouth switched from a content smirk to a frowning crescent, dipping at the corners. "There are six-hundred euros here, not there." His accent was Russian. Even in French, she could tell the difference between her own Polish accent and his. He smiled. "Come, I'm bigger than any of these Paris frogs. You have nothing to fear from them."

With a reluctant caution, she followed.

In the shaded passage, thorny hawthorn branches hung low and spiky holly leaves bulged into the path. She assessed which direction would be quicker for escape.

His hand pressed on her lower back.

She spun around. "Don't touch me. Please do not touch me."

He came in close. His eyes were the color of a gray rock, dense and rough. They made a sweep from her hair to her face to her chest. "Don't worry, sweetheart, nothing bad will happen. It's all good."

The holly leaves scraped her neck.

"You know, you're cute. Do you want to make extra money? I've got work for you."

"I'm not interested."

He half-smiled. "You've got nice eyes. The rich ones always want big-eyed girls."

"This is ridiculous. I need to go. Do you want the flowers or not?"

He grabbed her arm and yanked her body to his chest. "Yes, flowers." His hand was spread wide, clutching her rear.

In a snap, she said, "Let go of me."

He pressed her torso to his crotch.

She felt sick. With a breathy struggling voice, she said, "If you want the flowers, let go of me, now."

With both hands, she pushed on him hard and broke from his hold. He stumbled, laughing. "I love a spunky Polish girl." He took out his wallet and waved a wad of bills. "Come, spicy cookie."

In a brittle reluctance, she inched forward. As she put the bag of flowers in his palm, she snatched the money.

He laughed. "You're quick like a mouse."

She stepped far back and counted the bills, her face flush. There were six hundred-euro bills. As she put them deep in her coat's breast pocket, she said, "Listen, the flowers will only last two days. Fifty or so hours at most. Don't wait to use them, don't be stupid and accidentally kill—"

He yanked the lapels of her coat to his face. The vein in his forehead was raised.

She blinked.

"Who are you calling stupid?" His face locked into a fierce frown. She felt his breath on her lips.

"No one."

He poked her clavicle hard with a finger. "Don't call me stupid. Ever. Understand?"

A brown mole clung to his ear like a blob of mud.

Her mouth felt lax. "Yes."

"I'm not one of your fancy customers or whoever the hell you sell to. I'm Vlad, do you hear me? And I'm not bossed around because I am boss. I'm Vlad. I run this operation." He sneered, giving her a rough jolt.

She stumbled, losing her balance, worried she'd fall in the grit.

With a parting glare, he walked away, out from under the trees into the lighter silver sky. She wanted to jump after him, scratch his eyes out, kick him in the crotch. Instead, she straightened her body, retied her coat, and smoothed her lapels. Wiping her mouth, she marched out of the park, checking that she still had his money.

THAT EVENING, the door to Saint Ignace church was unlocked. Renia went inside. The tall cathedral was quiet, candlelit, its stone walls rising in a cloistered glory. The arches curved over her head like a mother curved over a child. She sat at the back, below the stained-glass windows, the purple flowers rising in a cheery geometry to heaven. Renia absorbed the noble architecture, the dignified respect to God, and rested in the safe silence.

An elderly woman in a plaid coat entered and dipped her hand in the holy water. With her wavy hair, low-heeled pumps and modest dress, she reminded Renia of her mother at Sunday mass. Mama once told her of how, during nursing school, she'd had a professor who liked to pinch her rear end and often tried to kiss her. Renia had had her own brief encounters with men of his kind but not in years. The feel of Vlad's hand on her backside, gripping that private place . . . her head swam. And the feel of his crotch against her stomach. She shivered. She'd been mildly, what, assaulted? She didn't feel justified using the word because she thought of Estera and what that word had meant for her. She went to the oil candles and lit one before placing it at the feet of Mother Mary.

The metallic scent of the candle oil rose in the air. She'd smelled it once before, in darkness, in an open area, not in a soaring house of worship but a cramped apartment. Not with marble floors but shag carpeting. And not with stained-glass but a blocky picture window. No straight pews, no flowered altar. Instead, a smooshed sofa, a buzzing light, the flame of a candle on a windowsill.

Estera had opened the door but did not appear. Renia inched into the apartment. The sitting area was dark, the curtains half-open, a liquid candle burning. A chipped painting of a sailboat hung crookedly over the sofa. A lamp on an end table, as if batted, leaned against the wall. Clothes lay scattered amidst an overturned ashtray on the floor. Bread crumbs littered the sofa. In the kitchen, dishes sat mounded in the sink. The warm light over the stove was splattered with grease. The room smelled of wet socks and metallic oil.

"Steri, where are you?"

"Here." She hid behind the door. In the dim, she was a meek outline of long hair and terry cloth robe. The pocket was torn and dangling. Her hair seemed wet, like she had come from the shower. Her right eye was swollen and blue.

"Is that a bruise?" Renia said.

Estera neither nodded nor shook her head. Her eyelashes tremored, her lips pinched shut.

"What happened?" Renia guided her to the sofa. She set the lamp upright, found a chain, pulled it. A yellow light illuminated pillows smashed into the couch, the scrunched fast food wrappers on the coffee table. They sat. Estera's chin was cut, her eye swollen, but the worst evidence was her neck. It had red burn marks at either side as if hands had been grinding it.

"You're hurt."

"It's nothing."

"Steri," Renia whispered.

Estera hung her head, covered her mouth. Her body trembled.

"Did he do this?"

Estera's eyes answered, a half-lidded disappointment.

"Oh Steri."

Estera wiped her nose with a sleeve. "Don't worry, it's nothing."

Renia wanted to dart up and pace around, to scream that her sister didn't deserve this life. She forced her voice to stay gentle. "I want you to be safe."

"Well, it's my fault. I started it."

Renia ached. That was a lie. "What was it about?"

Estera tilted her head as if the ceiling with its cracks and crooked light fixture could explain. "It was about my sweet violet."

She waited.

"It won't bloom. I've been fertilizing it, watering it carefully so it dries out enough, you know? I keep it on a tray of wet pebbles, in indirect light. I do all of the things it's always liked and yet . . ."

"It's probably tired. It needs to rest and go through dormancy."

Estera shook her head. "It's autumn, it blooms in autumn."

"Is it here?"

"No, at Biały Manor. But . . . Zbiggy doesn't understand. He doesn't understand a plant grows however it wants."

"Maybe it's best to give it away or . . ."

"No." Estera's face soured with resentment. "I can't believe you'd suggest that."

"I'm worried for you. Zbiggy doesn't take care of you."

"He does in his own way." Her tone sharpened. "But he spends too much money on his 'head candy.' We don't have a scrap of food in this apartment but every time he works he stays at the club afterwards to party."

They sat in silence.

"Estera, come home with me. Think about what to do next." Renia made sure not to mention their parents' names.

Estera's mouth drooped. "Tata thinks I make it worse because I go drinking with him."

"Yes, I know."

Estera slumped over.

"Listen," Renia said, "let's get you dressed. Leave him a note and come with me, only for tonight. You don't have to decide anything."

Estera nodded. A hair strand was stuck to her cheek. She made no move to leave. Renia rubbed her arm. She knew if nothing else, Estera would do it as a favor.

Finally, Estera went to change in the bedroom. Renia ran hot water in the kitchen sink and poured in soap. She washed the burnt butter off a pan, dried grease and tomato sauce from bowls and glasses, silverware. She scrubbed each plate and cup as hard as she could. There was one plate, smaller than the rest, that was particularly pretty. She didn't recognize it but knew Estera had chosen it. It had a weave of vines and grapes along the edge. Purple and green. A Tuscan pattern one had to inspect closely to appreciate. As Renia scrubbed it, she knew full well that even though Estera would leave with her tonight, she couldn't talk her out of returning tomorrow. Grime was clouding Estera's judgment and Renia yearned to clean that away, too, so her sister could rediscover who she truly was.

CHAPTER TWELVE

A few days later, Renia went to work in Valenton. There was no other way. She'd promised herself that what had happened at the square Boucicaut would never happen again. She'd promised herself to never call Zbiggy again. So, she merged into the crew at Les Racines Nursery and got to work. Her first morning, she loaded perennials onto trucks bound for Marseille. By lunchtime, her back ached and her feet had blisters. In the afternoon, she picked orders for clients, hauled perennials and shrubs from greenhouses onto trailers, then drove the loaded tractor-trailers to the office, wondering how Uncle Feliks had done this physical work for decades.

The day before, she had gone to the EDF office and paid her electric bill. At least she'd avoided the lights going dark and did have most of November's rent. But even if she scraped up the rest by working at both the shop and Les Racines, she'd have a mere forty euros to eat, for a month. She could stretch and only buy rice, bread, tea. She'd already eliminated her Sunday visits to the *boulangerie* and the occasional bottle of wine weeks ago. But the garbage bill would come in five days and that was two months overdue as well. The heating was one month overdue. She still needed to earn several hundred euros. As she unloaded the last order into the holding area, she considered taking what was left of the emergency cash from the Le Sanctuaire safe.

She arranged the plants in rows, double-checking she'd pulled every plant on the order list, debating whether to ask Uncle Feliks for an advance on her paycheck. He'd say no. He'd had to work hard and suffer deprivation as a young person so Renia would have to as well. When she'd called him a few days earlier, he'd said, "What, do you want a job?" And she'd had to say, "Yes. Yes, I do." He'd said, "I need you to work in the field for a couple of days. After, you can work in the office." She agreed. He was paying her a few dollars more than the other workers, but he wouldn't do anything as indulgent as pay her before the work was completed. So, she went to the office to get another order list.

Later, after she'd transferred the shade perennials to the covered houses and the sun perennials to the office for the year-end sale, Renia changed her shoes and fetched her purse. Though Feliks was too busy to take her to the train, Paweł, the manager, in a quiet act of sympathy, clocked out and drove her. He was a stout, late-thirties man who wore faded overalls and long underwear shirts even in summer. In the van, she told him how thankful she was for the ride but he waved her off and they sat in silence until reaching the station. An hour and a half later, she arrived at the Gare de Lyon, exhausted and stiff. She strained to haul her bike off the train, then flinched as she lifted a leg to get on. Riding to Saint-Germain was like riding up Mont Ventoux. She pedaled at such a slow speed, she feared she'd wobble and fall off.

At home, she yearned for a bath but without a tub had no choice but to shower. Once the water warmed, she sunk down and sat on the tile, letting the merciful heat spray her body. The tendons and muscles loosened. Her face refreshed. When she was done, she dressed in her warmest fleece and fell into bed.

The next morning, she woke late. Her eyes felt like swollen clods of clay, her hurting body in need of more sleep. She hit the Snooze button three times and finally, dragged herself out of bed and got dressed. She wanted to feel grateful because she'd put in an honest day's work, but she was too worn out from feeling pain.

As she came downstairs and out of the building, she noticed the shop door wedged open. The lights were on. There was no shelf unit of plants on the terrace nor the bistro set or other plants. Schumann's piano concerto played on the outdoor speaker. The flutes and French horns cantered in a bold march as if to announce a monarch.

Inside, Madame Palomer sat behind the counter, typing on the desktop. Her pale face frowned in concentration.

"Oh, Renia, thank goodness you're finally here, I can't get this email program to work. It won't send. I've been wrestling with it all morning."

The wall clock read ten-fifteen.

"How long have you been here?" Renia said.

"Oh, all morning, all morning, since early, I don't know. But look at this, I can't use this, the screen keeps resetting itself."

Renia studied the screen. Palomer had sent her sister-in-law an email, seven times.

"It's been sent. It cleared the screen because you were finished."

"Ah, such silly computers. I'll never understand how these CEO men are millionaires."

With a sigh, Renia set her purse in the cabinet behind the counter. She wanted to ask Palomer why she'd come, why she'd come so early, and why she'd come and nearly locked them all out of the business's system, but she was too surprised by her presence.

When Palomer was satisfied that she'd found the Exit button and had closed her email program, she said, "*Alors*, we must discuss a few things, my dear. For instance, this morning, where were you? I came to the shop at nine o'clock and no one was to be found."

"Well, we don't open until ten."

"But there's a display to prepare. It's October. People expect a festive atmosphere. The hay and corn and all else was inside."

Renia stayed silent, listening to the tinkling piano, soft and forlorn. She wasn't sure whether it felt better to defend herself or collapse on the floor. "I'll do it right away."

"What would have happened if I hadn't come? It's ten-thirty. The door was locked. I was appalled when I found a locked door. How often are you late?"

"Never," Renia said. She pushed the tiered shelves outside, biting her tongue, her wrists throbbing with pain, her arms jittering. She could not afford for Palomer to fire her. On the outdoor speaker, the clarinet repeated the piano's melody. She set out the bistro table and chairs, the shrubs, the corn, all of the festive autumn warmth she felt an odd resentment toward.

When she finished, she yearned to sit on the stool in the atrium. It was the only other place to sit. Her back felt as if a knife was stuck in her spine. As she was about to slip away, Palomer said, "And Renia, I have another question."

Her face blazed, her voice, short. "Where is the emergency cash?"

Where was the cash? "What cash?"

"The one hundred euros I keep in the safe."

Renia chewed her lip, remembering. *I gave it to Minh so her mother wouldn't die.* "Minh needed it, so I gave it to her."

Palomer's face contorted with surprise, then shadowed with resentment.

"She had to drive her mother to a special therapist, so I gave it to her for the fee and gas money."

Palomer shifted. "Apparently you don't understand, my dear, how to manage money."

Renia nodded. "She really needed it. I was going to pay it back. I was going to take it out of her paycheck."

"I came by today to specifically take that money. I need it." She pinched out the last words, as if her struggles were urgent. Who knew? Perhaps they were.

Renia stared at the floor, they were on opposite sides of the counter, Palomer sitting on the stool, Renia standing across, feeling trapped by a blocky partition.

"I'm sorry. I'll withdraw money from my personal account and pay it back today."

"Oh, never mind," Palomer said. "I already went to the bank and took it from the business account."

Of course. On another day, a day when she hadn't felt so damn fatigued, Renia would've been furious. Palomer had gone to the bank but blamed Renia anyway. Now, all she felt was a vague disappointment at herself for not pointing out her boss's unpredictable ways.

"And the atrium," Palomer said. "I was under the impression your sister was picking up her plant, but that wall is still in place."

Like Minh, Palomer thought the Violet Smoke needed special growing conditions.

"Yes, I'm sorry. She needs more time."

"But we're losing storage."

Storage we don't need. "She hoped to pick it up in December." That was a lie, but perhaps by December she could find a new home for it, even if it meant building a temporary nook in the apartment upstairs.

"And another thing, my dear." Palomer pointed at the fountain.

The goddess poured cool water that made a soothing music.

"The fountain is crawling with brown mold. I assumed you had cleaned it weeks ago."

"Yes, sorry," she said. She noticed the goddess staring at her bare feet, lost in her own reserved thoughts, content to ignore the humans in the room. "I haven't gotten to it, I will."

Palomer let go a huffy breath. "But when?"

"I had planned on it today, in fact," Renia said. She went to the plug at the wall and yanked it. The dribbling water slowed to a drip.

"Okay, yes, well, good. I have to go, my dear. I take it you and not the Japanese girl will be here today?"

"Yes, Minh is off." *We're not paying her if that's what you mean.*

Palomer tugged her purse onto a shoulder. "Well, I have to get home. If I'm out for more than two hours, Julo gets anxious. The other day he wet my entry rug. I think he did it on purpose, naughty dog."

As Palomer limped past the fountain, Renia stared at the water in the bowl. It was still and reflective. The outline of Renia's head and shoulders was surrounded by plants as if in a ghostly jungle. She imagined climbing in the water and disappearing.

As Palomer opened the door, she paused and said, "Oh

and Renia, can you bring the rent to my apartment, next week, dear? I won't be able to stop by the shop. The doctor changed the appointment."

"But next week is not the end of the month," Renia said. Her voice was more insistent than she realized. When Palomer shot her a look, she calmed her tone. "I mean it's only the 28th then."

They eyed each other.

Renia was too tired and in the right to yield. Palomer had to give her this one thing. "I mean, I could really use until October 31st or even November 1st to pay." She didn't share that she didn't have the money. "I've been working for . . . my uncle to help supplement my income." She smiled. "And my paycheck only comes every two weeks."

The idea of Uncle Feliks registered well. For whatever reason, Palomer liked the old codger. "Alright," she said. "You can have until November 1st, but please, Renia, do wash that disgusting fountain."

AFTER PALOMER DROVE AWAY, Renia clicked off the *Ouvert* sign and put on rubber gloves. Why not use the flower on Palomer? Erase the idea that Renia owed her any rent money at all. That was irresponsible, and it wouldn't last. She baled the fountain's water into a bucket before detaching the statue from the pipe. She lay the goddess with her urn on the floor and with a groan, lifted the heavy bowl to carry outside. When she came to the curb, she tipped it in the street, then got on her knees and with lemon soap, scrubbed it with a brush. Palomer was right, the bowl had succumbed to brown slime.

Black boots approached on the sidewalk. She rinsed the grime with a bucket of water, then scrubbed and rinsed again. Water splashed. The black boots backed up. *What*

fool walks toward splashing water? They were work boots, not
for hiking but made of black leather with sturdy laces for
lasting impact and scuffed with lime dust. She looked up to
see who was inconveniencing her. A man in canvas pants, a
black jacket, hazelnut hair. He was in his mid-thirties, six
feet tall or more. A face as bold as her feelings right then.
Round eyes, tan complexion, plump lips. She wanted to
ask why he didn't move, wave a hand at him, ask him to
step around and leave her alone, but as she opened her
mouth to speak, she felt nervous and said nothing.

"Excuse me, Mademoiselle," he said, "I'm looking for
Madame Renia Baranczka." His voice was husky. He
pronounced Baranczka with the proper Polish *ch* sound
though he spoke French with a faint American accent.

How dangerous was it to reveal herself?

His face was relaxed and open, on the square side with
deep-set eyes shadowed by a low brow. His nose was simply
a nose, neither flat nor pointed, but his mouth, his broad
mouth, which dipped down in the middle, reminded her of
a child's mouth. It was as if that mouth wanted to pop
open and share dumb opinions. His hair, a short cut of
untamed waves, seemed too messy to be upstanding. In
fact, he had a whole brutish nature stuffed inside controlled
clean clothes and a courteous approach that didn't seem
natural. She concluded he was one of Zbiggy's thug
friends.

She tipped the bowl on edge and let the last water
drain in the street. Then again, he seemed too polite and
patient to be Zbiggy's pal. Still, better to be careful. "Who
wants to know?"

His surprised eyes said he wasn't prepared for that
answer. "Um, well, I would. I'm from the horticulture
university. Madame Baranczka asked for our assistance
with a botanical matter."

He pronounced her name correctly again.

She set down her brush and wiped a strand of hair from her face. "I'm Renia Baranczka."

"Ah," he nodded. "Andre Damazy."

Again, that voice. It was soothing in a brusque but disarming way.

He held out a hand and she showed him the wet gloves. "Come in."

She bent down to take the bowl but with an easy motion, he lifted it instead.

"Oh, thanks. Inside here," she led him to the fountain base. The column sat like a decapitated torso covered in concrete vines. He set the bowl in place, checking that the short pipe slid into the opening in the column. Meanwhile, she locked the door. "It's back here."

Once more, the bulk of a man was in the snug lean-to of the atrium. Her heart beat fast. She told herself that Professor Bankole was a professional, so this man must be as well. Nothing to fear. She took off her gloves and shut the door. He watched with a polite expression. Though he was slightly shorter than Bankole, she felt the room shrink. Maybe because his face was closer to her height, she didn't know. Regardless, she left him to stand and watch as she set her crow bar in the wall. With an assured crank, she pulled the panel back. She handed him the bar and he set it on the counter. She took hold of the loose board and lifted it. It tilted toward her, the giant panel about to fall against her head when his hand shot out and grabbed it.

She glanced upward. His body leaned far over hers. There was no going around it.

"Does it come fully out?" he said.

He smelled like stewed raspberries.

Air caught in her throat. She nodded.

He scraped past her, his belt buckle, an antique brass,

brushed her hip. Worried about his next move, she bit her lip. He said, "Excuse me," and reached gently over her with both hands, hoisting the panel and setting it cautiously against the stone wall.

She let go a relieved breath.

Atop the weathered table, the Violet Smoke sat in a damp Wardian Case, the venting windows having been closed for two days. Moisture droplets clung to its ceiling. Six blooms sat in two clusters.

"Oh my," he said. He bent down, his hands on his knees, as if watching television. His eyes worked their way from the flowers to the trunk and through the branch structure. "It looks like a *Saintpaulia* . . . tree."

"That's what my assistant calls it, an African violet tree. The leaves and flowers resemble that, though the flowers are larger, less frilly, more cupped, and it has woody branches."

"Yes, woody branches. Very unique. Very."

Estera would have liked this guy.

Damazy knelt lower to see the leaves' undersides. "Canescent there too . . . so Edo tells me it emits a powerful gas."

"Yes," she said. "I'd like to know what chemicals the gas contains."

He was mesmerized by the plant, unable to take his eyes from it. "Are the branches at first green and then turn light brown? Or are they greenish brown when they emerge?"

"They're green and lighten to that sandy color."

"I see."

He leaned in, his nose nearly at the glass, his eyes bright.

"We can take the greenhouse off," she said.

"That would be helpful."

"But you have to put on this." She held out a mask.

He smiled. "Is the gas toxic?"

"Well, it gives some people headaches."

She put on her mask.

His mouth was half-open in a faint smile. Once he put the mask on, she noticed it was too tight. She reached up and loosened the strap. In a calm patience, he waited for her to be finished, her fingers touching his hair, which was soft and cool.

"Can you smell anything?" she asked.

"No."

"Good."

"What does it smell like?"

"Burnt apricots."

"Ah." He turned to the plant, his mask swinging down like an exotic elephant. "Burnt apricots could mean it's related to *Streptocarpus*. But that genus has fewer longer leaves, and these are *Saintpaulia* leaves. Huh." He let go a long sigh.

Renia hoisted the glasshouse. When he reached to help, she said, "I've got it," and set it on the floor.

He was already measuring the leaf diameter with a small ruler, carefully studying its underside, counting the numbers in a whorl. He mumbled the words "hirsute" and "metabolites," then asked more questions, some of which Monsieur Bankole had asked, and asked his own, mostly about the plant's history, whether a "chemotaxonomy analysis" had been conducted, whether it had always given off a scent, whether its scent was stronger at night, whether it ever smelled without the inflorescences, whether he could speak with Pan Górski, and finally, whether he could take "tissue."

His way was serious yet gentle. Often, he stuck a hand in his hair when thinking, then pulled it out to leave a ridiculous tuft sticking up at the mask's belt. He asked twenty-five or thirty questions, some even about Pan Górs-ki's personality. She explained he was an old loner whose soft spot was plants. "I've known men like that," he said. He asked whether Górski traveled and quizzed her about the conditions of the orchid house in Poland. What other plants grew there, what plants Górski liked, what plants he might have used to develop it. Renia recalled that it was heated with high humidity though to what degrees day and night, she couldn't remember. She told him Pan Górski had passed away. She knew he'd exhausted his questions when he finally said, "This plant . . . I mean, it blows my mind."

She couldn't help but smile at his boyish awe.

"May I take a cutting?" he said.

Something about the vague desperation in his voice pressured her toward consent. He was genuinely stumped by it. "Let me think about it."

He stared at the plant like a father stares at a newborn baby. After a minute, he said, "Wow, this mask gets hot."

"Do you want to take it off?"

He nodded. "Very much."

"I'll put the greenhouse back," she said.

He lifted the case and set it over the plant, careful not to let his fingerprints press on the clean windows.

"Hold on," she said and swung open an atrium window. She switched on a tiny fan clipped to the counter. Cool air rushed at their bodies.

"I have a friend in London who's a plant explorer," he said. "He's quite experienced. He may be able to identify it."

Renia took off her mask, unable to suppress a coy smile.

He tilted his mask back to sit atop his head. "What is it?"

"That's what Monsieur Bankole said about you."

His cheeks were shiny with dew. His hair flailed out at the sides. "Well, I'm more of a breeder. I have a few ideas about what it's crossed with, but they don't fit. My friend explores for plants almost every year in Asia and South America. His knowledge is immense. It's really the best I can offer. I hate to say I don't know what it is, but I don't. It's a relative of *Saintpaulia*, that's all I can say for sure."

She felt momentary shame in calling him out. "Yes, I understand."

He gave the plant another quick study, circling around, his mouth slightly open, his eyes far off as if his mind churned with thought.

"Can you at least tell me where the scent comes from?" Renia said. "What it is? If it's poisonous?"

"Well, usually flowers send out a scent to attract a pollinator but *Saintpaulia* reproduces asexually through small plantlets, like those." He pointed to a cluster of young leaves branching from beneath the plant's main base. "That's what doesn't make sense. Why would a plant that produces asexually want to attract a pollinator?" After a second, he answered his own question. "It must be in its hybrid nature, whatever it was crossed with . . ."

"You can take a cutting and flowers, whatever you need." She surprised herself in saying it. A sudden trust in him overcame her.

"That would be enormously helpful," he said. "I brought a kit."

He took out a small case with a pair of snips, a paper pouch with an alcohol wipe, and three plastic tubes that clipped shut. He ripped open the cloth's pouch and like a scientist, thoroughly wiped the blades. He set the mask over his face, waited for Renia to do the same, and lifted the glasshouse off the plant. He cut a fresh petiole with a leaf and then a stem with a flower. A tiny woody branch with leaves. Renia filled his tubes with water and capped them. She gave him a waxed paper bag. When he secured the samples inside the bag, he set them on the table, his hand touching hers. It was warm, incapable of harm.

Her heart vibrated. To stop it, she said, "When will you know?"

He placed the case over the Violet Smoke.

She fanned the air with a folded newspaper.

After a few seconds, he lifted his mask.

"Woah," he said. Alarm glowed in his brown eyes. "I can smell it a bit."

"I know."

"It does smell like burnt apricots."

"Yes."

"That's a strong odor." He covered his nose with a hand, blinked a few times as if resetting his vision. "That may be dangerous. Has anyone ever been hospitalized from inhaling it?"

Renia thought carefully about how to answer. *Yes, of course. Well, no, not really. There were doctors involved. But not directly because of the scent.* Give the honest answer or the simplest answer? Somehow with this man, she felt compelled to give an honest answer, but that answer would open a Pandora's Box of history and emotions, maybe even legal liability. "Well, not exactly, but I know someone who inhaled it a few times and sh—they seemed fine."

"Huh. I'm surprised to hear it. Just a trace made my eyes water. I can't imagine inhaling that scent more than once."

. . .

AFTER DAMAZY LEFT, she fetched her bucket and brush from the curb. At Vida Nova, the sandwich board listed *linguiça* as the special. The smell of garlic and sausage wafted across the street. Delicious. Her stomach rumbled. She heard Damazy's words: *More than once*. Yes, someone she knew had inhaled it more than once. A few times. Actually, who knew how many? Only Estera did. The smell of Vida Nova's special reminded her of bratwurst cooking on a grill. That charred fragrance. Sizzling sounds. Water running. Shouts and songs. A band. A band of brass and drums and celebration. Last Oktoberfest.

In the church's courtyard, enormous tents lined the square. Beneath, long tables, beer barrels, sauerkraut, pierogi, pickles. Smoke everywhere. People ate and danced and sang. The odors of broiling sausage and hoppy beer wafted through the air. A folk band with a piano and tuba played. Renia roamed past the dining tents and beer vendors and food stalls to the carnival. The Ferris wheel, outlined in white lights, rotated in a twinkling innocence.

She searched the crowd for Estera, hoping to find her before Zbiggy. Too late. The two stood by a target shooting booth, holding ceramic steins, Estera leaning against the wall, Zbiggy leaning into her. He held her chin with his fingertips, whispering words that made her smile. As Renia approached, Estera's face lit like a match. "Renka! Look what I found." She held a twenty złoty bill.

Estera's eyes, swollen and purple last week, had faded to yellow and blue. The neck scars had healed to a scattering of pink dots.

With a curt nod, Renia greeted Zbiggy.

"Hey, twin sister," he said. "Staying long?"

"Maybe." She held his gaze, stifling her disappointment at seeing him.

"All of a sudden, I'm thirsty. Give me your stein."

Estera handed him the vessel.

"The same?" he said.

Estera nodded.

"I'll be back." He wandered away.

Estera watched him with loving eyes. Renia watched him, suspicious.

When he was out of earshot, Estera's face settled into a crinkled resentment. Her voice was sharp. "Why don't you like him?"

Renia blinked. How absurd. "Why don't I like him? Because of what he did to you."

"Did what? You mean bring me here, to have fun?"

"No." Where was her outrage? Her pride? Her dignity? Even her misguided forgiveness. "Because of his behavior last weekend."

"Last weekend?" She smiled. "What happened last weekend?"

"Estera, you forgave him and went back after two days."

Her face relaxed, her eyes shifted with confusion. "Forgave him for what?"

She truly didn't remember. "You don't know?" Renia said.

"No, enlighten me."

That she forgot had only one explanation.

"Have you looked in a mirror lately?" Renia said.

"Yes, this morning, after I showered."

"Was the mirror steamy?"

"I don't know. Why? Do I have food on my face?"

"Food? No."

Estera's mouth slid into a curious smile.

"Have you looked closely at your eyes?" Renia said. "Like leaned far into a mirror and looked?"

"Why?" She put a hand to her temple, "Ow, that's odd."

"Estera, he hit you last week."

Her smile opened. "Zbiggy? You're mistaken."

"I'm not."

Estera searched her sister's eyes.

"Come with me," Renia said and took her hand.

They went around the corner to the bathrooms inside the church, passing a bouquet of drooping crocuses at the Virgin Mary's shrine. Once there, Renia brought her to the mirror. "Do you see what happened?" Her voice echoed. She lowered it. "Lean in, under the light."

Estera inspected her image. Her smile faded as she noticed the swollen discoloration. The red marks on her neck. A small cut at her lip. "I saw that yesterday. I thought I'd bumped into a wall during the night."

"No," Renia said. "You two argued and he hit you. He tried to strangle you."

She scoffed. "No, he didn't."

"Yes. He did."

Estera stared at the sink, blinking.

"Last weekend at your apartment, I came over. You were in your bathrobe?"

Estera's eyes closed, fists went to her forehead. Her body sank. "Now I remember."

Renia's chest tightened. "I'm sorry."

"Why did you remind me?" Her voice whined with bitterness. "You reminded me and now it's back."

Because it's the truth. "I'm sorry."

"Nice, Renia, really nice."

"Did you use the flower?"

She stomped her foot. "Yes, I used it. I always use it. Oh, and now you ruined things. I was fine. We were fine. But you reminded me."

"You can't live a lie, Steri."

"I'm not."

"How often do you use it?"

"Oh, stop with the brain damage drama."

"It's possible. How often?"

"I don't know. Whenever I need to."

"It's dangerous, Steri."

Estera's face shriveled. "Go home, Renia. Go home, I don't want you to stay. Zbiggy and I were getting along better than ever until you came. You always want to push us apart." She slapped the sink. "Now I have to use another flower to forget the memory again and we'll lose that money." Her voice was taut with resentment. "All thanks to you and your piety."

CHAPTER THIRTEEN

On November 1st, Renia rode her bike to Madame Palomer's apartment and knocked on the door. No answer. She slipped an envelope with rent money underneath, guessing Palomer was out shopping. In the last several days, she hadn't pressured Renia about a financial plan nor had she mentioned firing Minh. Renia wondered whether, if she sat down with Palomer in her favorite café and calmly spoke to her about spending too much, she'd change. Minh was convinced she would. Renia, not so sure. Convincing Palomer to change would be like chasing a feather in a whirlpool. She remembered Alain once saying, "The way to deal with her is to tell her what she wants to hear but quietly do what's best for you."

She rode back to Le Sanctuaire, thankful to be among plants again with their reliable ways and glacial actions. The fountain's goddess poured clean water in a reassuring stream. Across the street at Vida Nova, diners in overcoats sat under heaters and ate lunch. Renia couldn't afford to eat there but she didn't resent João for his success. He was an immigrant from Brazil who'd built his own business.

He'd created a warm atmosphere where people could eat long delicious meals and visit with friends. Renia yearned for that, but with the way things were going, didn't expect to experience it.

Her phone rang.

"Hey, Polish girl, it's been a long time. Like, how have you been?"

"I've been busy, Zbiggy," she said. "I'm working two jobs. You know, working hard—something you might not be familiar with."

"Oh, but see, I've been working hard too. In fact, I've been working so hard that my buddy and I need to order more scarves from you."

You mean Vlad, your lowlife boss? "I don't have any scarves," she said. "They're all . . . out of season. Sorry."

"I'll bet you do since it's been a couple of weeks since I talked to you. Your inventory must be bigger since then."

"Not lately," she said. Her voice was light and vindictive.

"Well, hey, think about it, like soon. You know my buddy won't settle for 'no.' He loves your scarves. He wants to pay you a lot of money for some scarves. It's getting cold out now, you know what I mean, Polish girl? We all need to stay warm for winter."

"Your buddy doesn't know how to behave," Renia said. "When I met with him, he was late. Then after he was late, he didn't know how to treat a lady. And I don't work with men who don't know how to be nice to people."

Silence.

She waited, wondering if he would lash out. She speculated that Vlad might be listening to their call.

In a crisp, fast voice, he said, "You better watch what you say."

"But it's true. I'm not inclined to work with anyone

who pushes me around. I have to go to work now Zbiggy, at an honest job where I work all day and am given money. I'm not sure you would understand but you should try it sometime. *Do widzenia*."

AFTER MINH ARRIVED, Renia left for Valenton. As she rode her bike from the country station into the pastoral road, she felt insignificant under the huge sky. Its blue plane was scattered with gauzy clouds, arcing over everything: the village houses, the buzzing fields, the windblown trees. Grazing horses. She enjoyed the silence until she steered into the gravel lot of Les Racines, careful to watch for uneven ground, passing the office trailer by the road side, and pedaled past the parking lot scattered with trucks and cars.

A man in a flannel shirt rode toward her on a bike. It wasn't Paweł, but a teenager she hadn't seen before. She was about to call out and ask where Feliks was, but he veered into a side lane. She pedaled past the greenhouses, hearing African soukous music from transistor radios as workers divided plants. The air smelled of cow manure. Beyond the greenhouses were a half-dozen hoop houses, one being covered with rolls of plastic by workers. The lane's end was capped by two perennial fields, still blooming pink coneflowers and purple asters and yellow goldenrod. They colored the earth like a rainbow around Feliks's cottage.

She slowed to a coast as Maya trotted up to her, barking an excited hello. She pet her head before setting the bike against the chopping stump. An ax had been thrown and was stuck in the wood. At the door, she knocked and waited.

She knocked again. Silence. She called into the kitchen

window, then realized Feliks would be at the office so she rode there. Inside, Paweł tallied a receipt for a large shrub order. When he saw Renia, he nodded. She peeked into the interior office but only found Mathieu, the part-time assistant, on the phone. He gave a wave and covered the phone. "He's in House 8."

She climbed on her bike, her muscles stronger from last week's work, and bumped along to House 8. Inside, she walked among the last of the tall bamboo, about thirty large plants whose leaves rustled like paper as she passed.

The sprinkler box shot forward. She ducked. It skated past and halted at the house entrance.

"Uncle Feliks?"

Dozens of emitters sprayed a monsoon. A triangular pattern of water pounded the plants. She turned to avoid the oncoming spray, but the water stopped and the system ceased moving. It groaned and died, a plume of smoke streaming from the engine box.

"Ahk. Overheated!"

Behind her by the front door, Feliks frowned at a control panel, shaking his head at an array of buttons and switches. A small panel hung detached by its wires. "I can get it to spray, I can get it to move, but I can't get it to move on the timer. I can only manually slide it." He pressed a big red button. The box shot along the pipe, lunging twenty feet.

Renia jumped from its path.

"Such a headache." He rubbed his eyes. "All day I've worked on it and nothing."

"Uncle," she said softly. "Can I work in the office today?"

"It will have to wait."

Her shoulders slumped. "Again?"

His voice snapped with a stern coolness. "Yes, again.

The plants are dry. I have no irrigation. I need you to water here first." He pointed toward the office. "Second, Paweł needs you for packing these onto the truck. Then," he shrugged, "about a hundred other tasks."

THAT NIGHT, Renia's body felt broken. Though she was tempted to take a taxi home on the shop credit card, she didn't. Palomer examined the charges every month, so she rode her bike. The pedals resisted as her feet pushed against them. She swerved into traffic, then into parked cars, her arms like trembling noodles. Her hands had chapped from the nursery's harsh soap and despite the multiple washings, her fingernails were still rimmed with dirt. She'd loaded sixty trees and thirty shrubs onto a truck bound for Marseilles. Afterward, she'd carted pots of shrubs from fields into hoop houses before trimming back dozens of perennials to ready for winter storage. Her legs ached, her shoulders hurt. Her head swayed as she watched the asphalt road roll beneath her. The route home floated in her mind like a vague idea.

She steered into the Rue de Vaugirard, feeling sorry she had such a harsh uncle. He could have respected how hard she worked. Instead, he always insisted on more. Her lip trembled as she imagined what a French uncle might be like. She'd had a French aunt, Nanette, who had often hugged her as a child. She sang songs with her. As she rode along the Jardin du Luxembourg, vowing to call Nanette, a black BMW pulled out from a No Parking zone. It trailed behind. At first, she thought it a coincidence but knew after the sedan didn't turn at any intersection that the following was intentional.

Two men sat inside the car, their dark forms stone-faced in the reflection of the night's lamplight. One may have been Vlad. She curved into the Rue Sereine, her breathing shallow. *Don't jump to conclusions.* As she neared Le Sanctuaire, she hopped off the bike, yanking the front tire to the sidewalk. Maybe she could slip in the building before they caught up. She leaned the bike against a post and frantically searched her bag for keys. The sedan drove twenty feet past and halted. In a flurry, she batted her wallet and brush and mirror around, feeling for those keys. They weren't there.

The sedan's door opened. Zbiggy. Oh, of course. But so soon? They had spoken that afternoon.

She checked the bag's side pocket. Empty. Too late to escape.

He sauntered down the sidewalk as the sedan idled. Its tail lights glowed neon red, its tailpipe fumed exhaust.

Renia leaned the bike against the building and searched her coat pockets, feeling the keys.

Zbiggy neared.

"I told you not to come here," she said.

"But we need to talk, face to face."

She eyed the sedan. "I don't want your friends knowing where I live."

"You live here? I thought you only worked here."

She pinched her eyes shut, regretting the slip, opened them. "What do you want? I'm tired." She debated whether to lock her bike to the post. Her pack and boots were tied to the rack.

"Look, Polish girl, I won't keep you. I can see you're all sweaty and tired. Do you always ride so far at night?"

"I only rode . . ." she closed her mouth. He may have thought she'd been in Paris. They had only seen her by the Luxembourg. "Sometimes I do."

"You look nice with messy hair. Like your sister."

"What do you want?"

He stepped in, obstructing the space between her and the door. He smelled like icy soap. "We need flowers —tonight."

The air was warm. Her body felt hot, her mind, anxious, wanting to get rid of him. "I told you they're not in bloom."

"I'm sure you can figure something out."

The black sedan emitted a low rumbling noise. "Is your Russian cousin in there?"

"No, Renia."

"Is Vlad your Russian cousin?"

"No, Renia. I told you, my cousin owns a bar."

"Yes," she said. The cousin she'd never seen. "I forgot."

Inside Le Sanctuaire, the light was dim. She left on an amber lamp in the back corner every night as a deterrent to theft. If she sold him a flower, he'd leave. It was the quickest way to get rid of him. "I don't think I even have a bud on that plant."

"Can you check?"

"I need to put my bike away."

He gestured to a sign post. "Please."

"No, upstairs."

"Lock it here for now."

"I don't want my pack stolen. You know, there are people in Paris who will steal things when you're not look- ing, Zbiggy."

"It's such a shame," he said. He was handsome in a dastardly way. With a curled mustache and top hat, he'd be the scoundrel in a Victorian novel that swindled a rich woman out of money.

She unlocked the store and walked the bike inside, expecting his thugs to emerge from the car and follow. "Wait outside." Saying it didn't mean he'd obey it, but she felt strong giving a command. She slammed the door and flipped the lock.

The door's shade was down. She decided against turning on the lights and shuffled through in the dark. The tips of stiff ferns scratched her arms. He peered in the window. As if she didn't care, she went to the atrium and shut the door, then leaned against it and let go a long, stabilizing breath. *Merde*. He'd come after her. They all had. She considered opening a window and climbing out. But where would she go in that confined courtyard? Who to contact for help? Yes, the opposite wall had two windows, up high, but they were always covered with closed blinds. She had no choice. She'd already allowed him to see where she'd gone.

The glasshouse windows were steamed, blurring the Violet Smoke. She lifted the case off the plant and felt a spread of moist air. The plant had one budded flower, nine petioles emerging. He didn't deserve that one flower. He'd never deserved Estera. But now, as then, she had no choice. She snipped the bud and watered the soil, then replaced the case, leaving the vent door open. After she repositioned the panel, she put the flower in a waxed paper bag, took off her mask, and went in the store.

Zbiggy watched her through the window, his hands cupped around his eyes. She opened the door. "Stand there," she said and pointed to the space behind it.

"Why?" he said.

"I don't want anyone to see you."

"You're as smart as Estera."

"Shut up. I have one bud. No flowers. This will open later tonight. Keep it in the wet paper towel. I can sell you this. I don't have anything else."

"Show me the plant," he said. "So I can tell Vlad you don't have more flowers."

"Not a chance."

"I need to see it."

"Not a chance."

"You know, I could crush that little Polish head of yours and take the damn plant if I wanted."

"Then you wouldn't know the combination."

"The combination to what?"

"To the lock of the safe where I keep the flowers."

His face twitched as if unsure whether to smile or frown. He gave her the money. She gave him the package.

"When will you have more?" he said.

She opened the door. The smell of carbon dioxide wafted in.

"Never."

"Can you make a dozen?"

"No."

"Come on."

"No."

"I know you can."

"I can't." Even though she probably could.

"Come on. We know a guy, he wants *twelve* flowers."

"I'm familiar with how many flowers are in a dozen."

"That's over 1400 euros, Renia."

She stayed silent. In the dim, his face was a series of slanted lines: his hairline, his sharp brows, his mouth . . . crooked, like his personality.

Still, 1400 euros would clear away all of the late bills and cover next month's rent. "Why does he want so many?"

"We've got a group situation."

"A group? Why you would use them all at once?"

"Why not?"

It's a lie. "What group?"

He smirked in self-satisfaction. "In a prison. Don't ask.

It'll work." He looked at the sedan. "But I don't know if Vlad can wait. Things are getting . . . tense between the boys."

Renia rubbed her neck. She disliked the idea of multiple people using the flowers at one time, in one place, let alone in an institution with barbed wire and guards and guns. And plus, Vlad was behind it all.

Still, if she could only deal with Zbiggy and not his thug employer . . . that would be safer, cleaner. And a dozen flowers . . . it did mean over 1400 euros. Still, the risk. What if someone got caught and traced the sale back to her?

"Not worth it," she said.

"It's big money, Renia. They'll pay one-fifty each."

"One-fifty?"

"Yep."

That was more like 1800 euros. Renia could cover the bills, the rent, and not work at Les Racines. The throbbing ache of her knees reminded her of that. The rumbling hunger in her stomach reminded her she also needed to eat to survive. "I can't go to a prison."

"No, no. I'll deliver them across town, to their contact. No one will know you're involved. Me or Vlad will even meet you at your park."

"No Vlad."

"No? Okay, just me then. And no one will suspect anything 'cuz this guy will bring in flowers to the prison." His eyes, his close-set eyes, were like two round buttons stuck in a scary doll. She resented that Zbiggy was even in Paris. He'd claimed to be staying at his cousin's apartment, but that may have been a lie. Before they'd moved in together, he'd told Estera he lived in an apartment by "the river." It turned out he lived in a cramped one-bedroom on the Pradnik, a tributary of the Vistula, and across the street from a vandalized cemetery. Nothing he said could be trusted.

With a brewing hate, she said, "You tell Vlad that I'm not interested in doing business with him. Tell him to get his own flower. Tell him to F off and die."

Zbiggy's face solidified into the insult. "So that's how you want to do things, huh?"

"Yes, it is."

"I thought you were smart like Estera. She could always see the solution in things."

"Estera's choices were self-preservation."

"You think so? You're wrong. She loved doing business. She loved all of it. Not just the plant, but the money, the party." He motioned to the sedan. "My friends."

Renia swallowed. The idea that Vlad had groped or assaulted Estera made her sick.

"You're a terrible liar," she said.

"No lie." His voice was light. "She loved doing business, any kind, any kind."

His words rattled her. Yes, Estera didn't think of consequences but the idea that she'd sell her body . . . if Zbiggy had let those scum friends have their way with her. . . Renia's stomach convulsed.

"I'll tell Vlad you're thinking about it," he said. "We could get a great business going, you and me, like me and Estera. We were a great team."

"You weren't a great team."

"Sure, we were. Always."

He ambled out the door. The rain tapped on the windshields of the parked cars. Tap, tap, tap. In her mind, she saw Estera sitting inside Tata's car, stone faced.

"When things got tough, you abandoned her!" Renia yelled after Zbiggy.

"You don't remember it right," he countered.

The street tree bounced in the wind. The smell of rain on warm cement, now as it was back then.

"Oh, my memory of it is very clear. I saw her that day, in my father's car."

His eyes dulled. "Don't be that way, Renia. Don't force us into a difficult situation."

"Leave. Now."

"So *merci*, and all that."

"Yes." As she slammed the door, she said, "*Et va te faire foutre.*"

A draft of cool air hit her body. The smell of rain on warm cement. Petrichor. She saw Estera in her mind again, shivering. Last October. In the driver's seat of Tata's car at their apartment complex. A violent wind shook a leafless tree in the distance.

Renia got in the car and slammed the door. "It was warm and sunny an hour ago, now it's terrible out."

"Yes," Estera said, "and terrible in here." She stared at the rain, a bruise by her ear. A new bruise. Every other week there was a new bruise.

Renia leaned back, her head hitting the cushion harder than intended. She breathed in, calming her pulse. No, she wouldn't lecture. But it was so damn frustrating.

"We're breaking up," Estera said. Her voice was monotone.

Renia squeezed her forearm. "Oh, I'm glad. He doesn't deserve you."

"He kicked me out."

Her mouth opened, words did not come. "He kicked you out?"

"I'm in trouble, Renia. I'm in trouble. I need to save money. I have to . . . I'm in trouble."

"What happened? Did the plant not bloom?"

Estera sniffed, her nose wet. "No, it bloomed. I sold the flowers."

In the back seat, untied garbage bags of clothes, a box of toiletries, dresses on hangers tumbled over each other. A pillow. A pointed shovel. A tub of gloves and trowels and pruners. Boxes of food. It reminded Renia of the city dump.

"When Tata learns the news," Estera said, "he'll be furious. And Mama will be heartbroken . . ." her chest heaved, "I've torched my life, Renia. It's all going up in flames." She let out a meek howl that dissipated into a sob. Her forehead fell on the steering wheel.

"Relax, take a breath." Renia grabbed at her shoulder, tried to wrench her back. "Tell me what happened."

"And I've no place to live. I can't go home. Tata hates me for being with Zbiggy in the first place. And now, if he finds out, he'll kill me. Mama too. It crosses the line. Oh, God. Where will I go? Where will I go?"

"Estera, what's the problem? Tell me so I can help you."

She shook her head, her mouth drooping. "Zbiggy says I was stupid and careless."

"Estera, what is it?"

"And I was."

"Estera, tell me."

She gulped air. "I'm pregnant."

Renia's eyes locked on the tapping rain. "*Chryste*. How long?"

"Three weeks."

"Are you sure?"

She nodded.

Renia gnawed on her lip, thinking. Where could she go? A shelter? A pregnant girl to a shelter? The shelters were all Catholic. They'd force her to bring it to term, then give it up. And the stigma. Maybe she could find a secular one, but most likely not.

Renia wanted to slam a fist on the dashboard. She wanted to say, *You were careless? What about him?* She stopped herself. Pretending she could fix it by judging him was pointless. Estera would have to come home. But there was still time. They didn't have to tell their parents. Not yet. When they did, Tata would ban Estera from the apartment. From his life. The two could find a cheap apartment but if they both worked, they had no one to care for the baby. And neither had money for a baby. Renia felt sick. They could sell flowers. God, no. She did have 1800 złoty in the bank. Her "someday" money. *Someday I'll buy a car. Someday I'll get my own apartment. Someday we'll move to Paris.*

That money. It was enough for a procedure.

"I have a plan," Renia said. "It will be difficult, but I have the money."

Estera's eyes widened a little. "A plan? Is it a good plan? An escape plan?"

The fog of their breaths on the windshield had mixed with the rain sliding down the glass, melting her vision of the objects outside. What was a streetlight now looked like a bent gray stick. What was two tan cars looked like a sandy mound. And what was a straight road out of the parking lot looked like a circular dead end.

"Kind of an escape plan," she said. "But not the one you're thinking of."

CHAPTER FOURTEEN

I n early November, Renia resolved to do whatever was necessary to keep Le Sanctuaire afloat. She brought in free cedar branches from a friend of Uncle Feliks's. She drew ten botanical sketches of holly and ivy and berries. As Christmas neared, new customers appeared, which boosted her hopes of being in the black by December, but they purchased small items like poinsettias and candles. Higher-priced sculptures and containers weren't selling. The inventory was old, so with reluctance, she put a price tag on the goddess fountain, hoping the elderly lady who'd admired it last summer would buy it. She'd be sorry to see the stone goddess go. The statue was disciplined in her task, content to be alone.

One evening, a couple weeks after Zbiggy had visited with his friends, she took the glasshouse off the Violet Smoke and let it air out. She didn't wear a mask because the plant only held one cluster of four tiny buds. She mixed potassium fertilizer with water and flooded the pot. She knew light would trigger the most flowering, so she rotated the plant, then paused. Guilt washed through her.

Was she fertilizing to make those twelve flowers? No. Yes. Maybe. If it made a dozen flowers at once, she would take it as a sign. In the meantime, she had no intention of seeing Zbigniew Wójcik again.

Still, her private promise to honor Alain's memory remained. And it wasn't only for him, but Estera as well. The toxicity question. She took out her phone and scrolled to Professor Damazy's number.

He answered, conversing voices and the hum of a fan in the background. When she asked whether he'd learned anything about the Violet Smoke, he said, "Oh, sorry, no. But I'm going to London this weekend. I'm meeting with my friend who's a plant explorer, the one I sent tissue to."

He sent the tissue? In the mail? To London? Across the channel? Where customs agents had inspected it? Where another botanist had received the package? She exhaled the worry in her heart and said, "Oh. I didn't expect you to travel for this."

"No, not at all," he said, "this is a close friend I'm visiting anyway."

"I see."

"He received the tissue a few days ago and asked another explorer in New Zealand about it."

"New Zealand?!"

The surprise in her voice must have startled him.

"Oh, uh, yes, but don't worry," he said. "He didn't send the tissue, he emailed photos. My friend and this other explorer collected specimens there years ago. He's a legitimate professional. Don't worry."

"So," Renia said, "you haven't learned much else?"

"No, unfortunately not," he said. "But if you'd be willing to take a few more photos of the branches and close ups of the bark and send them to me, that would help."

The last thing she wanted was the Violet Smoke to

become well known in the worldwide horticulture community. She knew it was highly uncommon for those papery branches to grow in a loose, twisting pattern. What other tropical did that? And the bluish-green tone of the leaves, almost smoky, but more blue than green. And then, the fine peach-fuzz hairs along the stem and leaf surfaces. Renia knew that was unusual in some way but she couldn't put her finger on it. Regardless, Estera was right. The plant was spectacular.

"Alright," she said, "I'll send them. And I was thinking . . . the leaves on this plant may offer a clue. Their color and texture and that fuzz, it's unusual. I haven't seen it on other plants."

"Nor have I!" he said. "You're right, the clue is in those pilose leaves but what that clue is, is the question. Well, Mademoiselle Baranczka, I look forward to your photos. It's clear you have a considerable knowledge of plants."

Renia hung up, her face loose with happiness. But why was she happy? Because Damaźy had complimented her? *Considerable knowledge.* Because he thought the Violet Smoke was as unique as she did? She felt like a sunflower on a hot day, as if she'd been facing pure energy. An energy purer and more well-intentioned than other people's. Was the feeling radiance?

The door jingled.

Oops. She thought she'd locked it. "One moment!"

"*Allô?*" someone said.

The panel lay against the stone wall. The glasshouse, on the floor. The Violet Smoke, exposed.

She rushed out of the atrium and pulled the door behind her.

Officer Kateb waited by the counter.

"Good evening, Mademoiselle. I was wondering if I could ask you a few questions."

Kateb was back? Was this a good sign?

She maintained a calm composure. "Yes, about what?"

"Monsieur Alain Tolbert."

She shivered.

He took out his notepad—the same pad he'd used on the day Alain had died—and checked his scribbling. "Can you confirm that the last time you saw Alain Tolbert was on August 25th of this year?"

Renia thought back. She didn't know the date exactly. It was a Tuesday. That's all she remembered. "Is this now an open case? Are you investigating a . . . something?"

"We're gathering more information. Can you tell me whether that's correct?"

"I don't recall. It's already November."

He stopped, stuttered. "Uh, yes, I know. It's been awhile since Mr. Tolbert's death, but if you could tell me, to the best of your memory, when you saw him last that would help me."

She remembered that day. How she'd been sketching a rubber tree when he'd come in. When she'd moved to Paris, she hadn't brought any pencils or pads. But once Alain had seen her half-finished ballpoint sketches on a few sheets of printer paper in the apartment, he'd bought her a sketch book. That Tuesday, he'd opened the shop door, stuck his head in, and said, "Ah, it's freezing in here, excellent! It's like an oven outside. So, you'll be happy, my dear Renia. I have an enormous order for you."

She couldn't help but smile at the memory. "I saw him that Tuesday, probably the 25th, before he died. He'd ordered four dozen flower arrangements."

Kateb wrote notes on his pad.

"I thought his death was deemed a suicide," she said.

"It might be, but we're not certain."

"You're not?" Blood rushed to her face. Still not certain?

"Not quite."

"You think someone killed Alain?"

"We're not saying he was murdered. We're just not certain about the circumstances."

She bristled. Did that mean she was a suspect?

"Do you know whether Mr. Tolbert ever mentioned wanting to obtain opioids?"

"Opioids? Like heroin?"

"Not necessarily."

What else was there? Alain had wanted the Violet Smoke, that's for sure, but heroin? Could the plant be mistaken for heroin? "No," she said in a slow cadence, "he never wanted anything like that. The most he ever wanted was to have a good time. I mean, you know, to live happily."

"If you recall that he ever mentioned an interest in opioids, will you let us know?"

She nodded. "Sure. Did you find heroin in his blood? Is this new, from the autopsy report?"

"No, it wasn't about the autopsy, it was about what was found in his apartment."

LATER, Renia went upstairs and ate a dinner of rice and butter. From her dining table, she saw, diagonally across the street, Alain's apartment. The windows were shut and dark. Curtains closed. The orange petunias in the balcony planter had grown spindly, the flowers had withered. Armand had not rented the unit yet, or whomever lived there was gone. She imagined Officer Kateb putting drug paraphernalia, a spoon or needle, in a plastic bag. Alain had been too much of a fancy gentleman for opioids. She tried to take pleasure in the warm smell of the butter on her plate, but she couldn't. The idea of Alain carrying on a secret drug life gnawed at her.

But people did carry on a secret drug life. She thought of Estera and looked at her phone. The black screen offered no answers. Before Alain's death, she'd called Estera every Friday. Renia pulled up her sister's contact information. If she answered, Renia would begin with, "I'm sorry I ruined your life." But even with an apology, Estera still would not understand. And it was an apology Renia didn't even truly believe in. She set down the phone.

Last June, Mama had told Renia that Estera was doing better. But why had she taken Estera's phone away? And Tata returned it. With a tentative hand, she pressed Estera's number. Waited. One ring, two, on and on. A voicemail message clicked on. The voice was not Estera's but the computer-generated recording. Renia left a message anyway, saying that she was thinking of her and that she missed her—and that Zbiggy was still in Paris and she needed her help.

THAT NIGHT RENIA slept in a restless fit. She woke every hour, her thoughts wandering toward Professor Damazy. She admired the intense way he stared at the Violet Smoke, how interested he was in learning more about it, how polite and helpful he'd been. At one point, she slipped into a dream. Damazy lectured her on the flower's scent. "You see, this flower is full of heroin. One inhalation and the whole body goes into shock . . ." As he spoke, Alain came in the atrium, smiling sweetly as one might at teenagers holding hands, and said, "You two are made for each other."

In the morning, Renia floated toward consciousness,

feeling a strange elation she hadn't felt since childhood. It opened in her chest and spread in all directions. She hung on to the image of Damazy, of Alain, wishing they could both stay in her real life. As she got up to shower, her phone rang.

Minh.

"Are you awake?"

"Yes, what's going on?" Renia said.

Silence. A heaved breath. "Everything's in disarray."

"Are you at the shop?"

"Yes. I went next door to help Justine carry in a book-case when it happened. Oh gosh, I'm so dumb, Renia. I left the door unlocked, like a dummy, I left it unlocked."

"Justine, the travel agent? What happened?"

"Come down, can you come down soon?"

Renia threw on jeans and a sweater and went down-stairs. As soon as she came out of the building, she saw the mess. The tiered shelving unit lay in pieces, the plants and soil scattered. Broken branches and leaves everywhere. The bistro table and chairs were scrunched as if giant hands had bent them into tangled sculptures. The hay bale was busted and strewn, the corn flung in the street, and saddest of all, the pumpkins had exploded on the sidewalk. All twenty of them.

"*Merde*." The air drained from her body. Her breath gone, her head faint.

Minh rushed out of the store, pushing a cart, wearing work gloves. "Renia." Her mouth sat in a crimp. She slowly swiveled her head. "I don't know how it happened. I heard wheels squealing. I came out and a black car was driving away."

Renia crouched down. A black car? A terra cotta pot holding a coral camellia had been smashed against the cobbles. Shards littered the sidewalk. She looked around for anyone who might have seen what happened but the Rue Sereine was quiet. The lights at Vida Nova were off and the chairs stacked by the door. Three motor scooters were parked on the street. An elderly lady, a lady Renia often saw, walked her small terrier, far off in the distance.

The travel agency windows were dark. "Where is Justine?" Renia said.

"She went to buy me a mop."

"For inside?" Renia said.

With mournful eyes, Minh nodded.

Renia flew in the store. The soaps and books on the table were thrown on the floor, the cabinet behind the counter opened, the receipts inside strewn about. The armoire's drawers were overturned and the linens scattered. She sprinted to the atrium. Below the counter, the shelves were bare, all tools, gloves, soil, pots, lay on the floor as if an earthquake had tossed them. The trimmings basket had been dumped, the dried flowers and stems in a heap. The safe, thankfully closed, appeared kicked out of place. But the one thing intact, the one item that mattered and was unbroken, was the wall panel in the atrium. It stood solidly in place, un-shifted, untouched as if whoever had been looking for the plant hadn't noticed the wall was a false, removable board.

"Thank God," she said.

Outside, Minh picked up the pots that were unbroken. Many were cracked into small pieces as if someone had thrown them at the sidewalk and stomped on them. "I'll get these perennials transplanted straight away," Minh said. "We may be able to salvage a few."

Every small potted plant had been overturned and thrown against the window, now dying in a dark heap of crunched petunias, lavender, salvia, geraniums. The hydrangeas lay exposed and on their sides, yanked from containers, branches snapped and tossed. The mums, asters, anemones—they'd been smashed, stems cracked, flowers wilting, petals scattered in dirt from stomped root balls. A small Japanese maple had been swung like a baseball bat against the stone wall, leaving a huge soil mark and the thin trunk cracked. Its leafy head lay lifeless, like a broken broom, on the mangled bistro table. Renia moaned. The plants had suffered, in their quiet way, they'd suffered, and most would never recover. Their little green souls, gone.

"Someone must have taken a sledgehammer to the shelves," she said. Wood shards had been blasted far and wide.

"I know," Minh said. "I don't know how they accomplished so much in such a short time. I was only in Justine's storage room a few minutes."

"There was more than one person. There had to be. I'm glad you weren't here. You could have been hurt."

"If I'd been here, it wouldn't have happened," Minh said.

"I'm not so sure." Renia scanned the mess, what it would take to clean up. The reality of who would do this settled on her.

"It was probably some drunk teenagers," Minh said, "up all night and drinking."

"What time is it?"

"Seven," she said. "I came in early to study for a test before opening."

"You better go and study."

"No," Minh said. "No way."

"I'll clean it up."

"I'll help you."

Renia didn't have the strength to argue. The entire terrace was disrupted; pieces of wet squash were scattered from the doorway to the street. She picked up a camellia shrub and set it upright. Minh picked up pieces of pumpkin in between traffic. Renia swung between rage and despair. She wanted to bash Vlad's head in yet wanted to cry at the thought of telling Palomer. Even if she saved some plants, she had no furniture for display. The ceramic containers, gazing globes, and glass candle holders lay scattered about like a cruel glitter. She swept the pieces and Minh held open the trash bags. After Renia tossed the last chunk of squash in a bag, she trudged in the store with slime on her hands. It felt cold and permanent.

"What will we tell her, Renia?" Minh said. Her face was red, her eyes bloodshot. Desperate expression. Estera's face, months ago.

"What day is it?" Renia said.

"Friday."

"She doesn't come in on Fridays. So, no need to tell her."

"Ever?"

"Maybe."

"Why does it smell like alcohol in here?"

Renia searched the floor. Behind the counter, someone had smashed a bottle of whiskey. Thick glass sprawled to the corners. A long puddle. The bottom of a cardboard box soaked. "Because someone was drunk, and wanted to create a mess."

That smell. Pungent. Sharp. Out of spite. Renia recalled the medical clinic in Kraków, on the city's outskirts: a narrow storefront with no sign, between an auto garage and a liquor store. On the sidewalk, a smashed flask. Wet stain. Windy air. She and Estera had tiptoed through the glass shards to go in.

In the waiting room, Renia sat and Estera went in to see the doctor. The gray lights, the rough fabric of a chair, the clock with its red, spinning arm. Renia struggled to read a magazine. Carla Bruni wore a chic dress to a charity dinner. A handsome actor had played a vampire in a movie, a rip in the page splitting his face in half. Behind the reception counter, a printer droned. Nearby, in a creaking chair, a gray-haired man in a threadbare T-shirt and cracked vinyl jacket sat, drumming his fingers on his knees. On a window sill, a pink angel plant wilted. Also called a "nerve plant," she thought. And every time someone opened the door, the smell of whiskey.

After forty-five minutes, Estera emerged from a side hallway. Her sweatshirt zipped to her neck, a scarf around her throat. Her face was pale. What had been a smooth ponytail now hung loose with strings of hair at her ears. Behind her, a nurse paused, wished her good luck, and handed her a brown bag.

Estera stared at the floor, said nothing.

Renia got up and put an arm around her, guided her out.

Estera's hands were cold, her lips white. She stared at her hands as if they were two appendages she was unsure what to do with. "I've created a mess."

"This is the way out," Renia said.

Estera sniffled.

They came outside into the sharp wind. Renia helped her put on her coat. Estera waited like a mannequin as Renia buttoned the heavy, wool frock. Estera's eyes gazed in absent attention at a fire hydrant. A fast food wrapper skidded by. They waited for a cluster of cars to drive through before crossing the street.

"Did it . . . was it what you thought?" Renia said.

In the distance, above a clump of spruces, two birds flew in a circle.

"I have to go to work," Estera said. Her hands shook. She wiped her nose. "Wait, I want to sit down."

"We can sit in the car."

But Estera veered toward a bus shelter—clear, plexiglass panels and blue posts. There was a poster of a young man in shorts and tall socks, kicking a soccer ball on a field. He smiled a big smile, though someone had blackened his front tooth as if it had rotted and fallen out.

Estera sat on the bench, the paper bag in her lap. She eyed it as if she'd never seen a paper bag before, then tossed it on the ground.

Renia picked it up. "You'll need these pads."

For a minute, they sat in silence. The wind blew Renia's hair into her eyes, obstructing the cracked sidewalk, the weeds, the pads of scattered black gum. "Come, let's go home."

"I have to work," Estera said.

"I talked to Pan Gorski. He knows you need to stay home."

Estera licked her lips. They were chapped. She nodded. "I did lose it. They . . . they took care of the rest."

"So that blood this morning, it was . . ." Renia stroked her hair, feeling hollow, sad at the loss of a child that never was but also an ashamed relief. "I'm sorry, Steri. It's for the best though."

Estera turned away, put a hand to her eyes.

"Estera . . . " Renia reached out to hug her, then pulled back and patted her shoulder.

"Mama knows," Estera said.

"What?"

A motorcycle growled by, its giant pipe emitting stale smoke.

"She saw the test in the garbage."

The color in Renia's face drained. "When?"

"This morning," Estera said, "I told her. I thought I lost it."

A passing truck blew a dark cloud of diesel exhaust at their feet.

"What did she say? She must be relieved."

Estera leaned against the wall. Behind her hung a poster of a girl talking on a pink phone, the cord wrapped around her finger, red hearts floating in a thought bubble above. "She's furious. She thinks I'm lying so I can get an abortion."

"She wanted you to keep it?"

"Well, yes, maybe, give it up. I don't know. She hates me now. I'm forever soiled in her eyes."

An elderly man in a cap and wool coat approached, checked the bus schedule. Estera noticed him. He glanced at her with a neutral expression, then examined the schedule.

In a harsh voice, Estera said, "What are you looking at?"

He pretended not to hear.

She repeated herself.

"Let's go," Renia said.

"No, what are you looking at?"

The man ignored her.

Renia coaxed her to her feet. They lumbered in a huddle across the parking lot to the car. Line after line of white paint marked each slot of space, as day after day marked time. Renia yearned to turn back the clock to before Estera had met Zbiggy and freeze life there.

"You want to know the good news?" Estera said.

"Good news? Yes, of course."

A faint smile broke through her red face, her bloodshot eyes. "He wants to get back together."

CHAPTER FIFTEEN

The next Sunday, Renia worked at Les Racines. For three hours, she gathered perennials and ground covers for a massive order from a well-known designer in Nice. Then, after a lunch of baguette, mustard, and luke-warm water she couldn't drink fast enough, she hauled shrubs to the potting greenhouse before transplanting them, crouching to loosen roots and shovel soil into larger pots. She did this forty-six times. She counted. Afterward, she dragged a heavy hose into the field and watered twenty-eight privets, twelve camellias, eighteen euonymus, twenty-two viburnums, and twenty-three hollies. She counted those as well. By day's end, her shoulders ached, her stomach growled, and her body was covered in sweat. An explicable, constant pain throbbed in her right elbow. She felt like a wooden doll whose limbs had been yanked for fun.

She went to Feliks's office, too worn out to worry about judgment.

He was writing in his ledger at his desk. Behind him a

poster of maple varieties hung, the colors parched, the paper brittle.

"I don't want to work in the fields anymore," she said.

His face melted into a sardonic smile. "You don't want a job?"

"I do want a job. But I want the job that was promised to me. I want to work in the office."

"You look thin," he said. "Stay for dinner. Paquet gave me a chicken. It's in the fridge."

"Do I have to pluck it?"

Sardonic smile. "I already did."

"Can I manage the books in the office? That's where you said my talent lies."

He fiddled with his pen, sat back, and folded his arms, studying her. "Yes. You've earned it."

His stupid attempt to teach her a lesson irritated her. "Also, I'm exhausted. Can I have money for a taxi home from Gare de Lyon?"

Later, he fed her dinner, insisted she eat another helping of potatoes, and drove her to the train. He gave her a day's pay and an extra thirty euros for a taxi. She spent seventeen to get home from the station to Saint-Germain and considered spending the leftover euros to drink wine at Vida Nova, but as she strained to lift her legs up the hallway stairs, she decided to take a shower and go to bed instead. Under the warm blankets, she mulled over her future, how long she could manage this double-job situation. She had to find a cheaper place to live. She couldn't even afford an apartment in the 13th, in one of the high rises where Minh's family lived. She stared at the complex pattern of tree branches in the window, nervous about failing at this attempt at a new life, nervous about returning to Poland and all of the judgment, all of the pain, she'd have to face.

Her eyes closed. Her body relaxed, and she drifted to sleep. In her dark torpor, she shifted around in restless twists. Images flashed in her mind and disappeared. Her mother crossing herself with holy water, her father banging on a piano, mumbling. She dreamed she and Estera were girls again. They rode bikes in circles around a statue of Balzac on the Boulevard Raspail. Renia had ridden past the Rodin statue a few days ago but Balzac in her dream was Mama, in a hood and robes. She held an open Bible, reading condemning passages at each girl as they passed. On the third time around, Estera rode off and Renia rode after her, but Mama called Renia back. She circled Mama at a distance, her fingers clenched with worry, as she watched Estera ride farther away.

Renia woke, the window pulsing with her heart beat from the wind. Mama used to hum rhythmically when Renia was ill as a child. She'd stroke her forehead. She imagined Mama's soft hand, soft voice. She hadn't spoken to her in weeks. They were both too busy. She checked the time, midnight, and vowed to call in the morning. At that thought, she fell back into a deep sleep. Blackness. Then, pounding. Distant. Was it night? Where was she? Paris. Early morning. Maybe. Construction. Or a neighbor. She rolled over. Again, pounding. It came from downstairs. She listened to her heavy breath, ignoring the noise, not wanting to leave the warm bed.

A voice shouted her name.

More pounding.

"Renia!"

She blinked awake, went to the window. The sky was pewter.

Zbiggy stood at the center of the empty street. "Renia!"

She grabbed a coat and flew out the door, onto the

stairs. As her legs stomped down, pain shot through her knees. Her calves wobbled. In the foyer, she undid the lock in a frantic turn.

Zbiggy was at the door, a fist curled, ready to pound again. He wore dirty jeans and a stained T-shirt, no hat or jacket, sweating at the hairline despite the freezing air.

"What do you want?" she said.

He came in and shut the door. She hit the light switch, blinked at the brightness.

"You have to help me," he said.

"Help you? I don't think so."

"Why not?"

"Why not? You guys destroyed my store."

He seemed perplexed. "What? Where?"

"Right here. You and your pals destroyed over 2000 euros of merchandise! Broke my furniture and my plants."

"What? I didn't know Vlad was going to do that."

"I'm sure you didn't."

"I didn't. I mean I told them you didn't want to sell flowers anymore, but they said they were going to just talk to you."

"Yes, well, they definitely sent a message."

"I didn't know."

His eyes seemed too panicked and curious to be lying.

"Well, it happened," she said.

He stared at a dry stain on the floor in a trance. "I swear, Renia, I didn't know. When did Vlad do it?"

"Last Thursday."

"I was at work."

"As if you have a job."

"I do!"

"What is it? What is this job?"

"It's . . . it's . . . " He wiped his mouth.

She folded her arms, waiting.

"I work at a tabac, okay? A convenience store. I was there."

That he was embarrassed satisfied her. He always had grand plans, but the reality of his life was small. "Well, whatever."

He wiped his face. "Look, Renia, we've always gotten along, right? I mean we're Polish, we understand each other."

Ha. That didn't create affection for him.

"So Renia, I messed up. I really messed up and you have to help me."

"I'm not going to help you." Her voice echoed off the foyer walls.

"Why?" he said. "I would help you if you were in trouble."

She lowered her voice. "You've already gotten me in trouble and my store in trouble, and not to mention gotten my sister into serious trouble. And now, what? Let me guess. You got a new girlfriend into trouble."

"No." He combed a hand through his hair, flattening it. "Okay, Renia. I'm . . . " His eyes squished shut, then opened, "I'm begging you. I'm begging you."

His plea was pathetic but mysteriously authentic.

"If it's a flower," she said, "I only have one that might open tomorrow, the others are all buds."

At that, he covered his face with his hands and turned away. He hunched in the quiet of the foyer. His body trembled.

Zbiggy crying? His panic was real. She remembered how he'd cried when Estera had once broken it off with him. He'd knelt before her in their bedroom, crying, begging her to take him back. After that, he played the sweet boyfriend. Opened doors for her. Fetched her drinks at bars. Put his coat around her shoulders. The loser did try sometimes. Maybe he truly didn't know what Vlad had done.

"Alright, alright," she said. "I'll sell you a flower."

He sniffled, wiped his eyes with a wrist. "Okay, but . . . I need it, no charge."

"What? No way, your friends made me lose 2000 euros."

"Okay, I'll pay you. But I can't, until like, next week."

"You're such a liar."

"Renia," he said, his eyes widened and he stepped forward.

She stepped back.

"He's going to kill me," he said. "He's going to kill me. I'm screwed, okay? I owe him a lot of money and he's going to kill me."

"Who? Vlad?"

"No, our other buddy, Yuri. He and I have been running a side deal, but I've been . . . I owe him a lot of money."

She wanted to say "Surprise, surprise," but she didn't, worried he might slap her.

"How much," she said. If she gave him her pay from Les Racines and whatever was in her tin, she may be able to go back to sleep.

"Thirty-eight hundred euros."

"Thirty-eight hundred euros?" Again, her voice echoed off the walls.

"Shhh, don't say it, yes, I know. It's bad. I'm bad. I got into a habit with him and it was a bad one."

"A drug habit, apparently."

"Shut up, Renia."

"Don't tell me to shut up."

He half-smiled, that straight strong nose coming at her like a truck. "Please, Renia, I'm sorry, will you help me?"

She scoffed a smile. "You can have a flower."

"Okay, great. Great. But the problem is . . . Yuri, if he sees me . . ."

The weight of what he wanted soaked in. He not only wanted the flower . . . what he wanted . . .

"I'm not going anywhere near your problems," she said.

"I need you to come with me."

She closed her coat at the neck. "No way."

"Renia." He set his hands on her shoulders.

She slapped them away.

"Renia, you have to. You see, he knows me. He knows my face. I can't do it. Only you can."

"What if he knows my face?"

"He doesn't. I know he doesn't. He's always taking over when Vlad's gone. They're never in the same place on purpose."

This disturbed her even more.

"Please, Renia. Please. If you want, you'll never see me again. I'll go back to Poland, I promise."

"What a lie."

"I'll tell Vlad you accidentally killed the plant and I'll go back. I promise. You'll never see me again."

Renia mulled over the risk. If she ignored him, they would kill him. If they killed him, they'd come straight to her for flowers. And they'd already sent a message. Fury burned in her body. She inhaled a lengthy breath. In some ways, using the Violet Smoke on one of those thugs would be sweet revenge. He'd never get his money. She'd cheat him, and he wouldn't know it. And cheating one of them after how Vlad had treated her felt good.

She poked Zbiggy in the chest. "Alright. I'll do it, but you're going to go to my sister and get on your knees and beg her forgiveness. Then, you're going to assure her that what I did was not my fault. I had no choice. And to make sure, I'm going to ask my parents if you went over and did it."

His voice was breathy, innocent. "But I already did that, Renia. I saw Estera before I left Poland."

"And another lie."

"I'm not lying. Ask your father. I went over there, twice, and talked to her. It was really nice. She told me where you worked."

"She did?"

"Yes."

Renia wondered how much of a lie that was. She pictured Estera and Zbiggy chatting in the family living room. "No, she didn't."

"Yes, she did. I swear on my grandmother's Bible."

According to her parents, Estera threw a fit at the mention of Renia's name. "I can't believe it."

"Please, Renia. I'll go back after this. I swear, I'm out. And if you want me to say sorry again to Estera, I will. I love her."

She laughed.

"Please, Renia. You'll never see me again."

She mulled the idea over. It would simplify her life but if Zbiggy left, any chance at that extra income left as well. She paced. She wanted his dirty money and yet didn't. If he left, would Vlad and Yuri try to steal the Violet Smoke again? She imagined the destruction on the terrace. Wood shards and broken squash and crunched metal. These men spoke in violent gestures. She'd have to make sure Zbiggy convinced them the plant had died. She had to be careful —with all of it.

"It would have to be quickly done," she said. "And I don't want him to see my face."

"However you want to do it."

Her heart beat hard. She was sure these guys carried guns.

"But listen, Renia, Yuri . . . he's going to wake up soon, we need to get there before Vlad gets there."

"Right now?"

"Yes."

His eyes searched hers for a response. She said nothing.

"Please, Renia."

"How do you know he wakes up soon?"

"He goes to the gym in the morning. Every day."

She didn't want to risk her life for Zbiggy, walk straight into a criminal's lair. But she'd do it if he could get through to Estera. She stuck a finger in his face. "Also, you'll go back to Kraków and you'll give Estera money. She paid your rent for years, you loser, paid for groceries, your partying. You're going to give her 1000 euros. It's not enough but it's something. You'll give her 1000, and you'll never contact her again, ever."

"I know. I will, Renia, I will."

He wouldn't give Estera the money, but he might stay out of her life. She exhaled.

He lifted his eyebrows, guilt and hope in his face.

"Wait, here," she said, a bitter taste solidifying in her mouth. "I'll get dressed."

As SHE RODE with Zbiggy in his clunker to Clignancourt, she stole glances at him. Thank God Estera had miscarried and not made him a father. His own father had been absent in his life, in and out of jail for auto theft, drunk when he was home. Where his mother was Renia wasn't sure, but she was sure his grandmother had raised him. Maybe that explained why he vacillated between nice guy and mean jerk. Now he fiddled with the radio, switching from hip hop to electronica and back to hip hop. "Do you like hip hop? This is it, right here," he said and spun up the volume. As the music thumped, he drove on, wiping his nose in a restive tic and swearing every time they missed a green light. She was trapped with him, for better or worse.

"So," he said, "you know how to do this, right? Like do what I tell my . . . customers."

Her mind wandered to the first, and only, time she'd ever used the Violet Smoke. "Yes."

He sang along to a rhyme whose last line ended in the word, "*fou, fou, fou.*"

They hit a bump and the glove box door loosened. It rattled. Renia opened it to slam it shut when a slim box slid out.

"What's this?" she said.

"Chocolate. Have a piece of chocolate, Polish girl."

"How old is it?"

He rolled his eyes. "Just eat it."

She bit into a cherry, the smoky smell of cocoa strong. They zoomed along the Boulevard Ney, Renia noticing garbage collected at the bases of street trees. Smashed soda cans. Rumpled chair cushion. A red sweatshirt, socks. Wet newspaper. She saw the same view from her bedroom window in Kraków. The playground in the concrete courtyard. Steel climbing bars, a cracked slide. Two swings, one roped up where the chain had broken. At the foot of a tree, a bag of garbage lay. A child's shoe overturned. Beer bottles. Ripped snack bags. And the smell of chocolate as she chewed, waiting for Estera to return.

An enormous box of candy lay on the bed. Dark chocolates, milk chocolates, chocolates with nuts. Rich cocoa smell. They were nestled in silver foil, a box from Moutarlier, an exotic Swiss chocolatier who made candy so that couples like Estera and Zbiggy could patch their relations.

Estera entered the bedroom, closed the door quietly. "She finished the chores."

"Who did Zbiggy rob to get the money for this chocolate?"

Estera's face wrinkled.

"Sorry," she said. She chose a chocolate with nuts. "Is he really serious about changing?"

"Yes, he says he called a counselor."

He says he called . . .

Estera plunked on the bed. A twin bed with a yellow chenille bedspread, beside Renia's bed, which also had a yellow chenille bedspread. Embroidered roses wove into each other. "He's even talking about marriage, but he'll never get Mama and Tata's blessing, at least not with this . . . situation."

"It's a complication," Renia said.

"Yes."

"But why can't you do it?"

"I'm scared. There will be resistance."

"And I might make mistakes."

"No, you won't. It's easy."

"I'll do it on one condition."

Estera's eyes waited with eager anticipation.

Renia focused on the lamp between their beds. The base was ceramic with figurines, an aristocratic couple in wigs and fine clothes. They were frozen in a dance, a delicate rose in the lady's hand, their wrists lightly touching. "You choose the plant or him."

Estera smiled. "I can't choose. I want them both."

"He's caused you a lot of heartache."

Estera paced around, smiling. "I can't. I can't choose."

On the bulletin board above the dresser, a postcard of

the Arc de Triomphe hung, Renia's acceptance letter to the School of Economics, Estera's ticket to a David Bowie concert.

"Well, I can't help you," Renia said.

Estera ran a hand through her hair, rubbed her neck. "What if I keep the plant but clip the flowers? I'll cut them before they grow."

"That's risky. You might kill it."

"Until he gets into counseling and changes. Okay?"

Estera bit her nails.

Renia tilted her head to the ceiling, focusing on the cracks, the cobwebs in the corners. She closed her eyes as if she could make Estera's desperation disappear. Quietly, she said, "Okay, but don't forget."

Estera hugged her. "I won't." She handed Renia a scarf. "Here, you'll want to wear this."

"How?"

"Wrap it around your nose and mouth. It works enough."

Renia put the scarf around her neck.

From a large duffel bag, Estera took out a bag with a flower.

"Do you want me to say anything specific?" Renia said.

"Yes, here's a list."

She looked it over. It was short, to the point. "Afterward, do you want me to take you to your apartment?"

"Yes, please. I can't wait to see him."

Estera's face beamed.

"Alright."

In the living room, all was tidy. The TV was off. Tata, in bed. On the coffee table, the Bible sat atop a *Polityka* magazine. Crossing lines in the carpet meant Mama had vacuumed. The laundry basket, on the buffet earlier, was gone. On the table by the balcony door, Tata's houseplants were watered. His sheet music books were closed and neatly stacked atop the piano. Mama sat on the couch, in a sweater and slacks, knitting under the soft light. She hummed to Paderewski's 'Chant du voyageur,' playing softly on the radio.

Renia sat on the ottoman near her mother. She took the flower from the bag and set it on the coffee table.

Mama noticed. "What is this now?"

"Mama," Renia said, she lifted the scarf over her nose and mouth. "I need to tell you something."

Mama blinked a heavy blink, shook her head as if to clear the odor she inhaled.

"Mama, Estera didn't have a miscarriage."

Mama coughed, leaned forward, heaved in a breath, as if struggling to take in fresh air.

"Because she was never pregnant."

Mama wiped her nose as if it itched, opened her eyes wide.

"What?" she said. Her head bobbed forward. "No. Oh, Lord, our Savior." She blinked again. Her head bobbed. "I'm too tired."

"Mama, you're not angry with Estera. And Estera didn't bring shame to our family."

"No," she said. Her head nodded.

"She never was pregnant."

"Of course not," she said beneath her breath. She slumped forward, her chin down, eyes closed, hand still ahold of the knitting needles. The hump of a half-finished blanket prevented her from tumbling forward. In a soft buzz, she snored. Renia put the Violet Smoke in the bag and leaned her back into the sofa, set a pillow behind her head. Her face was peaceful.

Last week her face had been searing with rage. She'd come in the kitchen while Estera and Renia discussed the pregnancy. She'd slapped Estera's face, condemned her for living in sin with Zbiggy, warning her she'd lose her job because of her drinking, insisted that she'd reduced her good life to garbage, and reminded her that she was certain to go to hell. At least now Estera had a second chance.

ZBIGGY PARKED in front of a modern apartment tower, a checkerboard of washed out blue and white panels, built in the 1970s. Shades in random windows were creased or torn. Rust stains ran in streaks from chipped balcony railings. A droning call to prayer sounded in the distance. Graffiti covered the lower walls. Empty cardboard boxes and trash bags sat in a heap by the front doors, emitting a rotten smell. A dog barked. On the second story, a hole in a window, made from a rock or ball, had a spider web crack of glass. The hole was covered with duct tape. The end of the tape, like a tiny hand, flapped in the wind as if beckoning them.

At the courtyard, Zbiggy lifted a sagging metal gate. They went in, passing a meager patch of dirt where lawn once grew. A half-deflated ball sat beside a bench covered in spray-painted letters. At the bench's edge, a folded newspaper teetered. Renia grabbed it and stuffed it in her coat pocket. Inside, the foyer smelled of burnt wood and spilled beer. Spray-painted words danced on the walls like desperate cries. Messages of anarchy, gang symbols. Frantic scrolls and upside-down crosses. It reflected her own feeling of chaotic fear.

As they climbed the stairs, her breath quickened. If Yuri went to the gym every day, that meant he was strong. "Stay outside the door," she said. "If he hurts me and you leave, I will stab you in the eye when I see you again."

"Don't worry, I'll wait in the hall, ready the whole time. I've got my piece."

"Your piece?"

"Yes."

Their shifting shoes on the concrete stairs gave off a slight echo.

"You mean a gun?" she whispered.

"Yes."

"That doesn't make me feel better."

On the third floor, they came to a door whose faded sticker said 310. Renia knocked. Waited. The door had a peep hole. In the corner, a plastic toy car sat on its side, a scuffed flower on its dingy hood. After a few minutes, a beast appeared. Six and a half feet tall. A body packed tight with muscles. Sharp, wide-set eyes slanted downward. Shaved head. A tattoo of a dragon wrapped up his neck. His face said Slav and his eyes said "get lost."

"I'm your neighbor," Renia said. "This paper was delivered by accident to my door. I live three floors up."

"I don't get the paper."

She unfolded it. "But it says your name here. Isn't it what, Yuri?" She angled past him into a shabby empty apartment save for a chair, a standing lamp, large TV, and assortment of video games. "Let me see in the light."

"Hey, stay out."

She took the flower from her pocket and slipped it beneath the paper, lifted her scarf over her mouth and nose. She held her breath, feeling the flowers' fumes at her eyes. "Aren't you Yuri Yvegenov?"

"Maybe," he said. His eyelids drooped.

"You know, Zbiggy doesn't owe you money."

"Zibggy? Yes, he does . . ."

"You're mistaken. Zbiggy doesn't owe you money."

"No?"

"No," she said. "Zbiggy doesn't owe you money. He doesn't owe anyone money."

His head teetered to the side. "You're right. I forgot." He heaved in a breath and as he exhaled, his eyes closed. It was that quick. She was about to give him a gentle push so he'd land in his armchair, but as she reached out, his body collapsed with a thump. She bent over to see if he'd hit his head, but he hadn't—he'd galumphed onto his side. He lay like a giant slab of meat. Beside the chair, on an end table was a small stack of bills. All fifties. Renia was tempted, very tempted, but he was asleep, and she had to be satisfied with that. She put the flower in the bag and went in the hallway, turning the knob to softly close the door.

In the hall, Zbiggy lay passed out on the floor. He'd slid down the wall and keeled sideways. She jiggled his shoulder. "Zbiggy. Zbiggy."

He slept with his mouth ajar, his hands limp.

"Zbiggy, wake up. We have to get out of here."

She swore and shook him harder, considered leaving. But if she did and he woke, he wouldn't remember the debt, wouldn't remember his promise, and wouldn't return to Poland. Plus, if Yuri found him, sleeping in the hallway, who knew . . . She jostled harder.

In an apartment down the hall, a stereo played Arabic music. A baby cried. She checked her phone, already six-thirty. She hooked her forearms under his armpits and dragged him to the stairs, his weight heavy. Her legs creaked, her shoulders felt stiff. She rotated his body and kicked his legs flat so he'd slide feet first. "Wake up," she said. "Wake up."

After a few steps, she had to stop and straighten his folded legs. At the next landing, she changed her tactic. She faced him and lifted so his torso would move with her and his legs would dangle behind. His beefy chest thrust her backwards. She managed five steps as his boots thudded against the concrete. *Thud, thud, thud.*

At the next floor, a door opened. A lean man appeared. East African. He wore thin pajama pants and a sleeveless white undershirt.

"Sorry," she said. "My boyfriend, he's drunk. Again."

He surveyed the scene with a frown, scratching his stomach.

"We're going," she said. "My car's outside. Sorry to wake you." She tugged the body onto the next step.

With a pinched expression of disdain mixed with surrender to practicality, he marched down the stairs. His feet were bare. In a thick accent, he said, "Take the feet. I will take the arms."

CHAPTER SIXTEEN

For six days, Zbiggy did not call Renia and she did not call him. After she'd erased Yuri's memory, she'd driven Zbiggy's car to Belleville, parked near the Goncourt métro, cracked the window, and tossed the keys through the opening. Then she went home and pretended nothing had happened. Well into the evenings, she worked at Le Sanctuaire, and on every day off for Uncle Feliks. She knew she'd make enough to cover two bills but would still be short for December's rent. Her tea tin had 16 euros in it for food, and nothing to feel hopeful about.

On November 18th, as she finished a sketch of a snapdragon in her apartment, Zbiggy called. He wanted to buy those dozen flowers. But he couldn't remember his debt to Yuri. Renia reminded him of how they'd not only erased Yuri's memory but Zbiggy's accidentally too, that he'd promised to return to Poland and give Estera money. He didn't believe her. She laid out the facts and at mention of the Clignancourt building, he recalled the memory. But he wanted to do that big job before he left for Paris, he said. The prison sale would make them both some sweet money, he said. Because he'd skim off the top, she thought. He told her he was going to get three-hundred more euros up front from the customer. The guy was loaded. She debated what to do. She told him she had no blooms. That was a lie. Nine new buds were forming. The truth was the Violet Smoke was thriving.

She hung up, sunk her face in her hands. It was such easy money. But it involved a dozen people. And who would take the flowers into the prison? If the runner was caught, it may lead back to her.

Still, Palomer had withdrawn another two-hundred euros last week. Julo had eaten rat poison and she'd taken him to a costly emergency vet. Afterward, she'd stopped by the shop in a foul mood, berating Renia for not displaying the old shoes more prominently, pointing out her "lack of business sense." She'd said nothing. The next day, she'd worked another long shift at Les Racines, dragging and hauling burlap trees through mud. Her body was tired, her mind was tired, she had no time to even search for a third job. She wasn't ready to admit defeat but wasn't ready to deal with criminals. She decided she'd do nothing for now but verify that she indeed had nine buds.

As she emerged from the apartment building into the street, she caught sight of Minh, slumped forward in a café chair on the terrace. Since the vandalism, the two had positioned a cart of plants beside the one salvageable chair for display. Minh's mother had given her four silk lanterns to sell and she'd tucked them throughout the greenery. Renia had bought a new hay bale and fresh pumpkins and ten small pots of mums in maroon and orange—all with the company credit card. The display was meager, but it at least filled an empty space.

As Renia approached, she noticed Palomer's Mercedes parked by the travel agency. Her mood darkened. Neither

Minh nor Renia had told Palomer about the vandalism, thinking they could make up the inventory through more sales, but the sales hadn't happened. Minh sat in the café chair, just outside the door, her head hanging, straight black hair hiding her face. Three tiny rosemary shrubs, trimmed into conical shapes to resemble Christmas trees, stood wrapped with red ribbons at her feet. Beside them was a small nativity scene. The manger crib had tipped over and baby Jesus had fallen out.

Renia quickened her pace. "*Salut*, Minh," she said in a bright voice, "is something wrong?"

Minh didn't respond, only stared at a basket of cyclamen on her lap. The silver-splotched leaves jittered from her shivering body.

Renia crouched, checked her face. Reddish skin. No tears.

"What's going on?"

Minh's eyes flashed desperation. "Madame Palomer fired me."

"Fired you?" Renia paid Minh off the books because the books in Paris demanded stacks of paperwork and strict regulations. To hire Minh had been easy, to fire her, also easy.

"Yes, she's not happy with me."

"Why? Did you tell her about . . . that Thursday?"

She nodded in a jump. "How could I not? She wanted to know where the shelf unit was, and the bistro set, and I panicked. I told her everything. I mean, I feel awful, I feel awful because I forgot to lock the door. It happened so fast, Renia, it happened so fast."

"Hush hush, I know," she said. Inside the store, the lights were on, Tchaikovsky's "Nutcracker Suite" played.

"This is all my fault, Renia, all mine. If I hadn't left the store, they wouldn't have done this."

Renia didn't think that was true. In fact, Minh may have been killed.

"I shouldn't have opened so early," Minh said, "but I did because I thought, 'Well, if I'm here, we might as well open.' I thought we might make some sales from early commuters. Gosh, I was wrong, so wrong."

"It's not your fault. Not at all. I'm sure those thugs had been waiting. I'll talk to her."

Renia went in the shop. Palomer was in the atrium, sitting at the counter, wiring together flowers. Orange lilies, red mums, fern sprays, and baby's breath were in clumps on the counter. Scissors, wire cutters, and a knife lay beside her hands. A roll of stiff wire was unfurled, corkscrewing in multiple directions. When she saw Renia, her face hardened into a glare.

"Renia, just the person I need to speak with. I noticed you used the credit card to purchase inventory."

"Yes." The alternative would be a bare sidewalk. A bare sidewalk before a plant shop at Christmas did not attract customers. "I thought you would want it to be festive outside."

Palomer shook her head in exasperation as if Renia didn't understand. As if she didn't understand the pressure Palomer was under. She wrapped a wire tightly around a collection of stems so that the flowers were smashed together.

"I'm sorry but Minh has to go," Palomer said. "She can stay through the week until she finds something else."

If Minh found another job that worked around her university schedule, it would be a miracle. "She needs that money for her mother's experimental therapy," Renia said.

"Speaking of conditions," Palomer said, "how am I supposed to recover from this horrible, horrible loss? The attack on us is unprecedented. Never in my thirty years of doing business has anyone ever attacked my store, and for no reason other than pure contempt. It's outrageous. I thought I'd have a heart attack when Minh told me. And how that child could be so absent-minded as to leave the store unattended . . ."

"She feels awful about it."

"Yes, I know. Anyway, I called the police and filled out a report by phone."

Renia imagined Officer Kateb scribbling notes frantically as Palomer explained the situation. "The police?"

"Yes, I don't see why you didn't. It's necessary for insurance."

Renia had dreaded the idea. She hadn't notified police because she didn't want Officer Kateb to connect her with a crime, even if she were the victim. But what to say, what to say? "I didn't call the police because I thought the incident would cause our premium to rise."

"Ah," she set down her wire cutters. "Yes. But I'm afraid we must. We must recover at least a portion of our losses." She studied her bouquet, positioned a fern frond to the left of the mums.

"Can't we wait a few weeks for Minh's sake? Her mother—"

"Renia, we lost almost 2000 euros worth of merchandise, we must let her go."

Minh's mother, innocent in all of this. Her sweet smile with a scarred front lip. How she struggled to move in her wheelchair. "What if I pay Minh?" She blurted this without thinking, then wondered if it were a mistake. If she had extra money to pay the full rent and Minh's pay, then maybe Palomer should raise the rent on the apartment. Quickly, she added, "I can take on a third job. I've got half of my nights free."

Palomer eyed her a moment. She took her cutters and

trimmed a wire with a crack. "You would take an extra job to pay for Minh?"

Renia closed the atrium door. "What if we cut her hours and she worked only when I'm not here? No overlap."

"But how would you get the inventory and accounting done?"

I already do it during the evening. "I'll figure something out."

Palomer wrapped the wire in a tight spiral, shook her head. "I'm sorry, my dear, but I can't sacrifice the more skilled person for the less skilled person. She has to go, but I'll give her another five days. It's nothing personal, it's this wretched misfortune. I tell you Paris is getting more and more dangerous. Every year, more deviants slip in from outside of France to wreak havoc and they must be stopped." With that, she set her bouquet in a vase of water, its bold chartreuse and faded white and sharp spikes and feathery forms all clashing against each other.

THAT EVENING, Renia found only broth in her kitchen cabinet for dinner. She heated the soup and sat at the dining table, fretting about Minh. Down on the street, a student carrying a backpack walked by. He dropped his wallet, stopped, and picked it up. Renia clutched her bowl as if its warmth could soothe the stark truth facing her: she had to sell the flowers to Zbiggy. She had nine buds and could probably create three more. Yes, exposing her dealings to convicted criminals was a risk, but she'd make almost 2000 euros—enough for January's rent and to keep Minh employed until the year's end. She could pay her in cash and not tell Palomer, make sure she worked on days Palomer was at the hairdresser or traveling. If she told her boss, she'd need an explanation as to where she'd acquired the money. She decided to get the cash first and worry about the explanation later.

She dialed Zbiggy. He answered with a grunt.

"Does your friend still want a dozen scarves?" she said.

Silence. Cough. "Yeah, absolutely. You have a dozen?"

"I will, within the next two weeks."

"Wow, okay. Let me give him a call and I'll call you back."

She finished her soup. The student came into view again, walking from the opposite direction, holding a wrapped box with an enormous red bow.

Her phone rang. "He's in," Zbiggy said. "Whenever they're ready. I'll give you the location."

"No, no. You need to come with me. Or deliver them yourself, like you said you would."

"Oh. See, I can't deliver them. This guy and I, we're on the outs."

"Again? Gee, I wonder why. You know, it's bad enough you're not in Poland."

"I know, but it's how it is. This guy doesn't like me. He'll like you, Polish girl. He'll have the money when you come, he said he would."

"I'm not going anywhere. Especially after our last visit. He needs to come to me. In the square."

"It's impossible," Zbiggy said. "This guy, Renia . . . he likes to do things his way. And he's touchy."

"Oh really?"

"Trust me, Renia. He's touchy."

"Well, I'm not going alone."

"I know, I know. You don't have to. I'll drive you there. And I'll wait for you in the car."

"Right."

"I will. I swear. I was going to anyway. But I can't show my face."

Renia considered it. "That's what you said last time."

"Well . . . okay, I'll tell you. It's nothing, okay? I dated his ex-girlfriend a few times and he's mad about that. But hey, she was free and she wanted to and—"

"That's enough," Renia said. "Is this guy Russian?"

"No, not at all. He's French. Cool. It'll take two minutes. You go in real quick, he gives you the money and that's that. We go. I promise. It'll be easy."

Renia let go a dubious sigh. "You better be right."

She ended the call, went to the kitchen and made herself a cup of green tea. She stirred in sugar for a faux dessert. As she sat at the table watching the Rue Sereine, she noticed each person briefly illuminated by the street lamp as they passed. A man in a suit coat talked on a phone, a couple arm in arm, a lone woman in a knit cap, baggy jeans, chunky boots, and a canvas coat as if she'd been working outside. As Renia inhaled the smell of the earthy tea, she remembered the library at the university in Kraków, the reading lights illuminating books. Hands turning pages. A trash can with a half-empty cup of green tea. Grassy smells. Estera, approaching, in a knit cap and boots and a canvas coat.

Her boots clunked against the wooden floor. Renia sat at a table studying for final exams. It was late November. Beneath her reading light, her book about probability glowed. Her attention had been swallowed into the ideas of financial risks and outcomes when Estera pulled out a chair.

The wood legs screeched on the hardwood floor. A nearby student looked up.

"Why are you here?" Renia whispered.

Estera's face seemed to have succumbed to the cold

outside, looking dull, gray. Her emerald eyes, faded. She wore denim overalls with work boots and a hefty jacket. Her pruners and holster were attached to her pants. She'd driven all the way from Biały Manor to downtown Kraków. The clods of dirt on the floor showed it.

"What do you think you're doing?" Estera said. Her voice rang in a strange blankness.

"I'm reading and taking notes."

"Don't ever touch my Violet Smoke again."

"What do you mean?"

"I mean stealing flowers from my plant."

"Stealing flowers?"

Estera's mouth tightened, as if ready to scream.

"I didn't steal any flowers," Renia said.

"Two blossoms are missing from the Violet Smoke."

"Yes?" Renia said. She knew at least one was supposed to be.

"I can't believe you came to Biały Manor and took them for yourself."

"Estera, I didn't. You were going to clip them last Monday. We agreed to clip the flowers until Zbiggy became more responsible. Remember?"

Her eyes raced back and forth, then she stared at the floor. "Yes, I remember. But I don't remember cutting them."

"I didn't cut them, honestly. I've been here for the last three days."

"But they're gone," she said. She rubbed her forehead, removed her hat. Her mussed bangs revealed a bump on her forehead. "I don't remember cutting them."

Renia touched her forearm. Estera shifted away.

"We used one on Mama," Renia said. "Remember?"

Her eyes gazed absently at her soiled hands. "Yes, I think so."

"Did you use the flower to forget that?"

"I don't know."

"You don't know?" Renia's voice bounced off the wooden walls. She lowered it and said, "I thought you recorded this stuff in your journal, every time you cut a flower. I thought you did that to keep track of how many flowers you had—and used on yourself."

Estera's face crinkled, as if she were unsure of what was true anymore. "But there's nothing in the journal about it."

Renia watched her strain to remember, strain to recall a memory she couldn't recall. And that bump, it was raised, and so bruised.

"Estera, you need to come home with me."

"No," she said. Her eyebrows wrinkled in struggle. "I can't remember right now."

"That plant is trouble. Zbiggy is trouble."

"How could you say that?"

"I'm worried for you. "

"I can't recall," she said, "I just can't recall."

"Well, maybe Zbiggy cut the flowers."

"No, he doesn't know where . . ." she trailed off, slowly closing her eyes. A second later, her eyes opened, her mouth opened. "Oh no, he's going to kill me."

"Why?"

"Two flowers were spoken for. The Russians will be furious." She tapped her fingers on the table, her face stern, her mouth open. "I need another flower."

"Estera, how many Russians?"

"This is terrible," she said. "What the hell am I supposed to do? I can't believe I forgot about this latest deal."

"Tell him the flowers dried up."

"That won't work." She dropped her head in her

hands. "Oh, hell. This is bad. Very bad. Nothing's worked as I'd planned. I've got to go to Biały Manor. I've got to grow more flowers."

IN THE ATRIUM, Renia soaked the Violet Smoke's soil with liquid fertilizer. Last November, she had helped Estera get the plant to produce more blooms. Now, she had to do the same for herself. It pained her, but she had no choice. She left the vent window open, checked the temperature in the nook. On Wednesday, she noticed the emerging buds had plumped. The nine existing flowers would open soon. Betting they would open by Friday, she called Zbiggy and arranged a meeting with the French buyer.

ON FRIDAY NIGHT, Zbiggy waited for Renia outside Le Sanctuaire. Getting into his junky car again felt like eating a rotten peach. A defeat, an embarrassment. Earlier that day, she'd told him she'd meet him at the buyer's "office," but he convinced her it was too remote for a bike. They drove on the Périphérique before heading north into the suburbs. The traditional French architecture gave way to angular structures and plain warehouses with broad yards of stored trucks and vacant lots. Train tracks. The light posts switched from short spiky lamps to tall slanted posts along roads cluttered with bits of tires, gnarled shrubs, and concrete barriers.

"Where are we?" she said.

Zbiggy shrugged with a loose tilt. "Out of the city."

He drove through a maze of streets and came to a dense shopping district, bouncing down a narrow trash-strewn lane. Store shutters, spray painted with graffiti, sat solidly shut and locked. A grocery store advertised sales in

Mandarin. Beside a tobacco shop door, a geranium grew, its coral blossom beaming in the night, but as they neared, Renia realized the plant was plastic. They passed ripped posters on boarded up windows, advertising a Turkish singer. Along a plywood wall, large looping graffiti showed a bent pitchfork, initials, genitals, and symbols Renia didn't recognize.

Zibggy slowed the car at a red light.

At the curb, a pile of dirty clothes lay. No, a homeless person sleeping. Behind them, a car, with its dented hood corded shut, idled. Inside were four men and thumping music.

"I don't want to do this," she said.

"We're almost there. It'll be over quick."

They went through a series of apartment buildings with plain iron posts, not like the decorative ones in central Paris, but plain pillars with heavy chains to separate traffic from pedestrians. A torn couch, its cushion foam exposed, lay near a dumpster. Zbiggy took a left and the neighborhood opened to an industrial area of one-story warehouses. Signs that read *Hydraulique* and *Véhicules* and *Euro Diffusion* flashed by until the street ended in a cement wall with barbed wire that bordered a shipping yard. They parked before a single-story warehouse whose door hung diagonally, closed, slightly off the hinge.

"This is it," Zbiggy said.

Renia inspected the sidewalk. It was cracked with a chunk of pavement missing at the middle. On the door's stoop, broken glass lay as if a bulb, once attached to a fixture, had fallen and smashed.

"I'm not going in there."

"You have to. It will take, like, two minutes."

Beside the car, shards of green glass and cigarette butts dotted the dirt.

"Are you sure this guy's in there?"

"Yeah. That's his office. He has little parties. He's probably got one going on now."

A party? She didn't like the sound of that. "What's his name?"

"They call him Antoine."

"Give me the car keys."

"What?"

"I want the keys."

"No. I gotta keep the motor running. It's freezing out."

The running engine did emit a welcomed but weak, dry heat through the vents.

"Then come with me to the door."

"C'mon, Renia."

"Do it, or else I'm not going in."

"Alright, alright."

He shut the engine and they got out of the car.

The door had a window covered in black privacy film. Zbiggy knocked three times, paused, knocked once.

Nothing happened.

"Okay, go in," he said, "you have to walk through the big room, take a right, and go all the way to the end of the hall. Say 'flower delivery.' He'll know who you are."

Her heart raced. "What does he look like?"

"Always wears green pants."

"Give me your phone."

"Why?"

"Because I want something of yours so you won't leave."

"What about yours?"

"Give me the phone."

He sighed and pulled it from his pocket. The plastic case was cracked. "I'll be in the car."

Renia knocked again.

No answer.

"Go in," Zbiggy said. He got in the car and started the engine.

She tried the knob. The door wouldn't open. She yanked and it gave. Inside was a dark, slightly less cold space. Dim sweaty air. A long window sitting high in the wall let street light through. Scraps of lumber lay about. Humped drop cloths and paint cans. She took out her phone and clicked the button so the camera's flash would light her way. She tip-toed past what was once a counter, stepping over scraps of dry wall, and found a hallway. The corridor wound several feet to the right and then right again, where she found herself in a larger room with intermittent posts and black walls.

She shivered. *Remember, 2000 euros.* In two minutes, 2000 euros would be in her hand.

Someone sniffed. A shoe slid across dry pavement.

To her left was an open doorway. A weak red light glowed.

"*Allô?*" she said.

A voice mumbled.

Her heart thumped fast. She came to a room where old chairs were clustered together in a corner. A man and woman, both rail thin, sat on the floor against the wall, one's head thrown back, the other's lazily swaying. Weak light from a window covered by a broken blind. Clicking sounds. To her right were three people, young men in jackets, laying in the corner. Beside them, a man and woman kissed in intense bursts before dropping into languid petting. After a few seconds, they'd kiss again in a sloppy embrace.

Renia's breath caught in her throat. More clicking.

Her heart beat hard in her ear. In a squeak, she said, "Flower . . . delivery."

A half-wall dissected the room and behind it sat a desk. A shirtless man, in camouflage pants, paced around. He was thin with ribs bumping along his skin. On his wrist a black leather band with metal studs hung like a diabolical watch. His hair was short, nothing memorable, and his face was chiseled with stubble covering odd red splotches on his cheeks. Aviator sunglasses hid his eyes in the dark.

He held a gun. A sleek pistol she had seen in spy movies. Rectangular. The man hiked three steps toward the wall, three steps back, pivoted, and pointed the gun in a random direction: at the ceiling, at his feet. He pulled the trigger. The mechanism clicked. The gun did not fire. He slotted a magazine into the gun's butt, pointed it at the floor, and said, "Boom!"

Renia's breath quickened. She cleared her throat, worried a sudden movement would set him off.

"There," he said. "On target."

Her fingers trembled, the wax paper bag rustled. In a slow effort, she said, "Flowers?" The word came out as more of the soft squeak of a mouse.

On the desk, a box of bullets was open. He paced and pretended to shoot his imaginary target, this time a post. "Boom. On target." He paced around some more, his arms waving in a frantic flapping as if wanting to urge a crowd to stand and cheer.

"Um, are you Antoine?" Renia said.

He spun around, took off his glasses. His limp blood-shot eyes stared through her. "Who are you?"

In a high-pitched song, she said, "I have flowers, for delivery?"

He pointed the gun at her. It clicked.

She jumped. Dropped the bag. She backed in the hall-way, not knowing which way to go. A voice said, "*Oh, putain,*" then a loud bang. A gun shot. For real. Searing her ears. She sprinted through the dark, stopped at a filthy toilet. Lazy laughter drifted from the other room. She took out her phone but couldn't find the flash so felt the air for obstacles. Finally, she stumbled into the large room where she'd entered. Huddled underneath the drop cloths were people.

At the door, she pushed hard but it wouldn't budge. She threw a shoulder against it, twice, harder. It swung open and she tripped into the night, hearing another gunshot. She flinched, checked behind her, and tore around the building, the cold air biting her face. When she came to a chain link fence with a dumpster, she realized she'd run behind the building and spun around, sprinted back, scanning the street for Zbiggy's car.

It was gone.

CHAPTER SEVENTEEN

Another gun shot rang out—or was it a clang from the shipping yard? Didn't matter, she ran, her gut in a knot. She searched ahead for a store or métro sign. After a few minutes, when she was convinced no one was about, she slowed to a walk, wrapped her raincoat tight, wishing for a hat and gloves, and hurried past the chunky warehouses that swallowed the city block. She took out Zbiggy's phone. It was foreign and greasy in her hand. Locked. That slime. She took out her own, launching the maps app. No métro stations nearby. The clunky image told her she was in Saint-Denis. In its most industrial section. At midnight. The nearest métro station was a mile away with train tracks and a canal obstructing it. She considered calling a cab, but she'd spend money she didn't have, and now really didn't have. Plus, would a taxi come to this neighborhood?

She swore, cold and alone, scanning behind and ahead for Zbiggy's car. All she saw was a dead animal at the corner, humped over. No, a dirty sweatshirt. She picked her way around puddles, the smell of stale water like musk.

She was sweating, beads rolling by her ears. She remembered Estera's sweaty body, her damp hair. Overhead, a fluorescent streetlight dimmed and brightened, dimmed and brightened, like the rectangular light over a hospital bed. Beneath the light, Estera lay unconscious. Covered with a cotton blanket, like a shroud. Dear Estera. Dear . . .

She was broken. Two fractured ribs, a concussion, two black eyes, a bruised hip. That's what he'd done. He'd been capable of more, but she was lucky more hadn't happened. Her torso was wrapped in bandages. Her hair was shaved above her ear, showing a row of stitches. Mama stroked her hair, wet and slick. In a low breath, she recited a Hail Mary, her rosary in hand. She sat in her down coat and winter boots though she'd been sitting in that warm room for hours.

When she saw Renia enter, she rose and led her outside the door. Her eyes sagged in sadness, her mouth clenched in anger. "He did this. He did it. He could have murdered her. I think he wanted to, I truly do." Her voice popped with disdain.

Renia wasn't about to defend Zbiggy. "I don't know what to do, I tried to talk her into leaving him. She won't."

"The only thing not bruised on her body are her feet. Her beautiful body, bruised all over."

"All over?"

"Doctor says she was hit with an object like a stick or pipe."

Or gun.

"And over something so stupid as a plant," Mama said. "Why does he want that plant? Does he make marijuana with it? What is he selling?"

"Something like that."

Estera's mouth lay open and lax. That her chest rose and fell was reassuring.

"Doctor had to give her a sedative. She kept howling for that mean moron. And now," Mama pointed at the hallway as if Tata were there, as if he weren't at work, "your father wants to kill him dead. He wants to chop off his hands."

Renia nodded. She thought of Estera's smiling face. Her delight when Pan Górski had given her the Violet Smoke. How happy her expression had been when she'd told Renia that she'd met Zbiggy. Now, the plant, combined with Zbiggy, had almost killed her.

"I've already filed a complaint against him. The court will order a forbiddance."

"You can do that?"

"When the victim is incapacitated, yes. She will come home with us."

"That's best," Renia said. Estera could heal with the three of them working together to watch her. They would take turns. When she thought of how outraged Zbiggy would be at learning of the restraining order, her relief solidified into anxiety.

"And the plant," Mama said. "He wants it, he phoned her about it, the moron. I will not allow him to speak with her. And so, to me, he says three words about her condition and the rest about when he could have the plant. But she wants to keep the silly thing." Her voice was pinched with frustration. "I told her, 'give it to him,' but she won't. She won't say where it is. Do you know where this plant is? We must find it, Renia, and Tata must break it into a thousand pieces and put it in the receptacle before it brings more harm. It's the devil's work."

Renia chewed her lip. Yes, she knew where it was but to destroy it . . . that meant destroying Estera. There, in the bed, Estera looked lovely despite the bandages and bruises. Her pale lips and pale skin. She lay like a fluff of cloud beneath the white blankets, under the white light, inside the white walls as if she were an angel sleeping in heaven. Despair pinched Renia's heart. If she didn't do something drastic, Estera would become an angel.

"I'll get the plant," Renia said. "I know where it is. I'll take care of it."

IN PARIS, Renia sat on the train, feeling like a dried leaf ground underfoot. The car was empty save for an old drunk in a filthy coat a few seats away. His head bounced every time the train flew around a corner. His bloodshot eyes registered little. In the tunnel, the lights screamed by. Why had the Violet Smoke come into their lives? Why Estera, why their family? Pan Górski could have given it to his daughter or Jan or sold it to a nursery. Why he'd kept it in that closet all of those years, years after he'd known its scent affected the brain, she didn't know. For whatever reason, its sad destiny had been with Estera.

The train slowed into a station and the doors opened. Now, over a year later, Renia had the plant, but no progress. She'd reached out, Estera had rejected her. How long would it go on? Estera adored the Violet Smoke, for its rarity, its purity, its unique power. It was the only plant in the world of its kind but after tonight, that wasn't enough of a reason for Renia to preserve it for her. This pet was no longer the key to their reconciliation. In fact, she resented the damn thing. Estera had lost so much because of it. Alain might have lost his life because of it. She rubbed her eyes, fatigued, hungry once again. She couldn't return it, wouldn't give it to Zbiggy. There was only one answer, a terrible answer she'd avoided but now couldn't: destroy it.

· · ·

THE NEXT MORNING, she woke with an anxious lump in her stomach. She got up, tried to ignore what had happened last night and went to Le Chasseur on the corner. She ordered coffee and brioche, wondering if she should chop up the Violet Smoke and put it straight in the trash. Too soon. Too impulsive. She needed more time. More time for what she didn't know.

As she ate, she noticed the windows of Le Sanctuaire, across and down the street, lined with white Christmas lights, lights she hadn't strung up. Minh must have. They cheerily illuminated the sidewalk. She'd failed to save Minh's job. Because she was a coward. When she'd seen the gun, she'd panicked. When the gun had gone off, she'd run for her life. Now, the flowers were gone. They were on the floor in that awful warehouse. She didn't have January's rent or money for her utility bills. The store had gained credit card debt and lost merchandise. There would be no lovely shop to manage, no cozy apartment in Saint-Germain-des-Prés, no belonging in Paris. It was over.

Later, as she paid the bill, she noticed a man standing in front of the shop. He was taller than Zbiggy but not as tall as those brutes Vlad and Yuri. A new thug friend? She put her purse over her shoulder, about to walk outside in the opposite direction, when the man turned around. Professor Damazy.

His identity was obvious. He stood with hands in pockets, not to intimidate and not to hide. His clothes, black jeans and boots and a hooded canvas coat, were the outfit of a man working in the weather. He was not a cosmopolitan sort but rather of the natural world. And yet his sophisticated personality was on par with the wealthy business men who came to shop at Le Sanctuaire.

As he knocked on her building door, she trotted across the street to catch him, waving, hoping with a sudden ache that he wouldn't miss her and leave. "Hello, are you looking for me?"

He glanced up, startled. "Ah, yes. Good morning. I hope I haven't come too early."

"Not at all."

His face, that serious low-browed face, softened into a relieved expression.

She hurried to the shop and unlocked the door. "You must have news."

"I do."

She led him inside and hit the lights.

As he waited for her to take off her coat, he studied the sketches on the wall behind the counter. "Wow, those are beautiful. Where do you get them?"

"I draw them."

"You do?" His voice rose.

"Yes."

"I mean, not that you couldn't but," he eyed the display of ferns and maples, an apple with a leaf attached, a lady's mantle in bloom, "they're very professional looking. I especially like the *Alchemilla*. You captured the fine details in those tiny flowers."

Her face warmed. No one had ever complimented her art before. "Thanks. I do it just for fun. So, about the Violet. I mean my plant?"

"Yes. Do you mind if I take one more look?"

"Not at all." She locked the front door and they went in the atrium. She got out the crowbar and this time he scooted out the panel in precise timing with her pressing on the bar to pry it loose.

Damazy lifted the board, careful to peek over so as not to bump her. She noticed his hands, the backs of which were tan, strong, and dotted with tiny scratches, perhaps from working with thorny plants. The scars were maroon and stiff, healing. He seemed not to notice them. His fingernails were clean and trimmed. His eyes, hovering over the panel, were the color of warm coffee. They were eyes that engaged with their surroundings, in a steady, perceiving presence.

She thanked him and handed him a mask. He put it on and lifted the Wardian Case before setting it with a graceful click on the cobbled floor.

As he crouched before the plant, he said, "Do you ever snip the blooms and toss them? To be safe? Or to water without a mask?"

She debated how to answer. "Yes, I remove them, sometimes."

"Well, that's probably safest."

That's the truth.

He took out a magnifying glass, floating it over the one last flower, the leaf stems. They were hairy and bendable with a slight pink tone, succulent, almost transparent. Delicate and yet sturdy. "Yes, the hairs grow in an upper direction. Wow, it is upper. It is." He smiled a loose, surprised smile. His teeth were wide and slightly angled downward, giving him a friendly air.

From his shirt pocket, he took a measuring tape and set it along the bud scars on the main stem. "Yes, that's at least two centimeters. Nes was right."

"What does that mean?"

"It means . . ." He set his tools on the counter and put the glasshouse over the plant. Renia opened the window. "It means," he said again, "this plant is an intergeneric hybrid between *Saintpaulia* and a rare species of *Vulleria*."

"I don't know the genus *Vulleria*."

"Not many people do."

They removed their masks.

"It's my estimation that you have a one-of-a-kind specimen, a rare cross. Its botanical name could be *Hybrid Sain-tulleria* 'Violet Smoke.'" He gave the shrub a loving look, as if its mere presence awed him. "And the scent is said to have a natural fentanyl-type of effect."

With an alarmed frown, she said, "Fentanyl?"

"Yes, I think a natural relative of it. And that might explain the headaches. So, your plant is very dangerous but potentially very useful. If you're inclined, there's a lab I've worked with in Switzerland that could assess it more thoroughly, do a DNA analysis to confirm its parentage and assess the gas."

She leaned against the counter, rattled. Fentanyl. That was serious. A lab to examine it? Utterly exposing it to the botanical world? Even more serious. "Well . . ."

"Think about it," he said. "In the meantime, Mademoiselle, I recommend you do everything you can to keep this specimen alive and well."

AFTER PROFESSOR DAMAZY LEFT, Renia paced before the Violet Smoke, wondering at serendipity. To destroy it or cherish it? She wasn't sure. But if she were to act, she needed to act soon. She covered her mouth and opened the vent and clipped the last flower. Then through the atrium window, she tossed it in the courtyard and closed the pane. It landed on the broken bench beside the broken boxwood, emitting scent into the empty space. A last flower no one would ever smell.

She watered the plant, let it drain, and set it inside a white garbage bag. After all, it wasn't hers to destroy. Loosely she tied the bag and cut holes at the top before finding an empty wine crate. She called a taxi. Minh would not be in to open the shop today, but she pretended that didn't matter. She would open later. If Palomer stopped by and noticed the store closed, Renia would say that she'd had to run an errand. Because there was no assistant, the store must be closed every time she ran an errand. She was in no mood to take a scolding.

At the Gare de Lyon, Renia struggled to carry the crate through the station. She regretted not renting a luggage cart. On the platform, as she was about to lift the crate from the ground to board, a mother and preteen son helped lift one end. The boy said, "Do you have to carry this all the way to Nimes?" She said she didn't. She was about to mention she was departing at Valenton but decided it best not to divulge her destination. She took her seat, the Violet Smoke at her feet, feeling a conspiratorial urgency.

She checked the car for Zbiggy or Vlad or anyone else who looked devious. When the train lunged forward, she sat back, feeling less like she was escaping and more disturbed at how she'd once done this before. The mix of guilt and an imperative to hide the plant flooded her heart. Like last December, in Kraków. Instead of a train through the countryside, Tata's car racing through traffic. As the train gained speed, she smelled pizza. Tomato sauce. A boy and his mother ate slices behind her. She'd grabbed a slice after her Macroeconomics class that day, eating in the car, hurrying to get to Biały Manor before Jan locked the gates for the evening. She made it, parking in the gravel area behind a stand of trees where workers parked, careful to hide the car in a nook of shrubs.

The orchid house was dark in the twilight. A dim room full of ghostly plants. She snuck in and went to the Violet Smoke. No blooms. She skipped wrapping her face and took the plant from its closet, put it in a plastic garbage bag. She hurried out of the greenhouse and headed across the lawn at the side of the house. A blanket of snow had dusted the grounds. Spruces held white powder poetically as if posing for a Christmas card. The tractor used to gather hay was outlined in fluff. Snow humped over the concrete birdbath surrounded by low yew shrubs. In the short distance, the house's chimney blew gentle smoke from the roof, as if in a painting. Winter had a reassuring silence. No birds. No cars. No airplanes. No voices. Only peace.

She wound down the path between the river birches, thankful for the trees' cover, figuring out what to tell Uncle Feliks about the plant the following week when she arrived in Valenton. Best to say it was a favorite of Estera's and that she needed to care for it a while. As she jogged down the path's curve where the trees opened to the gravel area, she saw Estera, leaning heavily on a cane, unsteadily as if she might tip and fall.

Her blood surged. *How had she gotten here?* Renia slowed her pace, deciding confrontation was better than avoidance. "What are you doing here, Estera?"

She was dressed in sweatpants and pajama shirt and cotton sweater, all covered by a mis-buttoned wool coat. The swollen skin around her eyes had receded but the bruises at her neck were clear. She wore a knit hat sloppily yanked to the side, showing the short patch of hair above her ear. Her face froze in a vicious crimp. "What are *you* doing?"

Tata's car was behind Estera. Renia would have to pass her to get to it. "I'm taking the Violet Smoke to a safer place."

"And where could that possibly be?"

Renia swallowed. "Away. For a little while."

"No, you're not."

She stopped to face her. "Estera, this plant is ruining you."

"Give it to me. It's mine."

She breathed in, eyeing Estera's cane. It looked bulky and solid, like it could crack a skull. "Mama and I decided it's best if we keep it for you while you recover."

"Keep it for me?" She said the words as if she were spitting.

"Yes, until you're well."

"I'm well enough to know I want my plant."

Renia swallowed. "Estera, don't do this. You can't see him anyway. Why do you want to see him after what he did to you?"

"He didn't do it."

Renia pressed the Violet Smoke to her chest. Estera had mentioned this before but Renia knew it was a way to let him off the hook. She always let him off the hook. In a solemn voice, she said, "Then who did, Estera?"

"I don't know who. I told you, I can't remember."

The concussion had made her memory hazy. Renia felt compelled to get her in the car and take her home. She marched past.

"Hey," Estera said. She hooked Renia's arm. Her grip was weak but piercing.

Renia paused.

"Don't you take that plant anywhere," Estera said. "It belongs in the orchid house. It's mine and I can do with it what I want."

"Not when it means losing your life."

Renia went to the car. With no other car in the area, she figured Estera must have taken a taxi to get there. She opened the hatch and set the plant in back, tucked in a towel to keep it from tipping. Renia had called Mama earlier that day to say she was taking the car to get the plant. "Did you hear my conversation today with Mama?"

"Maybe."

"Then you know I'm doing this for you."

"No, you're not," Estera said.

"Get in the car. I'll take you home."

"Not until you give me my plant."

Renia opened the passenger door, waited.

Estera limped toward the car. "Give it to me, Renia."

Snow started falling. Large, quiet flakes on Renia's cheeks and hands. "It's cold. Get in the car."

As Estera neared, she batted at Renia with her cane. Renia caught it and yanked it from her sister's hand, lunging her forward. She stumbled. Winced. Renia caught her, held her upper arms, they were frail and bony. Her body, wispy, like a thread.

Estera stiffened. With a brittle hand, she pushed Renia away. "If you take it from me, I'll find out where it is and steal it back. I'll find it, Renia, I will. Tata will tell me where it is."

"No. He won't," she said. "He wants to destroy it. Mama talked him out of it—for now." As she said this, she knew there was a strong chance Tata might tell her. It depended on his mood. She needed a better plan than to keep it in on Mama's desk at the hospital. "I'm not telling Mama or Tata where it is."

Estera's eyes fluttered. "It's my little dear. I love it. It's my Violet Smoke."

"I know, Steri, but it's too destructive, you can't."

"Give it to me," she said. Her voice cracked.

"You're addicted to it. And we can't risk him finding it and hurting you again."

"He didn't hurt me!"

"He did, Steri, he did. And he will again."

Estera's strained face hardened into resolve. "You are crossing a line, Renia."

"I'm sorry. I have to, but I'll keep it safe, I promise."

"You're crossing it." Estera folded her arms. Tears streamed down her cheeks, "If you take it," she said, her voice breaking, "I will never speak to you again."

"Estera, when you're better, I'll give you the plant back. I promise."

"You're not my sister." Her jaw chattered. "I may share a home with you, I may share a room with you, but I will never speak to you again. You're dead as far as I'm concerned." She got in the car and stared straight ahead, sniffling, wiping her face.

As Renia closed the door, she knew those might be the last words Estera ever spoke to her, but if she wanted her sister alive, she had to make the sacrifice.

At the Valenton station, Renia used the shop credit card on a taxi and arrived at Les Racines fifteen minutes later. In the parking lot, clusters of cut Christmas trees attached to crosses of wood stood in the front lot. It was an artificial forest of greenery. Workers bound the trees with twine, creating heaps of spiraled conifers, and tossed them on trucks for brokers to sell to offices and stores. The air smelled like fir and cedar. Renia took the Violet Smoke to the sales office. A few customers chatted about the weather as they paid their orders.

Uncle Feliks was at his desk in the interior office. His sweater vest was light green, the color of a pine needle. He talked on an old dial phone, holding up a finger at Renia.

When he finished negotiating the purchase of sixty *Arborvitae*, he hung up and folded his hands.

"I can't work today," she said. "And I need a ride to the station."

He nodded, pointed to the Violet Smoke. "Is this a present?"

She glanced at the outer office where a printer hummed as it shot out paper. She closed the door.

"This is Estera's plant from Poland," she said.

His face was blank. "And? You want to sell it?"

"No. I need to keep it here again."

He peeked inside the bag.

"I don't remember it. But I remember Estera asked about it."

"What?"

"She asked about it."

Renia paused. "Really? When?"

He gave a dismissive shake. "I don't know, July."

"July?!"

Maya pushed open the door and trotted in the office. She checked Feliks's face, checked Renia's. Satisfied, she lay at Feliks's feet. Feliks swiveled his chair toward the dog. With a pointed finger, he said. "You acted very poorly this morning. Digging a hole in the onions."

Maya wagged her tail, watching his finger.

He gave her a short speech about being courteous to his vegetable beds, then with both hands, scratched behind her ears. "I know. You were searching for a mole."

"Uncle, you spoke to Estera in July?"

"Yes."

"Did she mention me?"

"No. I only spoke a few words to her. She answered when I called your mother."

Renia wanted to know more but worried because the office door was open. In a quieter voice, she said, "Estera's boyfriend has come to Paris. He wants the plant. I have to keep it hidden."

"Is this the *mean moron*?"

Apparently, he knew the nickname. "Yes."

"Does he know about Les Racines?"

"I don't think so."

Feliks sat back, his hands on his tiny belly, surveying the crate and bag.

"It needs a warm house," Renia said. "And a place where it will be safe from accidents."

"What is it?"

"A cross between *Saintpaulia* and *Vulleria*."

"Never heard of it."

"I know, it's new."

Feliks tapped his pen on the table. "Put it in House 8."

"The bamboo house?"

"No. We sold the inventory. I've put the hibiscus in there for winter. It's set it to high temperature, high humidity."

"Is the sprinkler system fixed?"

"Momentarily."

"The leaves will shrivel if they get wet."

His voice hardened. "Then put it in the corner." He shrugged. "And water it yourself."

She lifted the crate. About to leave, she paused and said, "Uncle Feliks."

He wrote *Shipment Waiting* on an invoice. "Hmm."

"Is there a way to lock the greenhouse?"

He paused and scratched his forehead. "The workers must have access. No."

"At night?"

"Renia, you ask too much. It will be safe. Set it by the back door, draw a sign that says, 'Not for Sale, Do Not Remove.' I'll tell Paweł and the others you're storing it, and that it's expensive. No one will bother with it. It's too ugly."

He went back to writing. She went to the door, thinking how she'd have to snip the flowers as soon as the buds emerged. Yes, people had paid a price, it was expensive, but not in the way he thought it was.

.   .   .

When Renia entered House 8, she felt a blast of the tropics. Warm air enveloped her. She worried the air might be too moist as she carried the plant past potted hibiscus and cannas. Bougainvillea and jasmine vines twined around tall wooden latticework stapled to the pots. Windmill palms waved their wide hand-like fans, acacia trees bounced with their miniscule leaves. This was the stock that would be sent by cargo to the south coast come spring.

In the far corner, Renia flipped the crate upside down and set the Violet Smoke atop it. She took out paper she'd swiped from the printer and wrote two signs, one in French, one in Polish: it was not for sale and in Monsieur Baranczki's private collection. *Above all, don't water.* She set the papers' edges beneath the pot.

As she left the greenhouse, she glanced at the plant. A nervous knot in her stomach formed. What if a worker knocked it over? Was an anonymous plant in a commercial greenhouse safer than one hidden in a secret room? She wondered whether to put the plant in Feliks's house or a cold frame with a padlock. The first place was too dry, the second too cool.

A loud crack rang out. The sprinkler system churned and crawled on its track at a steady clip. Triangular sprays of water rained down. She hurried out to beat the spray, the heavy box gliding toward her. She made it to the door just as the system clunked to the end of its pipeline, the hose swinging back and forth. The engine box and watering arm glided backward to spray the rows again. She closed the door, hoping the Violet Smoke would survive it all.

CHAPTER EIGHTEEN

On Monday morning, a chilly rain drenched Paris. As Renia wheeled a cart of plants onto the terrace, she didn't see the neighbors she often saw: the young mother walking her toddler to school, João hosing off the sidewalk, Justine talking on her phone. The rain scattered the humans indoors as if shutting the neighborhood off to her. There would be no last nods of acknowledgment, no last goodbyes. She wasn't even sure she would see Palomer, who had a trip to Provence planned for the holidays. As she arranged the meager items on the terrace, she let the rain soften her coat shoulders, feeling heavy with failure. When she saw Zbiggy sauntering toward her, her sadness boiled to anger.

He wore his usual suit coat and hat, though now he sported a plaid scarf at his neck. His face was scrunched in thought. A five o'clock shadow had fuzzed his chin and he had a fresh scratch at his eye.

In a rushed tone, he said, "Where were you Friday night?"

"Where was I? Where were you?"

"I got hungry so I got some food. But I came back and you were gone."

"I was almost shot dead, so I left."

His face was blank. "Look, I need my phone—and more flowers."

She slipped past him to go in the shop. "We're done doing business here. All done."

He followed her.

"I don't have more flowers," she said. "You took me to a heroin den with a maniac who plays with guns. And I have no payment. We're done."

"I need another set of flowers. For Antoine."

"Antoine's flowers are sitting somewhere on the floor of his 'office'"

Zbiggy's face slid into a sneer.

She leapt toward him, ready to either slap or be slapped. "Don't you dare get angry with me. You took off and left me in Saint-Denis."

"I came back and waited for you."

She scoffed. "How heroic." She stormed toward the atrium, passing a statue of a gargoyle smiling.

"Hey," he said and grabbed her arm.

She yanked it away.

"I'm serious, I need more flowers."

"The plant is gone, Zbigniew. I chopped it up and threw it away."

His eyes went to the atrium. "Is it in there?"

"It used to be. It's not anymore." She opened the door and took the crow bar from the ledge. "Back up."

She threw her resentment into wrenching back the panel. It popped out easily. Zbiggy watched in dumb surprise. She tossed the crowbar on the floor with a clang and lifted the board. He jumped like a boxer to avoid bumping his head. The corner scraped his shoulder as he watched her maneuver it.

"You have to move so I can set it against the wall," she said.

He backed up, standing below a cement cherub that lay in three broken pieces on a shelf.

She set the panel with a loud clap against the doorway, pointed at the table. "There, it's gone."

The Wardian Case sat empty. A lone stem with a cracked leaf had broken off and lay inside. She opened the vent door and reached for it. "The garbage truck has already picked up."

He snatched the leaf, examined it. His breath quickened. He rushed at her, his hands waving. "Why did you do that? That was a cash machine for us."

"For us? All that plant has brought me is misery."

"If you don't have it somewhere, you're screwed, you Polish *dziwka*. Where is it?"

"It's dead. Gone. It's done too much—"

He pushed her, stuck a finger in her face. "I know you have it, you whore. You don't have the guts to get rid of it. In three days, I'm coming back for flowers. You better have them or a plant to show me, or this pretty little store of yours is over, do you hear me?" The smell of his icy aftershave filled her nose. "If the plant's dead, then you're dead."

He turned to leave, bashing the panel from his way. The board cracked, wavered, and fell against the case.

Renia flinched, her heart thumping.

He caught sight of her and kicked the table that held the case. The case shifted to the table's edge but didn't fall and shatter as he probably hoped. Renia felt a flash of satisfaction in that. He waved a fist at a short stack of terra cotta pots on the counter, sending them onto the stone floor, shattering.

She jumped, swallowing at the noisy crash.

He kicked a shard and stomped out.

Renia lowered herself onto the stool, breathing, grasping at control of her beating heart. The shop door slammed. She twitched. She was about to drop her head in her hands and cry, but instinct told her to run and lock the door.

THAT EVENING, the sight of Minh's family eating together made Renia smile with bitterness. They were crammed in at a small dining table in a tight nook. Minh introduced her mother and father, her two brothers, a wife and girl-friend, and grandmother. The smell of beef soup filled the room. Rice sat in a casserole dish, a bowl of vegetables steamed. Renia went to Minh's mother and shook her good hand. She leaned forward in her wheelchair and said, "Ren, Ren," as she patted her hand. Renia swallowed her guilt. Minh invited her to eat but Renia said she'd eaten already. That was a lie, but the truth was she had only a few minutes. She had to go home and pack her belongings to ship back to Poland.

They went to the kitchen and out of view. "Here," she said. She took an envelope from her pocket, money from the shop's emergency stash. "This is payment for one of the afternoons you would have worked. If you had been in the French employment system, you would've had more compensation for the short notice. Take this."

Minh stared at the money. "You don't need to compensate me."

"Take it. I won't have any more. I won't be in . . ."

Minh searched her face. "Where are you going?"

"Don't ask," Renia said. "I'll call you when I'm . . . when I'm . . ." she resisted saying "Poland" for fear Minh would protest. "I have to leave Paris for a while."

A steel spoon loudly clanged on a plate.

Renia jumped.

Minh watched her. "What's wrong? What's going on?"

"No, I'm fine."

"Are you leaving because of that guy? Your sister's ex-boyfriend?"

"No. Well, yes, but . . ."

Minh stepped in. "Renia, is he your boyfriend now?"

"No." She paused, her mouth fighting a smile. She considered telling Minh the truth about the Violet Smoke but thought it best to keep her ignorant of the whole thing. "But he is dangerous and has dangerous friends."

"They're the ones who vandalized the shop, aren't they?"

Minh was smart.

"Probably," Renia said.

"You shouldn't have to run from that guy. He should be arrested. We need to tell the police."

"I think Palomer did—"

Minh's mother called out in Vietnamese to Minh. Minh answered a few words.

"Listen, make sure to avoid the shop for now, okay? I'll talk to Palomer about my departure. Maybe she could hire you back after I leave." Renia said this to cheer Minh but Minh's mouth jittered in silence.

Renia hugged her, pressed the envelope in her hand, and dashed out, her throat too tight to say goodbye.

As she walked to the métro, she passed a café. The fragrance of newly brewed coffee permeated the air.

Beside the café was a club, The Crown of Thorns, where musicians hauled gear inside. A tall bald man carried in a hefty case. A chunky silver ring shown on every finger, a skull on his thumb. He wore a Black Sabbath jacket, jeans with chains at the belt, blood-red Doc Martens. He disappeared through an open door that led to a black hallway, painted with a mural of a coffin and cross. The club was closed but she heard pounding music in her memory. Winter chill. Dark misty skies. Idle chatter. The smell of hot coffee. Last December. Outside The Tomb.

Music vibrated her stomach as she ambled along a line of people, at least fifty deep, waiting to get in.. Students were on winter break and ready to party. As they clustered together in the freezing air, they fidgeted and laughed and snuck sips of alcohol in flasks. Renia kept her eyes at the ground, her scarf around her head, covering much of her face. She passed laced up boots and athletic shoes and high heels. It seemed every person sported a happy yet self-conscious expression. Beneath the eyeliner and piercings, she saw the eyes of young women, so young they must have only recently turned twenty-one. The boyfriends waited with arms slung around the girls, the tough yet indifferent stances, the arty way both smoked cigarettes or cackled at an unfunny joke. A cloud of marijuana smoke. The steam from the bouncer's coffee.

Zbiggy and another bouncer guarded the door, facing the crowd beneath the yellow glow of an outdoor light. They held giant flashlights whose beams illuminated identification cards. Zbiggy's partner was hefty and more muscular but one look at Zbiggy's high forehead and alert eyes said he was, without a doubt, the vicious one.

Renia rounded a clump of people standing behind a velvet rope. Zbiggy checked a young woman's driver's license. She twirled her hair, waiting. "How many?" he said. She pointed to two others. He unhooked the rope. The women teetered on spiked-heels through the tufted vinyl door.

Renia waited for him to notice. She didn't want to draw attention.

When his eyes landed on her, he said to the other bouncer, "I'm on break."

His partner, about to speak on a walkie-talkie, clicked off and said, "You already went on break."

"I'm taking my other one early."

The guy frowned, drank his coffee. "No partying."

Zbiggy bristled. "I'm not. This is my sister, I gotta give her something."

His partner unclicked the velvet rope for a man in a suit and a woman in a dress to enter, "Yeah, right."

Zbiggy led Renia a half-block down to the nearest alley. They hid behind garbage bins so headlights wouldn't shine on their faces.

"I have them," Renia said. "Where's the money?"

"Let's see it," he said.

"First, the money."

He checked around and pulled out his wallet. Counted out 10 one-hundred złoty bills.

She took the packet of flowers from her pocket. Ten of them. Lifted them to eye level so he could shine his flashlight on them. Inside the haze of the wax paper bag, he could see the purple flowers, each wrapped in a wet paper tissue.

He gave her the bills, which she put in a zippered pocket of her purse. She gave him the package, which he tucked in his coat pocket. When they came to the street corner, about to part, she stopped and said, "I'm throwing away the plant."

"Don't be so dramatic. Vlad and I want more flowers. We have a good thing going."

"Like your and Estera's good thing?"

He missed the sarcasm. "Maybe."

"I won't take responsibility for after-effects. There's nothing guaranteed about these anymore."

"Estera and I never got a bad report."

"Estera is the bad report."

"You were careless."

"You're an asshole."

"No need to be rude, Renia."

"Stay away from her. She'll never be the same, thanks to you."

He rolled his eyes. "So dramatic."

"And remember, make good use of these because I'm leaving Poland."

"Where you going?"

"None of your business."

"Paris? I know Estera likes Paris."

"Shut up."

"You know I have business contacts there."

She didn't answer.

"So, you're just up and leaving. Couldn't stand the pressure, huh?"

Renia thought of how for the last month Estera had been true to her word. They hadn't spoken. Estera hadn't even made eye contact. A complete full shunning that had worked. Renia couldn't take it anymore. It was agony to come home to that bedroom every night where the sibling who she'd shared her entire life with rejected her. There was nothing to do but move on and try something new. "Don't call Estera," she said, "or my family."

"But I already have," he said lightly. It was unclear from his canny eyes whether he was lying. "Just joking."

"Goodbye, Zbigniew."

He headed toward the waiting crowd. "Yeah, bye for now. I'll be in touch."

As SHE HIKED down the Avenue de Choisy, she felt nauseated. Tomorrow would be the last day she worked at Le Sanctuaire. How ironic that Zbiggy could stay in Paris and she could not. The thought of leaving the shop, the shop that had once gained a reputation because of what she'd done, made her wince. Goodbye to watering the plants in the morning, to listening to Chopin's Mazurkas as she ate lunch, to helping a customer find the gift they were looking for. Riding her bike to the wholesale nursery. To the quiet moments when the atrium filled with warmth on a spring day. Goodbye even to the pigeons on the ledge outside. She'd struggled to be Parisian but clearly wasn't, and never would be. It was a city for others to succeed in, not her. She was, after all, just a lowly girl from Poland. As she realized she'd never hear the soft trickle of the goddess and her urn again, she hung her head, her spirit wilted.

THE NEXT DAY, Madame Palomer asked Renia to help her at the wholesale, floriculture market. Though reluctant to go, she went, knowing she had to see Palomer in person to resign anyway. She steered the cart around as Palomer scanned the stalls. Roses, lilies, peonies, tulips, and cut greenery all leaned in rows of buckets beneath the transparent ceiling. Sweet scents and cool water filled the air. Renia watched how warmly vendors greeted certain customers, how easily they laughed with each other. When Palomer approached, vendors straightened up and spoke in complete, courteous sentences. In a formal exchange, they announced the price, at which Palomer often frowned, then paid, garnering polite but curt parting words.

Later, at Le Sanctuaire. Renia unloaded their wares while Palomer sat behind the counter, massaging her foot. She carried boxes of blooming Christmas cactuses and set them in the windows.

"The aisles of that ridiculous market are always so uncomfortable," Palomer said.

"Yes, I know," Renia said. "So, would you like to go for lunch?" Breaking the news to her boss over a meal might soften the blow. Her reaction would be more staid since they would be in public.

Palomer considered the offer. "Well, I am hungry—and so tired."

"How about lunch at the bistro across the street?" Renia forced her voice to sound breezy.

"Oh, I can't eat there. That man, he's a scoundrel. He raises his prices every year!" She shook her head, eyeing Vida Nova. A waiter picked up a balled up wrapper from the sidewalk.

Renia didn't argue. With a razor blade, she sliced open a box of candles and began unloading them. Her phone rang. It was Mama. Renia answered.

"Is Estera with you?" Mama asked frantically.

"No. She's not with you?"

Palomer said, "And now I should get back to Julo."

"She left a note saying she went to visit you in Africa, "Mama said.

"Africa? Are you sure she said Africa?"

"No," Mama said in a quiet clip. "I'm not."

Palomer headed for the door, then paused. "Oh, dear, I don't have anyone to help unload the flowers at the apartment." She noticed Renia was on the phone and waved a hand as if to say, "Never mind."

To Mama, Renia said. "I'll call you back, my boss is here."

She hung up.

"Of course, you can't leave the shop." Palomer sighed. "This is when I miss Alain so much." Her voice was breathy and fatigued. "He always used to help, and so gladly. He never hesitated."

Renia thought of how she'd witnessed Alain carry a bag of groceries to Palomer's car—once. She debated whether to volunteer. Her stomach growled. She was ready to eat a bowl of rice as soon as Palomer left. "Well, I could . . ."

"No, no. I'll manage. Keep the shop open, Renia. This is a lucrative time of year. We need to be open as much as possible. I was thinking we should stay open until midnight every night until Christmas."

Renia swallowed. She felt dizzy. She wondered whether to blurt out, "I can't afford the rent!" or "I have to leave Paris!" Instead, she kept quiet and sliced open another box of candles before putting the razor cutter in her coat pocket.

Palomer limped outside to the car. At Vida Nova, Christmas lights blinked cheerily in the windows. João held the door for a man on crutches. As Palomer got in her car and drove off, Renia realized she hadn't told her she was leaving Paris. Well, whether she told her boss in person or by phone or by note wouldn't matter. She was voiding any chance of a work reference later on simply by putting her own life first.

THAT EVENING, Renia kept the shop open until ten o'clock. She left a message on her mother's phone, asking when the last time she'd seen Estera was, and to call as soon as she

could. She thought of calling Palomer, but knew she went
to bed early. In her mind, she drafted her goodbye email.
She'd explain that she'd had to rush home to help her
ailing sister. Palomer would have twelve days to find a
tenant to rent the apartment by January 1st. That would be
easy. But no one to manage the shop. She'd leave Minh's
number and an argument to give her another chance. She
would have liked to have gone through the long bureau-
cratic process of quitting but couldn't risk the time. Zbiggy
would be returning soon and she needed to be out of Paris
when he did.

She locked the atrium door. Some of the more expensive items they'd purchased were in there. Minh would
know how to display them. She went outside, noticing Vida
Nova was still serving meals to a few diners on the patio
though João had left. Earlier, she had visited to talk with
him. He was a fifty-something Brazilian-Frenchman whose
father had come to Paris after World War II. Renia told
him she was leaving for a few days and asked that he keep
an eye on the shop. He waved a hand as if it were no
trouble and promised to check the window at night.

So, Renia had done all she could. The most she hoped
for was to work for Uncle Feliks for a few weeks before
saving enough to pay off the debt she knew Palomer would
come after her for, then on to Poland. Beyond that, she
didn't know. She hadn't worked out any plan. Plans never
seemed to work out as they should.

At eleven o'clock, after she'd done the accounting for
the last week, she locked the shop door. Le Sanctuaire was
no longer hers. With a deep sigh, she went to the apartment building door, admiring the ornate mailbox she'd
used for the last year. As she was about to step inside, a
hand shot out and yanked the door shut. A man pressed
against her. Frowning. The brute that Renia had put to

sleep. Yuri. He had tiny gray eyes and a wide chin, oddly small ears. "Let's go."

The words, French. His voice, growling.

"Go where?"

"Shut up."

The black sedan idled in the street.

"I'm not going with you," she said.

He jammed his hand under her elbow and shuffled her body toward the car.

"Let me go."

He opened the car door, about to shove her in when she said, "I'll scream. I'll scream so loud your ears will break."

He paused, yanked her. "Where is the plant?"

"It's dead."

He pinched her upper arm as he dragged her to the trunk. He checked the street. At the moment, the only person about was a young woman at the corner, smoking, talking on her phone. The tables of Vida Nova were cabled together on the terrace. All other businesses were shut down, their entrances covered by metal grates.

"Is it in here?" he said.

He hit the remote and the trunk popped open. Zbiggy lay inside, his hands and feet bound with plastic ties, his mouth gagged. His hat was smashed behind his head. One eye was swollen. Through the rag at his mouth, he tried to speak.

Renia shuddered.

"You take us to the plant, we'll let him and you go. If you don't, we'll let you both go, with a bullet."

Her gut loosened. She whispered, "Alright."

THE CAR SMELLED of leather cleaner and hair gel. It was a

locked luxury box. Yuri drove and Vlad rode in the passenger seat. She recognized Vlad's high forehead and stuck mouth. As they headed to Valenton, Renia calculated how long she had before they arrived at Les Racines. Her hands trembled. *Don't panic.* Once there, she'd give them the plant and they'd leave. In petrified silence, she watched the looming suburban homes give way to the openness of the country. The low carpet of clouds. They drove through claustrophobic *allées* of trees with thick trunk after thick trunk binding the roadway. An occasional street light illuminated an abandoned shed or parked tractor but was lost to the smell of cow manure and oncoming blackness.

Inside that blackness, she thought of how last December, only a few days after Christmas, she'd come for the first time to Valenton. She'd taken the train from Kraków and Uncle Feliks had picked her up in his work van. They'd driven this same route through the darkness. Then, as now, the terrain smelled of cow manure. She'd had two large suitcases and the Violet Smoke. That was it. He knew Renia had left Kraków because of an argument with Estera but knew few details. "Children will always bicker," he'd said. "It's natural."

Later that evening, they'd sat at the kitchen table and ate bread and cheese for dinner. Feliks ate as Tata did, wiping his mouth often, leaning far over his food as if someone might steal it. She wondered if she and Estera shared mannerisms. And she wondered if Feliks unconsciously remained estranged from Tata because he resented being a twin. He'd moved to France because he'd fallen in love with a French woman, but she wondered if he'd left because he'd wanted his own identity with his own face that no one else shared.

Before she'd come, Feliks had admitted it would be good to have company at Les Racines but reminded her

that she'd have to work the fields before doing the glamorous work in the office. Yes, *glamorous*, she'd thought. She
agreed, though she dreaded doing physical work in the
country. She wanted to manage a business in Paris.

Still, she worked for him for three weeks, quietly and
loyally. She watered, weeded, carried plants back and
forth, drove the tractor. Together they potted dahlia tubers
for the coming season. Orange cactus style dahlias called
'Explosion.' He whistled songs whenever they worked. One
evening, pressed with guilt but pushed by want, she
brought up the idea of moving to the city. They drank tea
in the sitting room, Maya snoozing by the fireplace. He
surprised her with his reaction.

"So Valenton isn't good enough for you?" he'd said.

"No, it's just that, it was always Estera's and my dream
to live in Paris."

"A folly," he said.

"Maybe."

The fire spit sparks at the screen, then hit the iron and
died.

She gathered her courage. "I'm going to look for a job
in Paris." The declaration was a betrayal, but after what
she'd been through with Estera she wasn't going to settle
for a life that made her miserable, she was already settling
for never speaking to her again.

"I can come on the weekends and help with the
books," she said, "or the field work, if that's what you
need."

He was silent, stroking his mustache. Finally, he said,
"This country life is not best for a young woman. Yes, your
Aunt convinced me."

After years of complaining about France's weather,
Aunt Nanette had moved to Portugal four years ago. Uncle
Feliks hadn't. But he visited her twice a year and spoke to

her by phone. A strange arrangement that somehow worked.

"Your future is limited in a small town," he said. "There's no one to marry. Ablik is the only unmarried man who's a gentleman but he's forty-five years old."

He was actually open to the idea. Hiding the thrill of it, she said in a controlled, casual voice, "I'll need to find a job. So, it won't be soon."

He frowned, set down his cup. "I have an idea." He got up and went to the bureau. Amidst a stack of papers and magazines, he pulled out an address book. "There's a woman in the 6th who I sell perennials to." He threw on reading glasses and flipped pages. "She's ill. She asked last month if I knew someone to help with her store. At the time, I didn't. But now I do."

Inside, Renia burst with joy. She was shocked that he was letting her go. The situation sounded too good to be true. In the 6th Arrondissement?

"She must have found someone by now," Renia said.

"I doubt it." He lowered himself into the chair, massaging his knees. "That old biddy is picky. Here's her number. Valentina Palomer, I'll phone her tomorrow."

Renia wanted to jump up and hug him, but he wasn't the hugging type. So instead she reached down to Maya's tummy and pet it with a brisk rub. In a low mumble she said, "Thanks, Uncle Feliks, I appreciate the help."

He took his mug in both hands and stared at the flames. In a tired tone he said, "I once wanted a better life too."

His eyes were absent, lost in thought.

With a tentative voice, she said, "Did you ever get it?"

He shot her a look. She wondered if she'd gone too far, been too invasive, made him angry. In a bright tone he said, "Yes, of course."

CHAPTER NINETEEN

As the sedan bounced down the drive of Les Racines, Renia warned Yuri to slow down lest he get a flat tire from the potholes. Instead, he drove briskly, bumping hard into the deep divots, kicking up a cloud of dust, revving when the car got caught in a hole. Renia prayed the noise would alert Uncle Feliks that dangerous people were coming. They drove past the greenhouses and perennial field where she glimpsed the last dahlias clustered together against the cold. Uncle Feliks might never work with dahlia 'Explosion' again and if he didn't, it would be her fault.

She wiped her mouth, smoothed her hair, told Yuri to stop the car, thinking she could go to House 8 and get the Violet Smoke. If she handed it over straight away, maybe they'd leave. It would be agony to hand away Estera's love, but she had to get rid of them. Instead, they drove to the drive's end and the cottage. The porch light was off. The chopping stump sat without the ax.

"Back up," she said. Her voice wavered, caught in her

throat. "It's in one of the greenhouses. No need to wake the owner."

They stopped the car. Yuri glanced at Vlad, debating what to do.

"Which one?" Vlad said.

"I think it's House 8 but I'm not sure," she said. "If you turn off your headlights and back up, I can read the house numbers better."

It was after midnight. The cottage was dark. Renia saw a flash of light near the bathroom, then stillness. Uncle Feliks may have been watching through the window. Did he have any weapons? What should she do? If he came out, there would be a confrontation. Her uncle wouldn't take kindly to gangsters. And then what? Talk? An argument? Would they kill him? She tremored in a cold sweat.

Yuri yanked the car into reverse, about to back up from the gravel parking area when Maya barked, an insistent warning, mixing a solemn, low-pitched growl with an occasional howl.

The outdoor lamp lit up.

Renia closed her eyes. "No."

Yuri shut the engine.

The three got out.

"Wait," Renia said.

The men loomed over her. They wore leather jackets and sharp boots.

"The plant is in the greenhouse. We don't need to involve the owner."

Vlad came to her, his body like a rock wall. "Where is it?"

Her eyes fluttered. "I'll show you."

The door swung open and light streamed out. In French, Uncle Feliks said, "Renia, is that you?"

He emerged in sweatpants and sweatshirt, hair rumpled.

Yuri drew a gun and pointed it at him.

He stopped. "What is this? What do you want?"

In French, Yuri said, "Shut up, old man, don't move."

Renia made a bet. It was a long shot but she said in Polish, "Vlad and Yuri have come for my precious greenery." She avoided saying the word "plant," a word she worried was similar in Russian and Polish. "I'll give it to them and they'll go away."

Uncle Feliks lifted his hands, staring at the gun barrel.

"Of course," he said in Polish, then to Yuri, "are you Russian?"

"Shut up, you old fool!" Yuri said in Russian.

"Do you want some tea?" Feliks said.

"Shut up," again in Russian.

"Renia, meet at House One Five," Feliks said in Polish. "Not the other house. Meet at One Five."

"What did he say?" Yuri said in French.

"Why One Five?" Renia asked in Polish. "The greenery is in the other house."

"Stop talking," Yuri said.

"It's a gift," Feliks said.

"Shut up!" Yuri said.

Yuri fired a shot at the ground. Maya barked. Her bold German Shepherd snout rose at the bedroom window and her paws clung to the sill. Her insistent barking crashed through the air.

"Shut the dog up," Vlad said to Feliks.

Uncle Feliks shrugged, as if he didn't understand. In English he said, "No one hears here."

Yuri shoved Feliks at the house and with the gun, struck his head.

Renia jumped forward but Vlad grabbed her. She wrestled against him.

"Don't hurt him," she said. "He hasn't done anything."

"The plant, you stupid whore."

"Don't hurt him, please, don't hurt him," she said. She panted. "I'll give you the plant, I'll give you the damn thing."

Through the kitchen curtain, she saw Yuri hit Uncle Feliks again. He stumbled out of view. Yuri opened the door. "Get some rope!" he called.

Vlad let Renia go and popped the trunk, revealing Zbiggy. Wide-eyed, sweating, his mouth stuffed with the rag. Vlad found a thick clump of rope by Zbiggy's feet and tossed it to Yuri. On impulse, maybe for Estera, maybe in hopes of saving herself, Renia tossed Zbiggy the razor from her pocket. *Don't be dense and lose it.*

As Vlad slammed the trunk, Zbiggy rolled onto the razor.

"Walk," he said.

They headed up the drive toward the greenhouses. The night bit at her face with still cold air, the sky bearing down with a dense net of stars. In her peripheral vision, she saw a rustle in the blackberry bushes behind House 18. As they came to Houses 16 and 15, she said, "I can't remember if it's in House 15 or 8," she said. She lightened her voice. "That's what my—the owner was trying to tell me. He moved it."

Her heart pounded. Her neck was covered in sweat despite the cold. Her breath clouded her face as they walked. She led him into House 15, which she knew had an alarm system, whether that alarm system was operating, she had no idea.

Inside House 15 were rows and rows of ground covers, purple carpet bugle and green periwinkle, all in tiny square pots on flats. It was as if an earthy carpet was rolled out before them. Renia scanned the area for the alarm.

"It's not in here," Vlad said.

Renia paused. A gun barrel poked in her back. Her voice quivered as she said, "There are a lot of plants in here."

"They're all small. Where's the big plant with the smelly flowers?"

She calmed her breath, pointed to the shed. "It might be in there."

He grabbed the back of her coat and brought her body to his face. "Don't mess with me. Take me to the plant or I'll put a bullet in your head."

Her heart thumped. No more stalling. Her mouth was dry. "Alright. Let's try House 8."

He swung her around and gave her a push. Once outside, she saw the shrubs rustle. Maya had gotten out. No. She was barking wildly in the house.

An icy wind blew. Renia wrapped her raincoat around her body and marched on. She picked her way around the puddles of mud. Her favorite boots would be ruined. As would her dress pants. Better them than her uncle.

"Where is House 8?" he said.

Before them stood the angular translucent greenhouses, metal roof flags displaying their numbers as if lined up for a game.

"It's the warm one, up here." She kept her voice light, thinking, if she wasn't serious, maybe he wouldn't be either, about killing her. "Wait," she said. "I'm freezing. I need to tie this." She stopped and knotted her coat belt, wondering how she could arrange her body so she could kick him in the crotch.

He pushed her forward. The wind chilled her neck.

"When I give you the plant," she said. "You must keep it in a warm place or it will die."

"Whatever."

"And every few weeks, you must give it fertilizer. And it has to sit by an east-facing window if you don't want it to get scorched. If it gets scorched, it won't bloom."

"Huh. Maybe I'll take you with it."

She shivered.

At House 8, she opened the door. As they went in, a gunshot cracked the air. The cottage. Renia slammed the door on Vlad's arm. He cursed, fired at the ground, dropped the gun. She slammed the door again and grabbed the gun and hurled it hard toward the plants. It skimmed across leaves, clunked against the back wall and disappeared in the palm trees

Vlad forced open the door and Renia sprinted away. She jumped over pots of purple heart and scarlet flames. He raced after her, tripping over them, stumbling as the pots toppled and formed a bed of slippery, plastic curves.

"You whore!" he yelled.

She pushed through a row of hibiscus shrubs, searching for the gun. Maybe if she gave the plant to him, he would leave. Maybe she'd survive.

"I'll kill you!" He yelled again

As she burst through the hibiscus to the jasmine, the back door opened. But she had to cut toward Vlad to get out. As she squeezed to the aisle, he caught her arm and slammed her body against him, locked her hands, and pressed a meaty arm around her neck. "If you do that again, you'll be dead. Now, where is it?"

She breathed into the pain. "In the . . ." she struggled to speak, "in the corner."

He shoved her to the rear of the house, past the giant leaves of fatsias and monsteras. The air smelled sweet, too sweet from gardenias and jasmine and oleanders. In the corner, the Violet Smoke sat on its crate where she'd left it, behind a half-dozen gardenias. The signs had scattered but the shrub seemed intact.

"Which one is it?" he said.

Maya was howling now. Howling high in alarm.

"There," she said. "If you let me go, I'll get it."

"Do you think I'm stupid?" He stumbled her body along the last row of palm trees to the crate. "Pick it up."

With his arm around her neck and hand holding her wrists, she said, "How am I supposed to pick it up without hands?"

"Go," he said and shoved her free.

She massaged her wrists, approaching the plant. Its leaves sagged with stress though they were still bluish green. She considered giving him a gardenia, but the flowers didn't match and the gardenia was blooming. She thought about how, as soon as she gave him the Violet Smoke, she'd never see it again, never witness the buds form on their delicate stems, never watch them plump and deepen to magenta before exploding into petaled cups of bloom, beaming that violet color, so dark and regal it was worthy of a queen's robe. It killed her to think Vlad's paws would be on it, letting it knock about in some car or apartment, ignoring it, bringing about its suffering. It was too innocent and pure.

As she lifted the pot in her arms, she saw a person slip through the back door.

Estera.

Renia warmed with shock, delight. Estera inched toward them, her arms extended and stiff, pointing Vlad's gun.

Oh, thank God.

"Back away from the plant," she said.

Vlad scoffed. "Hey girl, you came after all. I thought you were out of this deal."

"I changed my mind," Estera said. She advanced in a steady cadence.

"What deal?" Renia said.

"The deal where I get my plant back," Estera said. Her voice was calm. Her eyes stared in a focused trance.

"What do you want me to do with her?" Vlad said. "Break her neck?"

"Not yet," Estera said. "Not before we get the plant."

"Right," Vlad said.

"Me?" Renia said. "My neck?" She stared at her twin, frozen with shock.

The Violet Smoke's heft was in Renia's arms. Estera's wary eyes watched her. It was now or not at all. In a burst, Renia jumped, ducking behind the palms and sprinting along the house wall, straining to keep the pot upright.

"Renia!" Estera said.

She flew past the cannas, the bougainvilleas, the jasmine, the Violet Smoke's leaves jouncing with every step.

Vlad, unable to fit through the rows of tightly lined plants, paralleled her run down the center aisle.

Estera took a few steps, pointing the gun at Renia. But she didn't shoot.

A whirring noise groaned. Clicking. The sprinkler system woke.

At the front wall, Renia leapt to the system's panel. She wedged the plant with one arm into her hip and yanked at the little door. It wouldn't open. She found the latch and unhooked it. Inside the red button glowed. She punched it with a fist.

The engine box shot forward and hit Vlad square in the face. He dropped, giving her time to scurry to the door.

But as she was about to slip through, he landed at her waist, heavy, slamming her to the ground. The Violet Smoke sailed out of her hands and hit the gravel. It skidded out of the pot, a main branch breaking.

She screamed.

"Stupid whore," Vlad said and grabbed her arms. As she writhed around, he struggled to lift her. His nose was flattened, a cut at his eye dribbled blood. Renia wrestled as he got up, her knees on the ground, her torso at his waist.

A shot rang out.

Renia yelped.

Vlad twitched.

Another shot, and another.

She covered her head, glimpsing his shocked face. He opened his mouth, his eyes stunned. The full bulk of his body, his neck shooting blood, collapsed atop her.

Blood soaked her hands, her shirt, her neck. She heard him groan, saw his fingers clench and release and clench and release, and stop.

She tried to push him off, her heart pounding. His body was too heavy and her hands, too slick.

Estera crept over, the gun pointed at Renia. Her face, a strange blank. She stuck her boot against Vlad's shoulder and with a hard shove, rolled him back.

His eyes were open, his mouth ajar. He stared at the ceiling.

Renia sat up, panting. "Estera."

Estera's eyes were on Vlad, as if waiting for him to spring to life.

The sprinkler system hummed, clicked.

Renia inched toward her sister, her mind racing, her body chilled from the mud and blood in her shirt. "Estera, Estera." She got up slowly, her hand out.

Estera watched Vlad, her mouth tightly shut, lowering the gun ever so slightly.

A wet spray rained down. The sprinkler system with its long pipes and tiny emitters slid slowly toward the house's front. In a calm, programmed action, it passed over Estera, it passed over Renia, it passed over Vlad's body, soaking the ground with watery puddles of blood.

Renia heaved in a deep breath, wanting to reach out but frightened Estera would lift the gun again.

"Estera, it's me."

Estera, seeming satisfied that Vlad was no longer moving, lowered the gun all the way. Her long straight hair dripped.

"Estera, talk to me," Renia said, "I was worried. I didn't know where you were."

A siren wailed in the distance. Maya was no longer barking.

Estera examined the gun as if a foreign object had landed in her hands, then tossed it in the plants. She covered her face.

Renia climbed to her feet, her hand reaching in the space between them. "You're not really with them, are you? Can you forgive me, Steri? I only wanted . . ."

Estera's chest heaved up. She fell against Renia and squeezed. They trembled together. "No," she said quietly, "I'm not with them. I've come to visit you . . . and talk things out."

AT THE COTTAGE, all of the windows beamed with bright yellow light. The sedan's trunk was open and empty. Renia's razor lay on the ground, the blade broken off. As she approached the door, she noticed Yuri laying on his back in the tall grass, some twenty feet from the house. A puddle of blood at his neck, his throat slashed, his body, still. From the kitchen, Uncle Feliks hobbled out, pressing a towel to his bicep. The sleeve of his sweatshirt was sliced. Blood was splattered on his sweatpants. Renia urged him to sit. He blinked, checked that Yuri's body was in the grass, and sat on the chopping stump. "Where's the other one?"

"I think he's dead."

A medical truck roared down the driveway, its red lights flashing, siren sounding. As it slowed to the house, three paramedics jumped out. Renia pointed at House 8 and Feliks pointed to the grass. The last paramedic questioned Uncle Feliks, then Renia, then Estera. They checked Yuri's body, pronounced him dead. They checked Renia for cuts and bruises and gave her a blanket. Uncle Feliks brushed off her suggestion to go to the hospital. Instead, he went in the bedroom and let Maya out. She darted through the house and flew out the door, tearing through the tall grass. Feliks called her but her tawny fur melted in the woods.

A police car crawled down the driveway, its side spotlight shining bright. It parked, and two officers got out. Neither was Officer Kateb. Soon, another police car came, and a manhunt began. Four officers fanned into the woods with flashlights and guns drawn. After some high-pitched barking, Maya emerged, trotted to the police officers, barked, and sprung back to the woods. They followed her. After a few minutes, the paramedics' walkie talkies buzzed with scratchy communication, which drew them toward the trees with a stretcher.

Renia and Estera, with a broken Violet Smoke at their feet, watched as the head paramedic wrapped Feliks's bicep and treated the bumps on his head.

"Did you kill that man, Uncle?" Estera said.

He nodded. "I got a little help from your moron, but yes."

"How? With a knife?" Estera said.

"No, with the ax," Renia said.

Feliks shook his head. "It wasn't a knife or ax." He showed them the ax resting behind the stump. "It was this," he said and lifted his bloodied pruners.

"He thought he could take on a cousin of Czernicki," Feliks said. He smirked, then curbed his pride. "He learned."

The paramedics emerged from the woods, carrying Zbiggy on a stretcher. The tall grass flattened as they traipsed through. An owl hooted, a low distant chortle. A few clouds cleared, and a crescent moon appeared. Zbiggy was unconscious, a deep gash at his forehead. As the stretcher passed, Estera studied him as if studying an oddity, an artifact, an unfamiliar animal.

Renia asked about his condition.

"Trauma to the head," the paramedic said. "His face was cut from a rock, we think. He'd been running and hadn't seen the ravine."

"He's a wanted man," Feliks said to a police officer. "He bragged that he's wanted in France *and* in Poland."

"Wanted in two countries?" Estera said.

Yes, there's no one as wanted as Zbiggy.

The paramedics were about to load him into the ambulance when Estera said, "Wait."

She studied him, his limp mouth, his lidded eyes, her face in a tortured remove.

Just as Renia opened her mouth to remind her he wasn't worth going to the hospital for, Estera spit in his face.

The paramedics looked at each other.

"Now, you can go," she said.

CHAPTER TWENTY

In winter, the roof atop HortPolytech University was a windy place. A tall chain link fence covered in black cloth encircled the rectangular garden of raised beds and shed and greenhouse. The sun dropped below a blanket of pink clouds and warmed Renia's face. She wound through the garden, passing kale and carrots and broccoli, marveling at how one could grow food in cold weather, and knocked on the house door. A heating-cooling unit hummed in a loud purr. She knocked again. After a minute, she opened it and peeked inside.

The room was large and warm, jammed with growing tables holding tropical plants and blooming perennials and small potted trees. Bright grow lights hung from the ceiling. Vines spiraled over an arbor in the corner. There were plants that resembled ones Renia had seen and some she'd never seen: peace lilies with black flowers, philodendrons with purple leaves, a star jasmine bonsai, speckled hostas, white-leaved devil's ivy. A dwarf banana plant. It was a jungle she could have explored all afternoon.

Against the wall, at a small counter and sink, Professor

Damazy worked. Tools and plastic attachments littered the surface like a sprinkle of grit on a clean sidewalk. He wore canvas pants and a black flannel shirt, fiddling with an emitter and irrigation line. His face was at rest and involved, his hair combed back in a curve, his fingers moving like a boy's playing with toy soldiers. His jacket had been tossed on a nearby table, as had a leather bag and small cardboard box. The only noise breaking the hum of the heating unit was the slight squeak of the door in Renia's hand. She knocked harder against the metal frame.

He looked up, blinked. The serene expression drained into a pallid concern. "Are you hurt?" He set down the pieces and came over.

"What? No." She touched her face, remembering two days earlier she'd been fighting for her life. She realized she hadn't looked in a mirror that day.

"You have a mark on your neck," he said.

Those intense brown eyes examined her skin like a scientist, but his face filled with empathy.

"I'm fine. I'm fine." She said, feeling flush. "I must have bumped into something."

"It looks more like a scrape."

His eyes wouldn't shift from her neck. She wondered if her blouse was ripped or stained. It was fresh from the dresser but now she doubted her appearance. She had showered that day and brushed her hair, brushed her teeth. She hoped she looked clean.

"Sometimes I bump against sharp things when I work," she said.

He nodded. He seemed to be searching her eyes for a lie.

She swallowed, feeling self-conscious.

"Well, plants can be dangerous," he said. His eyes shifted to the plant in her arms and his face relaxed.

"Speaking of that, I see you've brought your 'Violet Smoke.'"

"Yes." She lifted the box with the shrub, wrapped in clear florist cellophane, missing its right branch.

"Here, let me take that." Gingerly he set his arms under the box and lifted. Their forearms brushed. "I see you pruned the branch stub off nice and cleanly." He went to the counter, setting the box down as if it were a crystal vase. With those solid hands, he removed the plant and put it on the counter as if afraid its properties would disappear at the slightest contact.

His attention couldn't be budged from it. His gaze shifted from the leaves to the branches to the soil. He squeezed a hand through the cellophane fold and removed a crispy leaf. "It truly is a wonder," he said. "My friend who's seen *Vulleria* in the wild is convinced this one's parent came from high in the mountains."

They stared in admiration.

"Are you sure about Switzerland?" he said.

She shrugged. She'd grown attached to the Violet Smoke, its alluring blooms, its odd beauty. Still, it needed to be studied. And it was too dangerous for a home. She and Estera had agreed this was the best and safest choice.

"If you're delivering it to the lab," she said, "then yes, I'm sure."

"I'll be very careful with it," he said. "I'm already thinking about how to best pack it for transportation."

"And watch for flowers," she said. "I'd hate for you to have . . . problems."

"Yes, there are native stories about the scent. The legend says the *Vulleria* flower can give anyone who inhales it temporary amnesia."

She smirked.

"But, of course," he said, "since *Vulleria* lives in such

remote conditions and dies off every year, no Western botanist has verified that."

I can verify it.

He must have read her expression. He seemed to know. "Is that why you wear a mask when it blooms?"

She nodded. Being honest felt like a weight lifted. And there was more, a lot more, but he didn't need to know. He was only an acquaintance.

"That means it's even more precious," he said. His eyes were wide. "It has a world of scientific potential. It's very exciting, I mean . . . you must be very proud to own it."

"Proud?" she said.

"I mean, as a plant person."

A wave of emotion overtook her. Her face burned. She wanted to say how ashamed she was. How sorry she was she hadn't told him the truth, that she hadn't sought him out on her first day in Paris. How sorry so many had suffered because of it. That two people were dead. How she'd used it for money when she shouldn't have. And most of all, how wrong this man was to believe she was someone virtuous when she was not.

"I did it to save my new life," she said.

"What?"

She swallowed. "And my sister."

He studied her fallen face, set a hand on her forearm. "Are you okay?"

Renia wiped her wet eyes.

"Yes," she said, feeling foolish. Life was unpredictable, and you couldn't control it. She'd tried her entire life to control it. She smiled at that. For the first time in years, she laughed. "Yes. I think now, finally, I am okay."

ON CHRISTMAS EVE, Renia unlocked the door to the shop

and fetched an herb table garland from the atrium. She hurried the bulky crate out to Madame Palomer's car, the scents of sage, thyme, lavender, bay leaves, and pepper berries all rising to her nose. Her boss waited in the driver's seat while Julo paced in the back amidst a blanket, bones, toys, and pillow. Renia carefully positioned it in the trunk between a wedged-in suitcase and enormous *bûche de Noël* in a box. Palomer was about to zoom away to Avignon.

"Renia, I'm too ill to help you unload the inventory from Marchaux today. I'm sorry, dear. You'll have to call the Japanese girl, just for today, to help you."

Renia slammed the trunk and strolled around the car.

"Oh, and the weatherman is predicting hail," Palomer said. "I'm worried about the atrium windows. Can you check on them tonight?"

Renia folded her arms. "The storm is supposed to pass through at two in the morning." She waited for her to say she wanted Renia to get out of bed, get dressed, and come downstairs to the shop in the middle of the night.

"Oh, is it that late? Well, could you anyway?"

For the past eleven months Renia would have said *yes* and *I'll take care of it* but today was a different day. A new day. A new era. She said, "Madame, I'm happy to check on the windows first thing in the morning but I'm not going to set my alarm, get dressed, come down, and go back upstairs for a two-minute window check."

Palomer's mouth opened in shock. "But the windows . . ."

"If the windows crack, there will be little I can do during the night anyway."

Palomer shifted her hands on the steering wheel, sniffed.

"I'll make sure to lock them tightly tonight."

This seemed to be enough. Palomer nodded, lifted a

finger. "Ah, and please put all jewelry on sale today. Gentlemen will be shopping for last minute gifts for their wives. We need to move merchandise and make up for the slow November. And please call me when you've done it, dear."

Across the street, João set a tray with soup and bread before a diner on the terrace. Their eyes met. He winked.

"Madame," Renia said. She held her head high, planted her feet firmly on the ground. "We would be making a mistake to mark down jewelry today. It's the day before Christmas. Studies show male shoppers don't care about price. If they need it, they will buy it. I'd rather not mark it down."

"Renia. I don't like your tone."

In a polite yet firm voice, she said, "Jewelry and gifts have been selling at a brisk pace at the current prices, so I don't think we need to reduce them. We'll make more money if we discount after Christmas. The past sales records show that."

Palomer blinked in an appalled frown. "Renia, your behavior is most—"

"I'm sorry, but this is the true me," she said. She relaxed into her strength. "And I have a request. Going into the New Year, I'd like you to consider opening a private bank account that I can transfer a fixed amount of money into every month. Otherwise, Le Sanctuaire won't stay solvent if you randomly withdraw varying amounts." She softened her tone. "You must remember from past years how unpredictable it is to do books this way?"

Palomer's nose flared. She glanced at the fountain inside the shop, seemingly unsure what to do. As the goddess poured an uneven but unending water, Palomer breathed in a huff.

Renia waited.

After a few seconds, her face calmed. "Oh alright, dear, you open it and I'll sign the paperwork. Whatever you think is best." She threw up her hands. "I'll leave it to you." She started the engine and Julo barked.

That was easier than Renia had imagined. She leaned in the window. "Lastly, one small thing: I wanted to let you know that Minh Tran is actually Vietnamese, not Japanese."

Silence.

Palomer rustled around in her glittery purse, as large as a suitcase, on the passenger seat, for a breath mint, avoiding eye contact. "Well, oh alright, dear, I'll make a note of it. *Joyeux noël, joyeux noël* to everyone . . . from everywhere."

LATER AFTER LUNCH, as Renia hung new sketches of hibiscus, jasmine, and oleander flowers on the wall, a dark-haired gentleman wearing a crisp suit entered the store. He wore a purple tie whose gray stripes matched the gray hair at his ears. Expensive Italian shoes. As he meandered around the fountain and came out of the window's shadow, Renia realized it was François.

They exchanged *bises*.

"I need your help," he said.

"Of course."

"Alain's birthday is in a few weeks. I want to plant something at his grave. I don't want to put a plant on top of his grave but rather inside the earth with him."

Renia thought about the choices. François wouldn't want a shrub to maintain, not a perennial to feed, not a big tree . . .

"What about lilies?" she said.

He smiled. "Do you have something pretty?"

"Better. I have something he loved."

She went to the atrium. With the false wall gone, the space was fully open. She'd reconfigured it for herself without apology. A shelving unit stood against the stone wall holding tools and inventory. By the windows, an array of plants hung from the ceiling or sat potted on the counter: dark ferns, chartreuse coleus, olive coral bells, sea green agave, pale angel wings, and a peace lily with black flowers that Professor Damazy had given her.

"Look at this! I never knew there were so many shades of green," François said.

She invited him to sit while she rummaged around.

"So, when you have a hectic day, do you ever come in here and take a break?"

His expression was impressed, his eyes, curious.

She thought of how many times she'd hidden herself in the atrium. She'd stared at the courtyard, cried about the past, and worried about her future, but had never taken "a break." And she'd certainly never grown a plant there. Now, she saw the space as reflecting her soul, a true *sanctuaire*. "Yes, I do."

She went through buckets of sand with loose bulbs and tubers, and then little boxes of trinkets and stickers and signs. Finally, at the top of the shelves, she found the two bags she'd retrieved from the storage unit. "Here they are." The bulbs were nestled in rough sawdust, as if hiding in a safe cocoon.

A strange hesitance flooded her body.

"Do you mind," she said, "if I kept one to remind me of him?"

François took the bag from her.

She blinked, her face warm.

"Of course not."

She nodded. It was difficult to speak.

"Renia."

"Yes?"

He took out a bulb and set it on the counter, nodded at it as if talking with an unknown being, an unknown person he'd been in a dialogue with. "I don't know if you know this, but I believe Alain . . . he took his own life."

Her mouth opened but no words came.

"Whether he died from cutting himself or hitting his head, we'll probably never know. But I want you to know that he didn't die from your flower."

"François," she took a step back, was about to say, *I don't know what you're talking about,* but his face was as serious as a stone.

"He tried to use the flower to forget I'd had an affair, but it didn't work for long."

"François, I never meant for it to bring on a break up."

"It didn't. I did. I was dissatisfied. And Alain had problems of his own. That depression he couldn't climb out of. That's why I left him, which, of course, made things worse."

He rested his hands on her shoulders. "I had always assumed you knew it wasn't your fault but last week I spoke to Alain's parents and they mentioned you'd been to see them in September. And that you had questions. I realized maybe you didn't know. I wanted you to know. He used the flower days before he died, not minutes."

Renia locked hands with his. "Thanks for letting me know."

As she walked him to the door, she thought of Officer Kateb and their last conversation. "François, did Alain ever use opiates?"

"No," he said. "Well, I mean, he had a prescription once for painkillers, but that was over a year ago when he'd had his appendix removed."

"Oh."

"Why?"

"No reason. Just wanted to double-check." She figured if it was an issue, Kateb would contact François.

She thought of the first time she'd shown Alain the Violet Smoke. They observed it through the closed Wardian Case. He'd clasped his hands together. "Renia, this could be the key to everyone's happiness," he said. "If you have a bad experience, a sniff of this makes it better!" Beaming, he wrapped his arm around her with pride as if she'd come up with some solution to save mankind.

"Despite all of his troubles and sadness," Renia said, "he really was quite an optimist."

On the first working day of the New Year, Estera arrived at Le Sanctuaire in Uncle Feliks's van. She and Renia unloaded primroses, hyacinths, and daffodils whose stems were emerging like straight spears of green light. She was glad to have fresh plants to sell, even if indoors. After they finished, the twins went to Vida Nova and sat at a table by the window. They talked about Feliks and their parents, and where they would travel on weekends now that Estera was living in Valenton.

After their brioche and tea arrived, Renia asked what she'd wanted to know for the last two weeks.

"Yes, Zbiggy and I talked in August," Estera said. "We met at a coffee shop. He apologized for everything, but we didn't get back together. He convinced me to forgive you though." She rolled her eyes. "Only because he wanted to make money again."

Renia thought of how she'd wanted to make money, thought of how she indeed had. She ate her bread in a vexed rhythm, thinking about what story Zbiggy would tell the police. She and Estera had told them Vlad wanted Estera's favorite, one-of-a-kind plant for revenge, which was mostly true. But if the police wanted more answers, she knew she'd have to face questioning, and even darker consequences. In the meantime, she decided to enjoy being with her sister.

"He wanted to make money and I wanted to see you," Estera said. "So, I begged Tata. He wouldn't tell me where you were. Then I overheard Mama on the phone. I should have known. Of course, you were in Paris."

Renia squeezed Estera's wrist.

"But I made a mistake in sending Zbiggy here instead of coming myself. I pretended that I wanted the plant back but really, I wanted to apologize. Unfortunately, Zbiggy had his own ideas." Her shoulders sagged.

"Yes," Renia said. "And so did his thug friends."

"I didn't know Vlad would go with him. And I didn't know that Vlad knew Russians in Paris. And some bar owner they call "their cousin." When Zbiggy told me you were selling him flowers, I had to come and put a stop to it."

"But you never called me back."

"I couldn't. I had to pretend that I was on those dumb gangsters' side. And by the time I got to Uncle Feliks's, you arrived the next night. When I saw Vlad's car, I knew what they wanted. I left the house so I could hide the plant. I was planning on promising Vlad anything, anything to get him to leave."

Renia thought of Vlad's small eyes and aggressive grin as he grabbed her in the square Boucicaut. "Well, we won't have to worry about him anymore."

"No," Estera said.

They were quiet.

"Vlad was the one who put me in the hospital," Estera said.

Renia straightened. "What?"

She lifted her cup to her lips. "That's why I had no problem pulling the trigger."

ON A LATE JANUARY MORNING, Renia walked down a frozen Rue Sereine. Rain had fallen overnight to leave a thin coat of ice on every sidewalk and street. Cars slid as they rounded corners, tires spinning in urgent efforts at control. Pedestrians, wrapped up like twisted pastries in thick coats and hats, tramped awkwardly, their hands windmilling when they lost footing. Justine and Monsieur Armand were nowhere to be seen, probably indoors. At the bistro, João had taken in the terrace chairs, knowing diners would prefer to eat inside the cozy warmth of Vida Nova.

Renia, who'd ridden the métro from her apartment in Batignolles, noticed icicles hanging from the balconies, reflecting the gray and white colors of the city. On Alain's balcony, a man stood talking on a phone. The door was open, but no music played. He paced in a brief circle, wearing only a shirt and slacks and socks but no coat. Somehow, he wasn't cold when everyone else was. It was as if he weren't human. He chattered on quickly, laughing and saying, "That happened, it happened! Do you remember?" He was so involved in his conversation that he didn't notice Renia and she barely noticed him, so she hurried across the street to escape the cold.

Once inside Le Sanctuaire, she noticed how loudly the fountain trickled that day. The goddess's stream created a large ripple, a ripple stronger and freer than she'd seen before. Renia clicked on the stereo and Satie's "Je Te Veux" rang out in a tranquil chime. As she brightened the lights, she caught the sweet scent of narcissus. Here she was, at last: in Paris, the entire Paris with its beauty and flaws, its triumphs and problems, no longer a childish dream but not a fleeting reality either. A person's home. *Her* home. She managed a thriving plant shop. Her sister lived nearby. Renia had started this life from seed and had worked hard to nurture it. Now, it had not only grown but, to her astonished heart, had bloomed.

ACKNOWLEDGMENTS

Like a plant, a story begins with a seed. For me, that seed is usually an idea or image. But the seed must be watered and heated to sprout, and then of course tended as a plant. Here are some folks who helped me grow this book.

First, my husband, who is my first reader and greatest supporter. Ethan, I couldn't have come this far without your deep love and unwavering belief in my ability (not to mention willingness to spontaneously watch the kids!), thank you. To my dear writer and editor friends who gave me thoughtful feedback and encouragement: Gretel Hakanson, Ann Hedreen, Larry Zuckerman, and Pierre-Marie Dufour. To my children, Trek, Pearl, and Hope, who always managed to occupy themselves when I needed just "20 more minutes." I appreciate your easy grace and patience.

To everyone at Magnolia Press, this vibrant publishing house whose founder, Nicole Tone, is nurturing into an impressively talented and professional organization. Thank you for taking a chance on this odd story about a flowering plant in Paris. To the creative Dionne Abouelela, who visually brought the danger alive, to my sweet fellow authors for their support, and everyone else whose contribution made the plant bigger and more beautiful.

Thanks to my author coach, Leigh Shulman, who helped me organize this whole mess called a writing career and is always at the ready with encouraging words and information. To Liz Culotti for her thorough advice early on. And to the writing community at large, the tribes that lift me up when I'm down: the people involved with the Goddard College MFA program, Women Writers, Women's Books, Writer Moms (in particular Autumn Lindsey), and the Women's Fiction Writers Association.

Lastly, I'd like to thank my early horticulture teachers, especially Timothy Hohn for his botanical eye, and all of my fellow plant geeks, the real life friends and online pals who share a passion for green life.

ABOUT THE AUTHOR

Karen Hugg writes literary mysteries and thrillers inspired by plants. Her stories are set in worlds where plants, real or imagined, affect people in strange new ways. A certified ornamental horticulturalist and Master Pruner, her passion is living green things and her aim is to entertain and inspire readers, to get them thinking while their hearts are pounding.

Karen has her MFA from Goddard College and lives in the Seattle area with her husband, three children, and four pets. When she's not digging or writing or all else, she sits outside and stares at the sky.

If you liked *The Forgetting Flower*, please help spread the word by posting a review on Amazon or Goodreads.

To read Chapter 1 of *Harvesting the Sky*, the next book in the *Botanique Noire* trilogy, please visit https://mailchi.mp/d8c2ffd1f6ed/botanicalstoriesinparis. You can also sign up for her newsletter there. Thanks!

facebook.com/KarenKHugg

twitter.com/karenhugg

instagram.com/karenhugg